A Forgivable Indecision

Shawn Jennings

A Forgivable Indecision

Cover watercolour painting by Pam Ling

tellwell

Tellwell Talent
www.tellwell.ca

ISBN
978-0-2288-2443-5 (Paperback)
978-0-2288-2444-2 (eBook)

Dedication

To all my former medical colleagues who taught, supported, and showed me love in my time of need

Table of Contents

Chapter 1
Bessie

Dr. James Wilson graduated from Montreal's McGill Medical School in 1911, in Quebec, Canada, at the top of his class, with honours. After a year of internship in Montreal, he set up practice in the small town of Rothesay, New Brunswick, less than an hour away from the city of St. John by horse. He was the first doctor ever to base a practice in Rothesay and the folks who lived in this small town were surprised and pleased when Dr. Wilson moved there.

A New Brunswicker by birth, Dr. Wilson was born in St. John, the only child of Matthew and Bertha Wilson. His father Matthew had a very successful wholesale business that shipped goods from overseas to central Canada and the United States, while his mother was a homemaker. James grew up in luxury but had no interest in being a merchant like his father and taking over the business; instead, he felt the call to a vocation where he could help others, and advancements in medicine interested him. He decided to be a doctor.

His parents brought James up in the Anglican faith and he was quite devout as a boy. At one point in his life, he entertained the thought of priesthood; but science fascinated him more. He gave up his clerical goal, thinking, *what better way to combine my love of science and desire to help others than through medicine?* Further, James pictured himself as a simple country doctor, riding dirt roads on horseback to see his patients, and so he turned his back on his privileged upbringing and decided to live a rustic life. But he loved working in hospitals too, and that is why he found Rothesay so ideal. The town was rural enough that he could become the community doctor he envisaged himself to be, yet it was also close to a hospital so he could learn from, and liaise with, medical colleagues. So, in June of 1912, he bought a farm in the heart of Rothesay and remodeled a section of the farmhouse into an office for his new practice.

His first year of practice was exciting and full of new challenges, a few disappointments, and much growth. Overall, he was pleased with how things went. But one day almost a year after he started, a patient walked into his office who would ultimately change his outlook on life forever.

James watched Bessie cry. He felt sorry for her; her distress was gut-wrenching. She sat on his examination table, rocking back e2and forth, clenching and twisting her small hands, her face hidden by long, brown hair. She wore a dark, brown, ankle-length dress and her stockinged feet dangled over the edge of his exam table. She looked innocent enough, except he knew different—this fifteen-year-old was pregnant.

He said nothing as she cried; he simply remained behind his desk, tapping his pen on a blotter. He had to be careful when examining a young girl. Any perceived impropriety would stimulate gossip: *Why did he open a medical practice in this small town? Why is he single? Is he not good enough to practise in the city?* The last thing he needed was gossip about him inappropriately touching someone.

As Bessie pulled a handkerchief out of her sleeve and wiped her nose, he felt himself flush in consternation, his high cheekbones lighting up like embers. He hoped she didn't notice; it was easy to see him flush because, unlike most men, he was clean-shaven. He was surprised by her situation. He had never dealt with pregnancy in someone this young before. He wondered if she could notice his distress. He was afraid he was glowing red like a bashful, grade-school boy being spoken to by his secret crush.

Rising from his chair, he walked around the desk and over to her. "Are you okay, Bessie?" he asked, lightly touching her shoulder.

"Are you sure?" she asked tearfully, without looking up. "Are you absolutely sure?"

"I'm sure," he said softly. "You're about six months pregnant." He bent over slightly to look into her eyes. "You're showing. You must have known."

"I was hoping with all my heart I wasn't," she admitted. "I prayed every night for God to take this away from me, but every morning when I woke up, nothing had changed. I felt my stomach getting larger, but no matter how much I prayed, nothing changed." She shook her head slowly from side to side and choked back another sob.

"Does your father know?" asked James.

"No. Pa's going to kill me. He'll call me a tramp, a trollop, and throw me out of the house." Bessie broke into tears again and covered her face.

James felt sorry for her, but he had to remain detached. *She has to pay for her sin, as we all do,* he thought. *It's not without risk to take a wild roll in the hay or an ill-advised walk with a boy in the woods; she might be a little temptress, for all I know.* But he knew her father, Amos, and he seemed like a very kind man. "I don't think Amos would do that," James said. "He'll probably be angry and demand that you marry the fellow right away, but—"

"*Marry*! I'm only fifteen," she pleaded.

"I know, Bessie, but a lot of girls marry young. Amos will insist. You have no option."

"I wouldn't marry that bastard—"

"Bessie!"

"I'm sorry, Dr. Wilson," she said, "but I wouldn't marry that guy and he wouldn't marry me." Bessie fidgeted with her handkerchief. "You see—" She hesitated, wiped her nose and then, dropping her hands into her lap with a sigh, whispered, "You see … I was forced."

"What?"

"*Forced*. You know… he did it to me and I didn't want to," she replied. "I struggled, but there was no way I could stop him. He had my knickers down and his thing inside me before I could do much."

Bessie stopped sobbing and looked directly into his eyes, making James flinch. He had never talked to anyone about rape or even sex before, except for in his medical classes. Embarrassed, he looked away.

"I suppose it was my fault," she went on. "I was at a church social one night last spring and Pa was getting bored waiting for me. Ever since Ma died five years ago, Pa keeps to himself much of the time and he can't abide too many people. You'd think he'd reach out for more company, but that's not Pa's way. Anyways he came to me saying he wanted to leave soon. I was having fun, chatting with my girlfriends, listening to the music and watching the older folks dance. I didn't want to leave with Pa, so I asked Pa if I could stay and go home with this relative of mine. The guy said that'd be fine and Pa agreed to let me stay …"

"You mean to tell me, Bessie," James inquired, "that a relative did this to you?"

Bessie looked at the door and then to the floor without looking directly at him. "That's what I'm telling you, Dr. Wilson," she said slowly, twisting her hands again. "I won't say who, but I trusted him and so did Pa. But as God is my witness, I'm telling the truth."

"So why do you say it's your fault?" he asked.

"Ma used to say, 'Don't be givin' a man temptation. Never be alone with a man you don't know.' I didn't quite understand what she was talking about when I was ten … but now I know."

James suddenly realised that he and Bessie were alone and he coughed nervously as he resisted an impulse to back away from her. "Well, a gentleman wouldn't behave in such a fashion, Bessie," he said quietly.

"Yeah? Well how can you tell who's a gentleman?"

He had no answer. He had never thought about it before. He wondered … *how* can *a woman tell who a gentleman is?* He knew fellows who had gone to visit prostitutes in Montreal back when he'd been a student, and to him they had seemed like regular old chaps—though he had been disappointed in their lack of morals. As for himself, he had never been with a woman. He intended to remain chaste and disciplined until he married … though he couldn't stop dreaming about the possibilities. He had no control over his unconscious thoughts.

"What happened next?" he asked.

Bessie stared at the opposite wall, avoiding his eyes.

"After the social," she recalled, "the man was as sweet as pie and helped me up onto his wagon. It was then I realised his wife wasn't with him. 'Where's … dah, dah, dah?' I say. '*Oh,*' he says, '*she didn't come this evening. Felt out of sorts—probably 'cause she's heavy with child.*' I didn't say anything—after all, he was my kin. I've known him since I was a little girl. Still … my Ma had told me to never be alone with a man. I should have left right then and there. I didn't. Should have known." She paused, rocked on the table, and hugged herself so hard her knuckles blanched. "I didn't think," she whispered.

"But you're only a young girl," James offered.

Bessie stopped rocking and looked at him with wet, brown eyes. At that moment, this little girl seemed mature beyond her years, but with the most lost expression he had ever witnessed.

"A *pregnant* girl," she muttered.

"You don't have to tell me the rest, Bessie. I get the picture." James felt a little nauseous. He walked behind his desk and opened the already-open window a little wider, letting in a cool, pleasant breeze. He looked out onto the Kennebecasis River, a shifting blue background behind the trees.

"No, I *want* to tell you, Dr. Wilson," Bessie said after a while. "I want to tell you it all. I want you to believe me. I'm no liar."

He turned and found a new girl sitting on the examination table, her face set rigidly in her determination to finish this tale. "All right, Bessie," he said resignedly. "Tell me the rest."

Bessie jumped down from the examination table. She seemed intent on getting comfortable before finishing her tale. She slipped into her small shoes and then sat down on a chair with her back to the wall, before continuing. When settled, she said, "Things were fine. He was talking about things—things I can't tell you or you'd know who I'm talking about—but I started feeling uncomfortable because it seemed to me his left hand kept leaving the reins an awful lot and brushing up against my leg. He seemed to have an itch on his thigh, but every time he went to scratch it, that hand kept finding its way to my leg.

"I inched over a bit to give him more room, if that's what he needed, but it made no difference—that hand found a way to my leg anyways. I was getting embarrassed, so I kept gabbing like an old lady.

"About three miles down the road, suddenly we turned off onto this small trail. 'Where we going?' I say. '*I got to show you something,*' he says.

"I should have jumped off the wagon right there. But then I thought maybe I was being foolish. I've known this guy a long time. So, I just sat there.

"Just a ways down this trail, he stops. He leans over me, puts his hand on my leg, rubs it like he was fixing to polish it, and says, '*You know I've always liked you.*'

'That's nice,' I said.

"Then he starts kissing me and his other hand is going up my leg and I start pushing him away, telling him 'no'..."

"Okay, Bessie," James interrupted, "I don't need to hear anymore." He coughed, as he was prone to do in uncomfortable situations, and sat down. He was sweating with discomfort.

"My Pa can never know who did this to me," she declared.

"He has to. He has to know the truth. He has to know the pregnancy was not your fault. You're a good girl."

"Doesn't matter. I'll tell him I was forced but not by whom. It'd kill him."

James fingered his stethoscope. "Bessie," he said. "We should bring this man to the authorities. He must be punished."

"And I would be punishing many of those that I love," she responded. "Besides, what makes you think they'd believe me—a young girl?"

"*I* do."

Bessie glanced at him, sizing him up. "Thank you," she murmured.

Trees rustled outside in the breeze coming off the water. It was a good sound, broken only by Bessie clearing her throat. "Dr. Wilson …" she said quietly. "I … I can't pay you right now, but I'm willing to come and clean the office, or your home. And I can bake. I can bake you a pie. Pa says my blueberry pie is the best …"

"That's not necessary, Bessie," James cut in. "Your father's been more than generous to me since I came to this community." Then he looked directly at her. "But I want you to tell Amos the truth. Truth is always the best policy."

Bessie was appalled. "Never! The truth would kill Pa … or he'd kill the guy."

"I think Amos can deal with it. Give me your word that you'll think about it."

She didn't look convinced.

He smiled at her. "You'll be okay, Bessie. You're young and strong. I'd like to deliver your baby if you'll let me, though there's a midwife on Rothesay Road by the boat club you can use if you prefer. But I'd feel better doing it myself, because of your age." Then he started to write on her new patient card where he recorded the date, reason for the visit, cost, and payment received. "I'd like to see you in about a month," he told her.

Bessie got up and walked to the door. She hesitated, her hand on the doorknob, as she looked back at him. "Thank you, Dr. Wilson," she said quietly.

"You're welcome, Bessie. I'm always here."

She opened the office door and left. He heard the jingle as she exited through the front door of the house.

James sighed and stretched backward, his hands behind his head. When he finished his stretch, he leaned forward, and wrote on Bessie's card, *July 10/13 Pregnancy.* Then he checked the entry to indicate 'payment made'.

He turned in the swivel chair and looked out the window. Bessie hadn't been as discreet about her assailant's identity as she'd meant to be. In mentioning that the assailant's wife was pregnant, she had revealed the identity of the rapist. Besides Bessie, there were only two pregnant women in the community, and one was

Bessie's aunt. James was quite certain that it was her own uncle, her father's brother, who raped her. *Wilfred.*

James looked out the window, watching the river flow by. He wondered if he should keep his word to Bessie and say nothing, or if he should tell the authorities. After all, she was just a child. He admired her willingness to take the blame and scorn for what happened to protect her father from the truth—remarkable courage for someone so young. He was ashamed he had thought she might be less than virtuous. He closed his eyes and prayed to God to help him make the right decision.

He got up from his chair and put Bessie's card in a file cabinet beside the window, deciding to give this problem more thought. Then he left his office to check the waiting room out front. No one was there, as he expected.

He hung a sign—*Office Closed*—in the window and left his office by a side door that opened into a small hallway that was in the personal quarters of his home. He walked to the stairs and climbed them, heading to his bedroom on the second floor. The room was hot despite both windows being open. He removed his jacket and hung it up. He undid his bowtie, unbuttoned the top of his white shirt, rolled up his sleeves, and then he poured water from the pitcher on his nightstand into a basin. He splashed the water onto his face. It felt good, though the water wasn't cold. When he was finished washing, he dried his face and hands and went back downstairs.

It will be cooler down by the river, he thought, as he opened the front door and was greeted by a blast of hot air. He grabbed his fishing pole from the railing of his front porch and as he walked down the front steps, he reached under the stairs for the bait can. As he continued across the yard toward the river, he glanced at his horse, Sadie, standing in a shade of trees inside her enclosure. He thought about taking her down to the river too, but she looked too comfortable. She stood, eyes half closed, lazily swatting flies with her tail.

"Hey, Sadie," he said. She snorted at him and stomped one hoof.

He started walking down the small dirt path at the end of the yard that led to the river, looking forward to the coolness of the riverside and the comfort of fishing. He needed to think. What should he do? Go to the police? Or do what Bessie asked him to do—nothing? *Maybe she will heed my advice and tell Amos about the pregnancy and being forced,* he thought. *Then Amos will coerce the identity of the rapist from her. It will be a shock to him, but he needs to know the truth.* The whole mess might get resolved without James even being involved. That would be a relief.

On the other hand, maybe she *wasn't* telling him the truth. Maybe she was covering up a lack of moral character by blaming someone else. He shook his head at the thought. *It couldn't be. Bessie seems like such a dear young girl.*

James arrived on the bank of the river. He lifted his head to the gentle breeze and squinted at the sun hanging over the opposite shore. *God's land is beautiful,* he thought, *but how could He let something like this happen to such a sweet child?*

He baited his hook and cast out. He prayed again for the wisdom and strength to deal with Bessie's situation. What should he do?

Chapter 2
The Meeting

JAMES SPENT A FITFUL NIGHT and felt uneasy upon waking up the next day. He kept replaying the conversation he had had with Bessie over and over in his mind. He dressed and prepared to do his daily chores. He went to the barn and gave Sadie fresh hay and water and then pumped a bucket of water from the well and carried it into the house to wash, shave, and use for breakfast. After cleaning up, he read a Montreal newspaper he had bought in St. John a few days ago. His first patient arrived at nine.

As the day went on, he found it difficult to concentrate on his patients; his mind kept wandering back to Bessie. He was still uncertain whether he should let Bessie handle the matter by herself as he had promised. He found himself being short with his patients as he pondered the problem and he chastised himself for getting annoyed at their questions. It wasn't their fault he was tormented by indecision, but he wished for some quiet time to think. Finally, as he was draining a boil on his third patient, a Mr. William Hawkins, he came to a decision: *I am going to tell Amos the whole story whether Bessie likes it or not.*

He was relieved that he'd finally decided and was now eager to put his plan into action, but it had to wait until tomorrow. Tonight, he had to attend the St. John Medical Society meeting. He had taken on a few patients who had doctors in St. John because they found it more convenient to see him in Rothesay, and while most of the local St. John physicians had welcomed him to the medical community, a few seemed resentful at the perceived intrusion. Some of the city doctors wanted to take away his privileges at the hospital, so it was important to attend the meeting to ensure that these few—especially Dr. George Peters, who seemed to dislike him the most—had any justification for doing so.

Dr. Peters did not attempt to hide his contempt and dislike of James and he treated him with such a condescending attitude that it made James feel like an intern on his first day. Dr. Peters seemed to interpret any comment or suggestion James made as a challenge to his authority. If it had been any other doctor, this would not have bothered James. Unfortunately, Dr. Peters was not only president of the Medical Society, but he was the chairman of the board of directors of the

St. John Public Hospital as well. Peters also had a lot of power in city politics and business and James knew it was important to smooth their relationship and show him that he was a responsible, good physician.

James found the St. John Medical Society to be a surprisingly progressive organization. At each dinner meeting, members discussed the latest medical research and assessed treatment and outcomes of specific cases at the St. John Public Hospital. But while James was impressed with the calibre and credentials of the physicians he was associating with, it surprised him that this progressive medical community had not recruited a surgeon. With the advances in anaesthesia, surgery was quickly becoming a specialty within medicine and these physicians knew that. Why had they not been active in recruiting surgeons?

He wondered if his pointing this out was why Dr. Peters was so disdainful of him. One night during a meeting, he asked the general membership of the Medical Society if they shouldn't be trying to recruit a surgeon for the area. Upon asking the question, Dr. Peters glared at him and did not even extend him the courtesy of a response. James looked around for support, but got no response from anyone else either—not even eye contact. Surgery seemed to be a touchy subject here, and it had something to do with Dr. Peters.

James wished his final patient of the day, Mrs. Beatrice Henderson, a good day as he saw her out. It was four o'clock; the meeting was due to start at six o'clock in St. John and he had to prepare to leave. He turned over the *Office Closed* sign, washed his hands, and went out to the barn. Then he saddled Sadie and left for the city.

He rode on the Rothesay Road to St. John. A train passed by on the tracks that ran between the road and the river. He felt the ground vibrate under Sadie; however, she didn't flinch. She was familiar with the twice-a-day run of the train. He patted her neck and then doffed his hat to acknowledge the Rothesay townspeople coming home on the train from a day's work in the city, though their faces were a blur and not discernable in the quickly moving train.

An automobile rambled by, kicking up a cloud of dust. The driver was wearing goggles that James found ugly and unnatural. Automobiles and their drivers looked and sounded like demons from the underworld to James. He didn't recognize the automobile; as far as he knew there were three in Rothesay, and this wasn't one of them. *Probably from the city,* he surmised, *friendly enough, though.* The driver smiled and waved. James coughed, waved back to him, and rode on.

James had resisted buying an automobile. He resented their loud, smelly existence. He thought he had left these smoke-belching behemoths behind in Montreal, but to his dismay he found the City of St. John was not far behind in accepting and accommodating these raucous demons on their roadways. His dream was to be a country doctor who rode a horse throughout the countryside to see patients; he didn't want an automobile. Ugly beasts.

He came to Marsh Creek and he said 'hello' to some boys who were fishing along the banks. He travelled beside the creek through some marshy, flat land, and then he and Sadie climbed a steep hill to finally arrive at the outskirts of the city. Once inside the city of St. John, they rode along dirt roads lined on each side by two-storied homes built close together. Children played in the alleyways and ran along the sidewalks. Some men and women stopped and looked at him as he rode along. He touched his hat in acknowledgement. He imagined many people knew him as the odd doctor who set up practice way out in Rothesay. *A most peculiar young doctor,* he could hear them say. He smiled.

A few automobiles rumbled by in clouds of smoke, curving and dodging to avoid mud holes. Many horses, snorting with effort, pulled wagons piled high with boxes and barrels. He assumed a ship with cargo must be in port because of all the activity. So many people and so much activity! He didn't miss this at all.

Homes evolved into stores as he journeyed further into the hub of the city. He passed a tavern and watched two drunken men stagger down the sidewalk as if they were on a rolling ship. *Disgusting.* This was one reason he lived in the country—to be away from the cacophony, foul odours, and too frequent sight of wasted lives. He appreciated the fresh air and gentleness of his small town.

Finally, he came to King Street and looked down the wide steep road full of horses and wagons. At the base of the street lay the harbour, and he saw he'd guessed right: A three-mast ship was docked at the wharf. The scene was active, and men carried cargo on and off the boat accompanied by noisy waves of laughter, shouts, bangs, and crashes. He looked across the water to see his family home, his parents' house, on a hilltop overlooking the harbour across from him. As a youth, he had spent many hours looking down upon this familiar scene. He imagined his father resting in his chair and looking out onto the harbour at this same time, not knowing that the fellow on the horse at the top of King Street was his own son. He reminded himself that he had promised to visit his parents this coming Sunday.

He rode down King Street and then led Sadie onto Germain Street to the Union Club, where the St. John Medical Society was meeting. Many cars lined the street. He hitched Sadie up to a wooden railing bordering the road. Most doctors drove automobiles these days. Only two horses with buggies were present and Sadie was the only single horse. He smiled. *No wonder they think I'm odd*, he thought. He patted Sadie on the neck and entered the Union Club.

"Well, if it isn't the 'cowboy doc'," said a man with wavy, red hair and a beard to match. Dr. Fred Madison worked across the harbour in West St. John and came to the meeting by taking a ferry that traversed the harbour.

"How are you, Fred?" James asked, shaking his hand. "And how is your charming wife?"

"Fine. We're both fine. Fit as a fiddle, as they say. Fit as a fiddle. And how are the fair ladies of Rothesay? I dare say you've had your eye on a few."

James blushed and coughed. "Really, Fred, I've been too busy—"

"Just joking with you, old man," Fred laughed, as he slapped James' upper arm. "Just joking. Come, let's go and sit down. You will sit with me, won't you?"

Fred placed his hand on James' shoulder and guided him into the room. They settled themselves at a table with two other physicians and were soon joined by several other doctors. The supper was served at six and during dessert, Dr. Peters called the meeting to order. After the normal business of the Medical Society was over, a specialist named Dr. Samuel Fletcher presented a paper on the pathogenesis of consumption. James listened attentively to the latest knowledge about the disease that was killing his father.

When the meeting adjourned, the doctors retired to the parlour for drinks and cigars. James had never tried tobacco and drank only occasionally, but he enjoyed relaxing and discussing medical matters with his colleagues over a glass of water. The parlour reeked of prosperity. Dark wood framed windows draped in green velvet and an ornate, gold fringe stretched across the two outer walls. A bar took up most of one wall, while a filled bookcase encompassed most of the other. Large leather chairs and dark mahogany tables filled the room. James was accustomed to this atmosphere. While he had chosen a simpler life for himself, his father—one of the most financially successful men in the city—had brought him here many times.

He walked into the room with Dr. Madison, the two of them engrossed in discussing the findings on consumption that Dr. Fletcher had just presented. Soon they were surrounded by a group of doctors discussing their experiences with consumption. When he felt a hand on his back, he turned to see Dr. Peters behind him. Peters was a small, portly fellow with slick, black hair parted in the middle, and a dense black beard that failed to mask his permanently haughty expression.

"My good man," Dr. Peters said. "You'll not ask me about seeking a surgeon tonight, will you?"

James was unsure if this was a joke or a challenge. "Good evening, Dr. Peters," he replied. "I promise. I won't say a word about a surgeon." Then, trying to smooth the waters by complimenting local doctors, he added, "I must say, I've found Dr. Bentley very knowledgeable about abdominal surgery and Dr. Adamson—"

"Precisely," Dr. Peters interrupted. "No need for a surgeon here. We have a very competent and knowledgeable staff and you will learn a lot from them. A surgeon would starve here. No need for one. No need at all."

Rebuffed at being cut off, James said, "I'm sure all the doctors here are very good, but it is hard to keep abreast of all the new surgical techniques and latest trends— "

Again he was cut off by Dr. Peters. "Dr. Wilson, not all trends are good or needed. I'm sure in the future a surgeon may come to our community when we older physicians succumb to the advancement of age and are gone. But meanwhile, those of us with experience are doing quite a good job with the community's surgical needs." Then he looked pointedly at James and said, "It seems the new doctors are not being trained to handle the simplest of surgical procedures. Too bad."

He turned and left before James could respond to the obvious jab.

Dr. Madison nudged him. "I don't think he likes you," he said out of the side of his mouth.

"I'm not sure what I ever did to anger him."

"I think he truly believes we don't need a surgeon here in St. John and you keep bringing it up, as if you are questioning his authority."

"I only brought it up once at a general meeting and I have never said another word about it. *He* keeps bringing up the need for a surgeon to *me*."

"James," Fred said, shaking his head and stroking his beard. "You have broached the subject to *many* people. You've asked questions and given opinions. Don't you think he hears? Don't you think he has any friends?"

James fumed at the thought. "This is so …"

"Childish?" Fred suggested.

"Yes, childish! Every hospital in Canada is embracing the concept of surgery as a specialty and recruiting surgeons. Surgeons bring new techniques and new ways of preventing infection to hospital communities. Specialized surgeons lower mortality rates. This has been proven."

"You don't have to sell me, old man. Nor most of the doctors in this room."

Dr. Madison took his elbow and ushered him out of the room. When they reached the hallway, Fred said,

"There are too many ears in there. I want to be honest with you, James. You're coming across to some doctors as a know-it-all, a young doctor fresh out of medical school who thinks the rest of us are stupid—"

"I don't think that at all!"

"I know you don't. I'm just saying you're coming *across* like that. Just give it a rest." Dr. Madison placed his hand on James' shoulder. "I'm only telling you this for your own benefit. I like you. I don't want to see you hurt."

He could see Fred was sincere and decided to trust him. He had to ask, "Why are they so scared of Peters?"

"I wouldn't call it 'scared'. They're respectful. He has done a lot for medicine in this city. He is one of the principle people responsible for the construction of the St. John Public Hospital. He's been the medical director there for over ten years. He developed funding for doctors to look after pauper cases and he is active in city politics and in the Church of England. He has powerful friends. He is no buffoon and is as aware of the research about the benefits of surgery as you are. Be patient. We'll get a surgeon someday, when the need becomes apparent. But for now, could you try a more conciliatory approach with Peters?"

He wondered what Dr. Madison meant by 'when the need becomes apparent'. *Will many have to die from dirty surgery? Needless deaths are happening now; statistics prove this,* he thought. But he resisted the temptation to argue further. "I'll try," he said. "Thank you for speaking to me so honestly, Fred."

He and Fred strolled back into the room, which was now filled with cigar smoke and the swelling jumble of voices.

Later that evening, James rode Sadie home at an easy pace. The sky was salmon pink. *It will be dark by the time I get to Rothesay Road,* he thought as he surveyed the sky.

As he and Sadie sauntered by Marsh Creek, he watched minnows jumping for flies. A few ducks swam along the water's edge, heading for their resting site. The boys were gone, their fishing ended for the day. He remembered those carefree days of his own youth, when he and his friends would fish in the harbour. At the end of the day, faces burnt by sun or wind, they would scramble up the banks of the harbour with wet feet to head for home. His mother would admonish him for ruining his shoes *again*, kissing his head and pretending to be annoyed as he tried to explain how slippery the rocks were. He remembered the majestic tiredness that would sweep over his body as he fell into bed for the night. Long-ago, carefree, busy days. It was good being a boy.

He rode over a small bridge that spanned the creek. The only sound he could hear was the clop-clop of Sadie's hooves. The Kennebecasis River came into view, still and dark in the waning light. He looked up at the majestic homes on the hill that faced the river, observing the warm, wavering shadows of kerosene lamps behind window curtains. Bessie lived with her father and siblings on a farm further inland; they were probably lighting their lamps at this moment. Perhaps Amos was sitting in his chair trying to make sense of Bessie's news, too shocked and dismayed to appreciate or care about the oncoming darkness. Or perhaps she hadn't said anything yet and was lighting the lamps as she always did at this time of day, carrying on with her chores as though nothing was different. He imagined her moving about the farmhouse doing needless tasks with a strained, forced smile.

His Medical Society business over, he was eager to visit them, but it was too late in the day now. He owed Bessie an explanation before he told Amos. Tomorrow. He would visit them tomorrow morning.

Chapter 3
Amos

JAMES HEARD THE TRAIN RUMBLE by and opened his eyes. It had to be quarter past seven in the morning. He panicked—until he realised it was Saturday. No office hours. He stretched his arms and yawned, grateful that he didn't have to hurry quite as quickly as he usually did.

He got up and shaved and dressed with less haste than usual. He was going to visit Amos and Bessie today, first thing after breakfast. It was the right thing to do. To discuss what had happened was best for his patient.

He was on his way downstairs when he heard a horse galloping toward the house. He opened the front door and stepped onto the veranda just as the horse and rider came to a sudden halt before the steps, a cloud of dust drifting behind them. It was Amos. "Doc!" he cried. "She's gone! Bessie's gone! Did she come here, Doc?"

Immediately, James knew Bessie must have said something, or else why would Amos have come to him? He looked at Amos, whose long, black, grey-streaked hair, was swept back straight from his face from the hard ride over. Bessie's father was about 40 years old, clean-shaven, and in good shape. A ruggedly handsome guy, he reminded James of cowboys he'd read about in novels. A six-gun on his hip would have completed the picture. This cowboy seemed very distraught. He remained on his horse.

"What do you mean—gone?" James asked.

"Gone. Not there. I got up this morning and *no Bessie*. I went to her room thinking she was still mad at me for last night, and I found this …"

Amos reached into his coat pocket, brought out a folded sheet of paper, and offered it to James. James walked down the steps and took the note from him. He felt an ominous sensation building in the pit of his stomach. He opened the paper and read:

Dear Father

I love you. I always will. I know you don't mean the things you said last night. It has been hard for you since mother died. I have greatly admired your courage.

You must believe me—I was forced. I am a good girl.

I don't want to go to Boston. I don't want to have this child. God forgive me, I hate the baby and the man who did it.

I'm caught. People won't believe me though, and I'll always bring shame upon you.

I can't tell you who did this to me, father. He'd probably deny it anyways.

Thank Dr. Wilson for me. He's so kind.
I'm doing this my way, Pa.

I'll always love you.
Bessie

"Jeez, Doc," Amos said. "What's she done? I should never have said what I said, but I got angry and ..." Amos bent his head and started to cry. "She wouldn't tell me who the bastard is who did this to her," he sobbed. "I got so angry—she wouldn't tell me anything. I kept demanding she tell me who this son-of-a-bitch was and all she did was sit there and not say 'boo'. I got madder and madder and ... and ... finally I called her a *slut*."

Amos dropped the reins, buried his face in both hands, and cried harder.

James' hands shook as he refolded the sheet of paper. *This letter doesn't necessarily mean suicide,* he thought trying to quell the rising panic. *She may have just run off to have the baby where no one knows her.*

"I never meant any of it," Amos finally mumbled. "I don't think Bessie's a slut. I was just angry is all. She—"

"She's probably run off," James interrupted, "to have the baby in private to spare you the shame. Don't read more into this letter than there is, Amos." He handed the letter back. "Here, you keep this. I'll gather my things and come with you to look for her. First, we'll check the train station ..."

Amos and James checked the train station, the ferryboat at the harbour, the hospital, the police station, the homes of Bessie's friends and they talked to all the neighbours, but no one had seen Bessie. The police told Amos the same thing James told him, that she'd probably just run away and would be back before long with her tail between her legs. They said it was a common situation, and not to worry.

"This time you must have *really* got her mad," a policeman laughed, clapping Amos on the shoulder as if the whole scenario was a joke. James felt like smacking the grinning constable, but he was probably right—she might already be home. *Please, God let it be so.*

They rode home from St. John together in the late afternoon, exhausted from their travels. They passed Marsh Creek. James noted the twisting swarms of midget flies floating in the shadows on the other side of the creek as he swatted at the horseflies that buzzed around his face.

At that, Amos said, "I gave up long ago."

"Gave up?" James questioned.

"Swatting horseflies. Seems as though they bother you more when you make that arm motion."

"My father always said that."

"I hear he's ailing," Amos said.

"Yes. Consumption has taken hold of him. I don't think he has much more time. He's failing fast."

"Sorry to hear that." Amos looked at him and slowed his horse down. "Dr. Wilson—"

"James, please. I told you to call me James."

"Ah yes, James. Well, James, I want to thank you for today. You didn't have to spend all day with me. My brother could have come."

"I know …" James said slowly. "I just thought it might be better if he stayed at home. You know … in case he was needed while you were away." He felt his face flush at the lie and he coughed. "Besides I had the day free and I'm concerned about Bessie."

"You're a good man," Amos said.

James cringed with the compliment and felt his cheeks grow hot.

"Bessie told me she saw you yesterday," Amos said.

"That's right. I told her she was pregnant, but I think she knew that already."

"Did she tell you who it was that did this to her?"

James looked away. "No … She wouldn't say." He needed time to think. He didn't think he should tell Amos that his own brother had raped the girl; Amos had too much to worry about right now. When they finally found Bessie, then he would divulge the disgusting situation to him.

"She wouldn't tell you either?" Amos asked. "Stubborn girl. Always was headstrong like her mother." Amos covered his eyes, clearly disturbed by the memory of his lost wife.

They trotted along the River Road in silence. James couldn't think of anything to say to ease Amos' worry. But truth be told, he was not feeling too good about Bessie's departure either. Guilt was building with each passing hour. He should never have let Bessie deal with this without his help. She was a child! His sad indecision might cost Bessie her life. *No. She* will *be home. She* has *to come home.*

He rode Amos home to his farm and was sad to learn from the rest of Amos' children that Bessie had not returned. He asked Amos if he wanted him to stay. Amos replied no, he wanted to be alone with his children.

"I can never thank you enough, James," Amos said. "Pray for Bessie."

Amos dismounted and gave the reins to one of his sons. He shook James' hand and went into the house with his arms around two children.

James turned Sadie for home. He was ashamed, because he was relieved when Amos did not accepted his offer to stay for a while. A good physician would sacrifice anything to help a patient, but he wanted to run and hide.

As he rode away from the farm and down a hill, he turned and looked back at the farm. He saw Amos in the living room, his head surrounded by little heads resting on his shoulders, their shadows dancing on an adjacent wall. Then a pregnant lady came out of the front door and stretched her back—Wilfred's wife. He nudged Sadie to quicken her pace. He felt so tired.

Chapter 4
Mary

James rowed away from the harbour's shore. His father waved to him as though he was not disappointed and hurt, but James knew otherwise—his father was heartbroken. Parting wasn't easy for James either, but he couldn't take his father's illness. As a doctor, not being able to do anything to help the man was tearing him apart. Further, even though he was dying of consumption, James' father continued to be the stoic man he had always been. It drove James crazy. For once, he'd like to hear his father complain or lament about the unfairness of it all, but he never did.

James glanced back for one last look and saw his father lower his arm and turn around to leave the harbour shore. He felt sorrow and a pang of guilt. He could never be as brave; he could never be the man his father was.

Suddenly, James heard a roar and he turned his head just in time to see a huge wave bearing down on him. The wave came from nowhere. He had never seen a wave like this before in the harbour. He sat paralysed as it curled and then poured down on him. He gasped, surprised by the coldness and ferocity of the water. He tried to grab for the side of the boat, but the sheer weight of the water prevented him from lifting his arm, pushing him over the side of the skewed craft.

He tumbled under the water, unable to comprehend his orientation under the surface. Somehow, after what seemed an eternity, his face emerged into the air. He gasped and took in a mouthful of water, then choked and coughed as he fought for another breath before the heavy currents forced him underwater again. Thrashing wildly, he fought his way to the surface once more as the water roared past the banks of the harbour. Then he was under again. Muffled sounds … above … under … His chest ached. He couldn't see the surface. He needed air.

James gasped and turned over to see his curtains glowing orange-red in the early dawn light. He needed air. This was a dream … water … something about his father.

It had been another restless night and he was surprised he had slept at all. Clearly the events of the past days were troubling him. His stomach tightened as he thought about Bessie. He hoped she had come home during the night—that would be a big relief.

He got up with that hope, and also was cheered by the thought of seeing Mary today at church. He had seen Mary O'Sullivan for the first time a few weeks ago. She had been away in Boston with her family for the past year. Her father was still there, but the rest of the family was back in Rothesay and expected him home soon. Mary's father was an important man. He owned O'Sullivan's Liquor Distributors in St. John, but James couldn't remember having ever met any of the O'Sullivan family when he lived there. If he had, he certainly hadn't noticed Mary.

He washed, dressed, fed Sadie, and prepared breakfast. He had to admit, besides giving praise to the Lord God, lately his motives for attending church included a chance to see Mary. He smiled and shook his head at his own foolishness. He had never even spoken to her; he had only watched her from a distant pew, planning, dreaming, and waiting for an opportunity to ask her father's permission to visit her when the man returned from Boston. Would he dare? Even now, the thought of speaking to her caused his chest to constrict. He was such an idiot around women.

He cleaned up and read a paper until it was time to leave for St. Paul's Anglican Church, which was not far from his house. It was a perfect summer morning with large billowy clouds drifting by and as he walked through a pasture on the way, he touched the grass stalks that swayed and flowed like water in the gentle wind. He wondered if Bessie was somewhere appreciating the morning at this same time, and suddenly felt nauseated and weak with worry for her. Then he paused, took a deep breath, and walked on.

At a crest of a hill in the pasture, he looked down and could see people dismounting from their wagons and carriages and talking in front of St. Paul's. Families were walking down the road with children trudging along in front, resisting the urge to run. They all seemed so happy, the comfortable townspeople of Rothesay on the banks of the Kennebecasis River. They were living the simple life. *The knowledge that one of their own is a rapist of children will soon put an end to their placid world,* James thought. He wished *he* wasn't privy to this horrible piece of information.

He walked down the hill and entered the churchyard, acknowledging many members of the congregation as he walked through the throng. He made his way to the pew he usually sat in, near the back of the church.

He said hello to Mrs. Mawhinney, a widow who usually sat beside him in church. She was a gossip, but pleasant enough. She gave him a lot of information about the community every Sunday—who was related to who and the news about various people. The information about who was related to who was of interest to him as a physician, as it could come in handy when treating people whose families tended toward specific ailments. However, he didn't care to hear about her impressions of other people, as he abhorred gossip. But she was harmless enough; just a lonely, elderly lady who liked to talk.

He suddenly recognised Bessie's Uncle Wilfred's voice behind him, talking to someone.

He turned his head and saw Wilfred smile and greet his fellow parishioners. Wilfred accepted their sympathy about his niece and thanked them for their concern and this made James burn with rage. He clenched his fists. *If only they knew the* real *Wilfred,* he thought. He tried to relax. He had to bide his time until Bessie was found, and then they would learn quick enough about their 'friendly' neighbour.

He watched as Wilfred entered the aisle, holding the arm of his very pregnant wife with his children trailing behind. He was a large man with thick farmer hands. His face was pleasant enough, round and jovial with no beard. For a moment, James again wondered if Bessie *had* told him the truth about being 'forced'. No, the girl had been so distraught and sincere; there was no way that was an act.

Wilfred nodded to James as he walked past. It was a wary nod; not the friendly greeting he was extending to the others. His smile seemed less natural, strained. *Maybe Amos told Wilfred about Bessie's pregnancy, and that she came to see me on Friday,* he thought. *Is Wilfred worried that Bessie told me the whole story?*

James frowned at him and Wilfred looked away and travelled down the aisle to his seat with greater haste. That clinched it for James. He was sure then that Wilfred *was* guilty of raping Bessie. He had no doubt. Once more he tried to relax his hands and breathe his way to calmness.

His thoughts turned to Amos. He probably wouldn't show up today, unless Bessie had come home during the night. James hoped that was the case and he prayed that Amos and Bessie would come sauntering down the aisle at any minute. He would grasp Amos' hand with relief and smile at Bessie with understanding.

Just as he was thinking this, Amos appeared. He was with his children, but Bessie was not part of the pack. James turned to Amos to ask him about her, but before he could say anything, Amos sadly shook his head and walked past.

I should have known Amos would still come to church, James thought, *even though he is distraught over his lost daughter.* Someone had told James that Amos was a very devout man. He would want to pray to God for her safe return. *No wonder Bessie feared telling her father his brother raped her; it would shake him to the core,* James thought. Amos was a kind, trusting fellow, who had been through many trials including the untimely death of his wife. Bessie was probably correct in thinking that this evil misconduct by his own brother might be the final straw that could break him. Mrs. Mawhinney had told James that Amos was never the same after his wife died. He'd become withdrawn, though pleasant. According to her, he was only a shadow of his former self. *Still, Amos deserves to know.* He would have to deal with the truth, as hard as that may be.

Amos and his four children filed into the pew where Wilfred and his family sat. Amos sat beside his brother, said something to him, and then knelt to pray. Wilfred squeezed his brother's shoulder as Amos rested his head on his hands while praying.

A wave of rage coursed through James' body again as he watched. He couldn't endure this outrage much longer. He clenched his hands, stood, and was about to leave church when Mary arrived. He sat down again. *Mary! Maybe today I will speak to her.* Mary was followed by a gentleman James had never seen before, who was escorting Mary's mother. *Her father.* Mr. O'Sullivan was wiry and small, with thick, wavy red hair, sideburns that swept down to the corners of his mouth and a long, thin nose. He laughed, bowing to the ladies and slapping other men's shoulders, as he entered the aisle from the foyer. He seemed like a jovial fellow. James immediately liked him.

"Clancy!" The man seated in front of James, Mr. James Henderson, whispered loudly to Mr. O'Sullivan and then he leaned over the side of his pew to pull on his suit coat. Mary's father turned toward Mr. Henderson. "Good to see you, Clancy, m'boy!" Mr. Henderson said. "You are a sight for sore eyes. When did you get back?"

Clancy shook the gentleman's hand and said, "A week ago. And it is great to be back, I must say. It was wonderful to see my brother and his family again, and Boston was a treat, but there is no place like home. I was anxious to get back and tend to business—even though my partner, Ainslie Stewart, has done a fine job looking after things."

Mr. Henderson pulled Clancy to sit down beside him and whispered something into his ear. They both chuckled. Mrs. Mawhinney huffed. She had shown similar disapproval of displays she considered to be frivolity in church before. According to her, laughing and joking weren't to be tolerated once a person passed into the doors of the sanctuary—though apparently idle gossip was not only allowed, but considered pious. James smirked. She was a character, that Mrs. Mawhinney.

At her huff, Clancy glanced back toward Mrs. Mawhinney and his eyes met James' eyes. James hoped Clancy didn't think it was *he* who huffed. He smiled disarmingly at the man, and then realised it was Clancy who had passed him on River Road in an automobile a few days ago when he'd been riding Sadie into town.

Clancy smiled back at him, then stood up and proceeded walking down the aisle to his pew with his wife and nine children. The O'Sullivan children ranged in age from toddlers to teenagers. Mary, who appeared to be the oldest, herded the youngest by touching their heads as they walked along. He thought she glanced at him out of the corner of her eye and he was inwardly thrilled, so thrilled he couldn't breathe. Mary was the most enthralling girl he had ever seen. Her features were sharp but delicate, and today her long red hair was tied back in a bun. She was a very pretty girl, about nineteen years old. She had an engaging manner that seemed at once gentle, caring, and thoughtful. He watched her looking after her younger siblings with kindness and love and admired the way she took control without direction from her mother. From what he could see, Mrs. O'Sullivan never said a word to her children—Mary seemed to be the one who kept care of them. He imagined she was a great benefit to her mother around the home, an uncomplaining, loving daughter. He wondered if she had a suitor. He hadn't seen her with anyone, but that didn't mean she wasn't betrothed—perhaps to someone in Boston?

Mary ably arranged seating for the little ones and then helped her pregnant mother get comfortable. Then she knelt down in prayer, encouraging her younger siblings to do likewise. She pressed together the hands of a very young sister beside her and James noticed Mary's delicate little wrists. He smiled when he saw the youngest one shake off Mary's hand as if offended that Mary thought she needed prompting to pray.

"Large family, the O'Sullivans," James whispered to Mrs. Mawhinney.

"Humph," Mrs. Mawhinney responded, as if she didn't approve of large families.

"Is that Mr. O'Sullivan?" he asked, nodding toward Clancy.

"Yes," she whispered. "Back from Boston. Been away for nearly a year. They have family down there, but I don't know why he was there for so long and why the rest of the family came back before him. I wouldn't be surprised if they were looking for a husband for Mary. She's of that age, you know, and I don't imagine most of the gentlemen around here are up to the O'Sullivan's standards. I shouldn't say that, but they *are* very rich. Money marries money, you know."

James chose to ignore the comment. Mrs. Mawhinney knew full well that his own father was well off. However, she seemed oblivious to the possibility that her statement might offend him. Instead she continued filling him in on the O'Sullivans.

"He's a liquor merchant," she went on. "He owns a liquor distribution business in St. John. But I imagine you know that. I can't say I approve of the family.

Liquor only causes misery, I say. I've never tasted a drop in my life." She straightened up and lifted her chin, clearly not caring if he took her words to heart. Then she asked, "Mind if I share your hymnbook? I left mine at home. I don't know how I remembered my prayer book and not my hymnbook."

James moved closer to her and opened his hymnbook as the opening notes of the first hymn started. They stood as the doors beside the sanctuary opened and the choir entered, singing the processional hymn. They marched down his aisle to the back of the church first, as they did every Sunday, before going up the opposite aisle to the front of the church. Mrs. Mawhinney gave it her all, especially as Reverend Philpotts walked by behind the choir. The Reverend gave James a knowing glance and smiled as if he was sympathizing with James for Mrs. Mawhinney's vocal assault.

When the choir finished and settled in their pews, James sat down and opened his prayer book. His parents had given him this well-worn prayer book many years ago. He stroked the rich brown-red pebbled cover. It gave him comfort.

James and the congregation spoke and chanted responses to Reverend Philpotts as he droned on with the familiar doxology. James hardly needed to glance at his prayer book as he stood, knelt, sat, and chanted in the same practised, orderly flow he had known since childhood. As the service progressed, he felt stillness enter his soul, a stillness he understood to be God's presence, and he found peace for the first time in days.

The Apostle's Creed ended the first part of the service, but the congregation remained standing to sing a hymn. As he sang, James looked up at the massive cross behind the sanctuary. The bronze cross was so simple and yet so inspiring. He hoped God heard his silent plea for Bessie.

The hymn finished and he saw Mary turn to admonish a young fellow to keep quiet by putting her finger to her lips and glaring at him. The young fellow pouted and put his head down. He must have pinched the brother beside him, because the other brother jumped and hit the young fellow on the shoulder. Mary reached across and pressed one boy's arm. The boys seemed to grasp that Mary was serious and settled down.

James thought she glanced at him before she turned back around. Was that a smile? He imagined touching her delicate lips with his finger, moving that finger slowly over their surface as he brought his own lips closer to hers …

Reverend Philpotts was finishing the Biblical readings but James had not heard a word. Mary was consuming his thoughts and he was indeed weak. He resisted the temptation to look at Mary again and instead concentrated on Reverend Philpotts, who was walking across the altar to enter the pulpit. The sermon was about to begin.

He tried to focus. He looked at the cross again and at the brass rails that separated the elevated altar from the floor. *Mary.* Then he looked at the massive wooden pillar that rose like a flower from the floor to blossom where it met the vaulted roofline. *Mary.* He marvelled at the craftsmanship, dedication, and hours it must have taken to create such structures. *But all I can think about is Mary.*

James saw Wilfred lean over to whisper something in Amos' ear and it jolted him from his thoughts of Mary. Suddenly he was ashamed. A young girl was missing and she may very well be in peril, yet he was thinking only of himself and his needs. He felt angry at himself. *I did nothing to protect that child.* He had not talked to her father, but instead had gone to the Medical Society meeting. *A meeting was more important than the safety of that sweet girl. My standing in the medical community was more important than Bessie. I'm a hypocrite!* Suddenly he realized that Dr. Peters was right—he was a self-righteous crusader who had never done anything to command respect.

He closed his eyes and concentrated on Reverend Philpotts' words. The reverend was speaking about duty to family, community, country, and above all to God. James cringed and closed his eyes. He had messed up in his duty to little Bessie. He had left her in her hour of need. If he could only take back those few minutes …

"And let no man take his duty lightly," Reverend Philpotts cried out. "For he ..." James did not hear what the Reverend said. He couldn't focus, couldn't control the intrusion of his thoughts. He gave up trying to follow the sermon and instead asked God to bring Bessie home to her father.

"Amen," Reverend Philpotts finished.

"Wasn't that a wonderful sermon?" Mrs. Mawhinney whispered.

"Quite," James lied.

The collection, a final hymn and the benediction were performed, and soon the congregation was filing out of the church. James felt a surge of excitement course through him as Mary walked by, even though she didn't even glance at him, leaving him feeling like a schoolboy with an infatuation.

As the church emptied, Mrs. Mawhinney kept chattering to him. "It was a lovely service. I wonder where they got the flowers on the altar? Probably from Mrs. Livingston. She has such lovely flowers. I recognize the black-eyed Susans ... but what were those yellow ones? Oh, there's Mrs. Livingston now—she'll tell me." She nudged James out into the aisle, squeezed past, and joined Mrs. Livingstone as she walked by.

Glad to be rid of her, James stepped back into the pew to allow people from the front of the church to file past him. When he left the church and stepped outside, he discovered the O'Sullivans standing beside Reverend Philpotts at the bottom of the stairs. Reverend Philpotts was saying goodbye to the congregation and talking to Mr. O'Sullivan at the same time.

James descended the stairs and shook Reverend Philpott's hand. "Great sermon, Reverend," he said.

"Thank you, James," he replied. "James, have you ever met the O'Sullivans?" He introduced him to Clancy O'Sullivan first and then to the rest of the family. As he took Mary's delicately extended hand, for the first time he saw her straight on. Her smile made his legs weak.

"Pleased to meet you," he managed.

"Clancy has been away in Boston for quite some time," the Reverend said. "We're glad he's finely decided to return home." The Reverend laughed and clasped Clancy by the elbow.

"I'm pleased to meet you, Dr. Wilson," Clancy said. "And we may be seeing you before too long." Clancy took his wife's hand and smiled at her. "As you can see, Rebecca's having a baby."

"That's grand, Rebecca," Reverend Philpotts said. "Congratulations, Clancy! I'm so happy for you."

"Congratulations," James said.

"I'd like you to look after my wife, Dr. Wilson," Clancy pronounced.

"Clancy!" Mrs. O'Sullivan exclaimed. "I don't need to bother Dr. Wilson."

Clancy patted his wife's hand. "Now dear," he said. "We've discussed this and you know how I feel—you had such a hard time with the last pregnancy. I'd feel better if a doctor was around."

"I've done this so many times," she said, "I think I could tell the midwife a thing or two."

James noticed Mary was blushing. He tried not to look directly at her as he said to her mother. "It would be no trouble Mrs. O'Sullivan. I think Mr. O'Sullivan is right. Let me check you over. If you wish, you can still use a midwife for your delivery. But I may be able to identify things about how your pregnancy is progressing that a midwife might not see."

"That is very kind of you, doctor," Mrs. O'Sullivan said. "If Mr. O'Sullivan insists, then I will see you. But it's a waste of your time—I'm fine."

Mary glanced up at him and smiled.

"Fine," Clancy said. "It's settled. You're not a spring chicken, Rebecca. You have to take care. Isn't that right, Dr. Wilson?"

"Yes, it's important for women of all ages to look after themselves with the utmost care, and some studies suggest that this is especially true for older mothers," James said. "In fact, there is a new medical field evolving that specialises in monitoring pregnancies. It's called 'obstetrics'. Doctors who specialize in it are developing new techniques that can ensure safety for mother and babe—especially if there's trouble."

"Well, I don't know," Mrs. O'Sullivan said. "I will defer to my husband on this matter. But I've never had a male attend to me in that way before …"

She was clearly nervous, so James said, "Don't worry, Mrs. O'Sullivan. If you're more comfortable with a midwife that's fine. But I assure you, I've attended a few women around here and many in Montreal where I trained."

"I'm sure she will be in to see you, Dr. Wilson," Clancy said, smiling at his wife in a 'no nonsense' way. "But right now, we must be going. It was a pleasure to meet you, Dr. Wilson." Clancy extended his hand and James shook it. Then the O'Sullivans said goodbye to Reverend Philpotts and James, and they left. James thought he saw Mary glance quickly back at him, but he couldn't be sure.

"They seem like a good family," James commented as he watched them walk away.

"Yes, a nice family," Reverend Philpotts said. "But I can't condone what Clancy does for a living—distributes liquor. I've only seen liquor create misery. And yet …" The Reverend shuffled his feet and looked down as he searched for the right words. "And yet, Clancy is a good man. I guess he's a good black sheep!" He laughed and bade James farewell.

However, as James turned to go, he called after him. "James!" James turned back. The Reverend took his shoulder. "I've heard that Bessie—Amos' girl—is missing. Do you know anything about it? The word is that she came to see you shortly before she ran away."

"I know a bit," he said cautiously.

The Reverend looked at him and, realising he was not going to volunteer any more information, finally said, "I can't imagine why she'd run off. She seemed like quite a happy child. She's been a rock for Amos since his wife died. A wonderful girl. I hope she's okay."

James murmured in agreement and left, but it made him think, *what would the Reverend think if he knew I'd done nothing for Bessie?* He had felt like babbling to the good reverend like a humiliated schoolboy, '*she made me swear not to do anything! What could I do?*'.

He headed across the road to the field. He walked along the path and when he reached the middle of the meadow, he had a feeling of being watched. He stopped and looked around the empty field but all he heard was the rustling of the tall grass in the breeze and the buzz of flies. He looked around and saw only the shadows of clouds drifting over the field. He searched the tree line. Nothing. He felt spooked, uncomfortable. Something *was* wrong, but he couldn't figure out what. He turned and walked home, imagining noises coming from the far woods and behind him.

Chapter 5
The Wilsons

LATER THAT DAY, JAMES RODE Sadie into St. John to visit his parents. Many of the city folks were leisurely strolling about town, dressed in their Sunday church clothes. To accommodate automobiles, more than half of the city streets had now been paved and James imagined that soon the whole city would be a network of ugly black asphalt, like Montreal. *And one day, the black asphalt snakes will probably reach out to Rothesay.*

He carefully guided Sadie over streetcar tracks in the road; he didn't want her to snag a hoof and sprain a ligament. The shops and warehouses were quiet as he rode around the harbour, the silence broken only by noise coming from the tenant housing nearby that housed the working poor, mostly Irish. There, children played in dirt yards, lines of laundry stretching above them from building to building, while adults leaned out windows to converse with others. They seemed happy enough despite their poverty.

As a child, he was never allowed to play on a Sunday like these children were. However, many times, he had slipped away from his parents to join his friends in play on a Sunday afternoon. He never saw anything wrong with it and he still didn't; he couldn't imagine God frowning upon children playing, even on Sunday. His parents probably knew where he was, but they never reprimanded him. They were loving and fair. He smiled.

He turned onto Douglas Avenue, where his parents lived. Douglas Avenue was the first residential street in the city to be paved. Tall elm trees lined the street of stately homes. The well-to-do folks lived here.

He rode into the backyard of his parent's house and tied Sadie to a post near the back door. Then he turned to look down at the quiet harbour that lay at the base of a rocky hill that fell from his parent's backyard, and was reminded of the dream he'd had last night. He shuddered. It made him anxious.

He entered his childhood home and met his mother in the kitchen. "I saw you come in, James," she said. "You look deep in thought." His mother was wearing a long white apron over a dark grey dress with lace sleeves and a lace collar. He noted the streaks of grey that ran through her dark hair.

"Hello, mother," he said. "I was reminiscing." He kissed her on the forehead. It was scary how easily she could read him. When she looked at him quizzically, he said, "I don't remember about what."

He sniffed the air and said, "It smells good."

"I'm cooking a roast of lamb," his mother said.

"Is father in the lookout?"

"Yes. If you're going upstairs, could you tell him to come down in fifteen minutes? Dinner is almost ready."

"Of course," said James, and then he asked, "How's he been?"

"Unfortunately, I think he's weaker, but he never says too much about his condition. You know him." She shook her head sadly and turned back to the stove.

James climbed the stairs to the second floor and then proceeded up another narrow flight of stairs to the viewing spot his family called the 'widow's peak'. Windows surrounded him, strategically placed in all four walls for a 360-degree view. His father sat by an open window, looking down at the harbour.

"Hello, father," James said.

"James, good to see you," Matthew exclaimed, turning around to smile at his son.

Matthew Wilson was an older version of his son, but where James had a full head of rich, youthful brown hair, Matthew's was now thin, straight and grey, parted on one side. He extended a frail, shaking hand to his son. James was surprised at how thin his father's face had become in the two weeks since he'd last seen him.

He grabbed the hand and bent down to kiss his father on the cheek. "Getting the air like your doctor told you to do, I see," he said.

"Yes, I spent most of the day up here, James. I find it too much trouble to go back down. I'm waiting for your mother to say, *'you're going to die of the cold, sitting in front of that open window,' as* if I won't die anyway."

He laughed until he started to cough up thick bloody phlegm. He reached for the cloths beside him and James saw the many bloody rags crumbled up in a basket nearby. "Looks like you've had a bad day," he said.

Matthew nodded and looked out onto the harbour. "Quiet day down there," he remarked.

James followed his father's eyes. A three-mast ship and two steamships were tied up along the docks, rocking quietly in the water. A fisherman was tending his nets by the shore. "The salmon catch has been good this year," James said.

"Aye," Matthew responded.

Neither said anything more for a moment, and then James ventured, "We discussed consumption the other night at the Medical Society meeting—there is nothing much new to treat it yet, though some research has been undertaken. Are you still taking the creosote capsules and Fowler's solution?"

Matthew made a face. "Yes. I'm taking both. But what's the good of them? I'm not sure they are helping. The tincture of morphia is a relief, though. That I know." Matthew shivered. "Would you mind passing me that blanket over there? That's a good lad."

James spread the blanket over his father, careful not to get too close. Today he had reacted before his brain said no and had lightly kissed his father's cheek. He knew the tubercle bacilli that was responsible for the spread of consumption—or tuberculosis, as it was now called—could be spread in this way. He felt sorrow that his father had the disease and wondered who he had contracted it from. The latest protocol for TB patients was to isolate them, and many municipalities were constructing sanatoriums to stop the spread of the deadly disease. St. John was planning such an institution at this moment, and James wondered if his father would wind up there. However, James had worked with many consumptive patients in Montreal and never contracted the disease, which made him wonder, *why do some people get the disease but not others?* It seemed he was immune—but nevertheless, he'd promised his mother he'd keep visits to his father short as a precaution. She didn't want to lose her son as well as her husband.

"I'm tired, James," Matthew said. "I've spent a year up here … reading … watching … and thinking. I'm tired of being sick, but I'm *more* tired of thinking and being alone."

"I know, father. It's a tough disease."

Matthew nodded, said nothing for a moment. Then turned and smiled. "How's it going with you?" he asked James.

"Fine, father. I've been busy." He looked away; his father could read him as well as his mother and would soon note that something was on his mind. Trying to distract the man, he asked, "Did you eat today, father?"

"An egg and some biscuits," Matthew said as he took another rag from his pile and coughed some more. His chest heaved as he struggled for breath after the coughing fit. James felt so useless. His father had financed his medical education and now he was a doctor, yet he could do nothing to help him the man he loved so much. It was unfair. Then Matthew said, "You do know we sold the business to Robert Beckwith this week?"

"I knew you were going to sell soon."

"No regrets? You like being a doctor?"

"Absolutely, father."

"Robert's done a good job running the business since I've been sick. I gave it to him for a fair price—I could have got more—but he's been so good to your mother and me. Besides, the money should be enough to keep your mother going for a long time and there will still be lots left over for you when she passes."

Talk like this embarrassed James. He hoped his father couldn't tell. He said, "I know the business meant a lot to you, and that it must have been hard for you to sell it. But I like being a doctor. And I have no interest in business."

"I know that. I knew that from the time your mother and I caught you cutting open that dead frog in your room. Remember?" They both laughed, sending Matthew into another fit of coughing.

"Dead frogs and selling goods aren't compatible!" Matthew said when he could finally talk. "I knew you were destined for bigger things. I'm happy, if you're happy."

"I'm very happy, father."

"Now you just need a good wife," teased his father.

James flushed a little and countered, "Leave me be, father! All in good time!" Then, pretending to change the subject, he asked, "Have you ever heard of a family by then name of O'Sullivan? They own a liquor distributing firm here in St. John."

"Yes. It's a good business, I hear," said Matthew. "They own the building on that sandy point over there." Matthew turned around in his chair and pointed. "But you must know that ...?" He looked at James questioningly. "They're nice people," he finally said when James didn't respond. "I believe they have a home out your way. I take it you've met them?"

"Yes," James said. "They go to St. Paul's church and Mrs. O'Sullivan is with child. She may need some medical attention and they spoke to me about it. I was just wondering if you knew them, that's all." Then, changing the subject, James added, "We better get downstairs. I promised mother we'd be down in fifteen minutes."

He shut the windows, helped his father down the stairs to his bedroom and got him propped up in his bed so he could take his meal there. Then James joined his mother in the dining room and stayed several hours after dinner to have tea with her.

James rode home later that night through a silent town. A fog had rolled in from the sea while he'd been visiting his parents. Other than a horse and wagon appearing out of the fog, going the other direction on Main Street, the night seemed too quiet. *Creepily* quiet.

He felt depressed and was very cold as he rode through the thick fog, and his thoughts turned to Bessie. *Where is she? Is she okay? Is she alive?* These worries, combined with the fact that his father was dying slowly before his eyes, made him uneasy. He felt empty and powerless. He wished he could fix things.

Chapter 6
The Discovery

THREE DAYS LATER, A POLICEMAN from St. John rode into James' yard while he was washing Sadie in the barn. James felt his stomach tighten.

The officer dismounted and started up the front stairs of his home.

"Officer!" James called. "In here."

The officer turned around and met James at the barn door.

"Dr. Wilson," the officer said, "I'm afraid we've found that missing girl. There's a dead girl in the Kennebecasis River."

James felt his stomach drop. He'd been hoping Bessie had just run away, but the awful truth sapped the strength from his body.

"I'd like you to see this girl and confirm who she is," the officer said. "Best you do it before we get her father too upset. You *did* know Bessie MacKenzie, didn't you? It was you came to the station with Amos MacKenzie, am I right?"

"Yes. Yes, I knew her officer," replied James.

"Then if you'd please follow me ..."

James went back inside the barn to saddle Sadie and then met the officer in the yard. The officer introduced himself as Officer Kimball. Together, they rode down the Rothesay Road until they came to Renforth Beach. Then they crossed the railroad tracks and left their horses tied to a tree on the edge of the beach.

"Over this way, Dr. Wilson," Officer Kimball said.

Kimball pointed to the end of the beach where the sand ended, and reeds grew. James could see a body floating amongst the reeds. A few people were standing around it. He followed the officer across the sandy beach, his feet slipping in the sandy slope. Waves broke upon the shore, sending ripples of stones falling into the river as they receded. The sound rolled down the beach towards the small form floating in the reeds.

The small crowd parted as he and the officer came close. "Drag her ashore now, fellas," Officer Kimball commanded several of the assembled men. They dragged the body on the beach and turned the small frame over.

It *was* Bessie. Her face was ghastly pale and swollen like dough. Strings of river-weed trailed from her lips.

Her glazed eyes were open, staring blankly at the sky. Her braids were soggy and loose, with bits of debris clinging to the hairs. She wore a white and blue dress, embroidered with little pink flowers. James imagined she and her mother had stitched these together, once upon a happy time … before sickness, death, and lost innocence entered their lives.

"So that's Bessie MacKenzie, Dr. Wilson?" the officer asked.

"I'm afraid so," James replied.

He was supposed to do something. He had to make an official pronouncement of death. Normally, he listened to the heart of the deceased with his stethoscope. He hadn't brought his. He dropped to his knees and felt for a pulse in her neck. He felt stupid taking the pulse of dead person. His face reddened and he bent his head. No one spoke; they seemed to be respectfully giving him time to complete his task. He felt like a charlatan; it took no great expertise to take the pulse of a corpse. He took his fingers away from her neck, closed her eyes, and removed the river-weed from her lips. He looked down and noticed that the pockets of her dress were filled with rocks.

Finally, he straightened and said, "I can't really determine the time of death." He didn't want to say, 'I now pronounce her dead'. A moron knew that.

"We'll take it from here, Dr. Wilson. Thank you for coming," Officer Kimball said, shaking his hand.

"Do you want me to tell her father?" James asked.

"You can come if you want, but it is our duty to inform the next of kin when there has been an unexpected death. You don't expect foul play, do you, Doctor?"

"No. She wrote a note," said James sadly, remembering Bessie's words.

"She meant business," the officer said. "You noticed the rocks in her pocket?"

"Yes."

"Hard to imagine what would drive a young girl to do such a thing." Officer Kimball took off his hat, scratched his head, and looked at him. "You know anything?"

James looked out onto Long Island in the middle of the Kennebecasis River. He had promised to tell all when they found Bessie. But it was hard. Two families would be devastated by what he had to say. Wilfred deserved punishment—but his family were innocent victims and they would suffer. *Amos!* How would he survive the death of his daughter and the knowledge that his own brother was indirectly and disgustingly responsible? He couldn't do that to Amos now. *Later,* he thought.

"Dr. Wilson?" the officer asked.

"Could I talk to you in private, officer?" James asked, putting his arm around the policeman's shoulder and leading him to the top of the beach. "I *do* know something," he said quietly to the man, "but I can't tell you now. You have to trust me. I will tell you in a week or so."

"You do know," Officer Kimball said seriously, "that it is an offence to withhold information?"

"I do. This was a suicide."

The officer assessed him with cautious eyes and said nothing for a moment. Finally he acquiesced. "All right," he said. "I'll be waiting to hear what you have to say, but I'm not interested in anything that isn't criminal activity."

"I know," James replied.

Officer Kimball told one of the men to take Bessie, and he and James went to deliver the terrible news to Amos.

Chapter 7
The Accusation

THREE WEEKS LATER, JAMES ENTERED the police station in St. John, determined to tell all. It would be hard, but it would also be a relief to share Bessie's secret. He had waited a respectful time to go to the police, because he thought Amos needed more time to grieve. But now, with Wilfred playing the grieving uncle and supportive brother to perfection, James could not remain silent any longer—now was the time to tell the truth.

"I'd like to speak to Officer Kimball," James said to the policeman at the reception desk.

"And who shall I say wants him," the officer responded.

"Dr. James Wilson."

"Just a minute." The officer left and went down the hall to the back of the building. He came back a few minutes later. "Second door on your right," he said.

Officer Kimball was sitting behind a desk in front of a window, waiting for James as he entered the room. "Come in, Dr. Wilson," he said. "I've been waiting for your visit."

He motioned James to take a chair facing his desk.

"I've been waiting to talk to you for Amos' sake," James said, "for what I have to tell you will hurt him very much. The information will either destroy him or cause murderous rage. I fear telling you the truth because of what it might do to Amos, but in the end, justice should be done—no matter what the consequences."

"I see," Officer Kimball said. He looked at him expectantly.

James' mouth felt dry. He had rehearsed this moment over and over in his mind. He hesitated. Perhaps he should spare Amos and let the whole matter drop—no one would ever know except him and Wilfred. No one would get hurt and life would go on. But could he live with the secret? Could he watch Wilfred and not be tortured? *No,* he decided. *Truth and justice are God's way, even if it is the tougher journey.*

Officer Kimball leaned back in his chair.

James knew his face must be flushing and true to form, he coughed. "Bessie was pregnant," he blurted out. "She saw me the day she disappeared."

Clearly the officer did not expect that. "Well I'll be …!" Officer Kimball said. "She was so young!" He shook his head. "She must have been humiliated and decided to kill herself. That's a shame, but hardly a crime. The children have such loose morals now-a-days—"

"It wasn't like that," James interrupted. "Bessie wasn't at fault. She was raped."

"She told you this?"

"Yes … the day she saw me … the day she disappeared."

The officer scratched his face and puffed out his cheeks. "Was she bruised? Cut? Did she have evidence of forced entry?"

"She was six months pregnant!"

"Really!" Officer Kimball stood up and walked around the desk with his hands behind his back. He leaned against the desk beside James and said, "I didn't notice and the funeral director made no mention of pregnancy."

"That doesn't surprise me. She wasn't very big for being six months along. Her father hadn't noticed either, and he lived with her every day."

"Does Amos know?"

"He does. Bessie told him the night she went missing."

"Mr. MacKenzie never told me," Officer Kimball said as he selected a pipe from a stand on his desk. Then he walked back behind his desk, opened a drawer, and took out a pouch of tobacco. He lit his pipe and asked, "And you believed her?"

"Pardon?"

"You believed the young miss? Don't you think a young girl like her would make up this story to cover up a lack of judgement, or loose morals, or to protect the boy?"

"I thought of that. Believe me, I was sceptical at the time and questioned myself for weeks afterward … but in the end, I believed her then and do now. It is hard to explain—you had to have been there—but I know she was telling the truth"

"And why didn't she tell us six months ago?"

"She was scared to tell anyone."

"Was she being threatened?"

"No. She was scared of hurting her father."

Officer Kimball puffed out his cheeks again and rubbed his rather large, pocked nose. "I imagine she was scared for herself … of what her father might do to her."

"Amos is a gentle and kind man," James said. "She was scared of telling her father who the rapist was because …" he shifted and coughed once more, "… because it was her Uncle Wilfred who raped her."

"Wilfred MacKenzie—Amos' brother? The gentleman with all those children, who was so good to Amos during the funeral? *That* Wilfred MacKenzie?" asked Officer Kimball in disbelief.

"Yes."

Kimball rubbed the back of his neck, and then his face. He sighed heavily, sat back, and looked at James. "Dr. Wilson," he said. "You have no proof. You have a little girl's say-so—a *dead* little girl's say-so, I might add—and your personal belief that she was telling the truth. I can't charge a man with no proof, let alone take him to court. Can you do better than that? Unless you can, it's conjecture."

James had not thought of what would happen after he told the police. "Can't you investigate?" he asked, his tongue tripping over his teeth.

"Investigate what? I supposed we could exhume her body and verify the pregnancy, but how would that lead to proof that it was Wilfred MacKenzie who put the baby there?"

"There must be *something* ... You could question him!"

"Dr. Wilson, even for a living woman to prove rape, there has to be evidence she fought to stop the man from raping her. There has to be bruises, broken bones, bloody noses—*something*. Without this kind of evidence, men can be falsely accused of rape when the affair is *consensual*. There has to be some protection under the law for men."

"I understand the rationale," said James, "but there must be times when the victim is unable to fight, or is in such fear for her life that she doesn't struggle, and no visible signs of violence are present!"

"I'm sure there are cases like that. But without physical proof, we can't take those accusations seriously. And even *with* physical evidence of rape, we get very few convictions."

James felt very tired. This was wrong.

"For all I know, Dr. Wilson, this might not even be a suicide. She could have been murdered. Maybe this was staged to *look* like a suicide. There were signs of trauma to the back of her head, but then again, she was in the water for three days and those marks could be from her head smashing against rocks. What I'm saying is, I can't be one hundred percent sure it was suicide and I can't prove it was murder. So worrying about whether she was raped is the least of my worries. Do you understand? I'm in a bind here."

James *did* understand. Officer Kimball was telling him that Bessie was unlikely to ever get justice for what was done to her, let alone for how she died.

"What did the coroner say?" James asked.

"She drowned. Apparently by suicide."

"Could it be possible Wilfred murdered her?"

"Look, Dr. Wilson," Officer Kimball said. "There's no proof of anything at this point. Right now, it seems a teenager died by putting rocks in her pocket and jumping in the river. I have no reason, except for your word, to suspect that anything more happened. So, while I can see you're upset, I suggest you drop the matter. Go back to your patients and pretend this never happened." Then Officer Kimball leaned forward and looked him in the eye. "And I'm not going to question Wilfred MacKenzie about raping the girl. I've no evidence to accuse him … and why put Amos through this turmoil if I can't do anything about it?"

James had nothing further to say. He felt stupid and was angry at himself. *If only I acted quicker.* He should have gone with Bessie and told Amos about the rape after she inadvertently disclosed who'd attacked her. *I was an indecisive fool!*

"Take heart in knowing that Wilfred is probably innocent, Dr. Wilson," said Kimball kindly. "But I thank you for bringing this to my attention."

James felt unworthy and embarrassed by the adulation. It was *his* fault that a young girl was dead; however, there was nothing more he could do. He shook the officer's hand and thanked him for his time. But as he left the police station, he vowed that somehow or other, Wilfred was going to pay.

Chapter 8

The Appendix

TWO WEEKS AFTER HIS MEETING with Kimball, someone pounded loudly on James' front door, awakening him in the middle of the night.

"Just a minute!" he yelled as he hurried down the hall, tying up his night robe while he ran.

He opened the door to see a fellow he had met but didn't know well, Mr. Thomas McGarrigle, standing there.

"Sorry to bother you, Dr. Wilson," Mr. McGarrigle said, "but my boy—Thomas—he's having terrible stomach pains and vomiting. He's been like that since late afternoon. We've been trying to hold off seeing you. We thought it might pass. But it's been getting worse. He looks awful pale ..." McGarrigle was very agitated.

"No bother," James said. "I'll come right away. Come in, Mr. McGarrigle. Please, just wait a moment while I put some clothes on … Ah, on second thought, would you be so kind as to saddle up my horse in the barn? I'll change and meet you there."

Mr. McGarrigle seemed pleased by the call to action and started running over to the barn before James had completely finished his instructions.

James dressed quickly and noted from his bedroom wall-clock it was a quarter past three in the morning. He collected his doctor's bag from the office and then hurried out to the barn. The late August air was cool, a welcome relief to the heat of this past month. He looked up and saw a million stars in the moonless night sky. At this time of night, the moon had settled behind a crest of hills, leaving the river valley James lived in quite dark.

Mr. McGarrigle was leading Sadie from the barn as James arrived, both of them mere shadows in the black night. "It's dark," McGarrigle said. "You follow me." He ran over to his horse and mounted it, and James followed him out of the yard on Sadie.

James knew very little about the family except that the McGarrigles lived about five miles upriver and young Thomas was named 'Thomas' after his father. He questioned the senior Thomas about the boy's symptoms as they rode along. McGarrigle said the pain began low in young Tom's belly, then he began vomiting and became feverish and confused. He had some diarrhoea, but no cough.

James hoped it was a simple case of catarrhal enteritis, diarrhoea caused by eating too many unripe apples, or perhaps by the quick change from hot to cool in the weather. Catarrhal enteritis would pass. But McGarrigle had indicated that the pain was more than just cramps—*appendicitis, maybe?*

As they rode, James reviewed the surgical technique for an appendectomy in his head in case he needed to perform this procedure at the McGarrigle home. It would be preferable to get young Thomas to St. John Public Hospital if he could, because the days of home appendectomies were gone … *despite what Dr. Peters thinks*, thought James. James was certain that the old ways should give way to the new, safer, better-researched ways of practicing medicine. He was old-fashioned about choosing horses over cars, but not about old ways when new ones were better for curing patients.

They turned off the road they were on and began heading away from the river, towards the McGarrigle home. They passed a field of hay on the right and a field of corn on their left, both swaying and rustling in the night breeze. Finally they reached the two-storey McGarrigle home. James admired the two large gables that rose up into the night sky above the upper windows. He could make out a large barn off to the side.

"You can hitch your horse up to the railing, there," Thomas said, indicating an area of the porch. James did so and entered the house with Mr. McGarrigle. He heard young Tom moaning as soon as he entered the front door.

"Oh, thank God you're here!" a woman said, coming towards them.

He assumed this was Mrs. McGarrigle. He didn't recognize her, though he was sure he'd been introduced at church. Though she appeared to be not quite forty yet, her hair was completely grey and was threatening to fall out of the loose bun precariously hanging to one side of her head. As she rushed over to them, wisps and straggles of hair floating about and dangling to her shoulders gave her a bedraggled look. Her face was round and James imagined it was usually pleasant and friendly, but at present she looked frantic.

Without introduction, Mrs. McGarrigle grabbed him by the hand and said, "This way, Dr. Wilson. He's been sick since this afternoon, and it's getting worse. I don't know what to do. He's in so much pain …"

Mrs. McGarrigle dragged him upstairs to Tom's bedroom. Tom lay on his bed curled up in the fetal position, moaning, rocking, and clutching his abdomen. His face was white and sweaty, with a mop of red hair plastered to his forehead. James guessed he was only about ten years old.

"Hello, Tom," James said. "I'm Dr. Wilson. I'm going to help you. I need you to turn on your back so I can examine your abdomen."

"I don't know if I can, sir," Tom gasped through chalky-pale, trembling lips. "It hurts bad if I move." He tried to turn onto his back and then with a cry of pain, froze.

"Listen, Tom," James said, "I'm going to help you turn over. I'll take your knees and lift them up as you turn your shoulders. Can you do that for me?" Tom nodded and James said, "Are you ready?"

Tom shook his head in affirmation. James completed the movement as quickly as he could, while poor Tom clenched his teeth and moaned. When the boy was on his back, he raised Tom's nightshirt and gently placed his hand on his abdomen. "Can you show me where the pain started, Tom?" he asked.

Tom passed his hand over the whole abdomen below his navel.

"And where is the pain now, Tom?"

"Maybe more here," Tom whispered, pointing to his right lower abdomen. "Mom thinks I was eating apples from Henderson's farm that weren't ripe. But I swear… I haven't ate any apples."

"I believe you, Tom," Mrs. McGarrigle said. "I was wondering at first, but not now." She looked at James with worried eyes.

James gently moved his hand over Tom's abdomen. It didn't feel too hard. There was no peritonitis or signs of a burst appendix. Then he slowly moved his hand to the right lower quadrant. He pressed harder when his hand was over the appendix, and Tom squealed. Then he took out his stethoscope and listened to the bowel sounds. They were diminished, but present.

"What do you think, Dr. Wilson?" Mrs. McGarrigle asked as James removed the stethoscope from his ears. She began wiping Tom's face with a damp cloth, every inch the worried mother.

James gently placed his hand over Tom's abdomen and felt for rigidity again. "It's definitely appendicitis," he said. He gave Tom's abdomen a final deep thrust and let go suddenly. Tom howled. "It hasn't burst," James said. "But it has got to come out."

"When?" Mrs. McGarrigle said worriedly.

"Tonight," said James. If the appendix burst, mortality was almost one hundred percent.

The parents looked stricken as James took a moment to consider what to do. He contemplated operating immediately, here in the home—the sooner the appendix came out, the less likely it was to burst—yet studies had shown far less post-surgical wound infections from surgeries done in the hospital. Further, he was not an experienced surgeon yet and would rather Dr. Bentley in St. John perform the operation than him.

Although he wasn't an accredited surgeon, Dr. Bentley had impressed James with his surgical skills and was the next best thing. Certainly he was more skilled and experienced at surgery than James, and it would be a good opportunity for James to observe, assist and learn.

"Do you have a good wagon, Thomas?" he asked with some urgency. "We have to take young Tom to St. John for an appendectomy."

"I do," Thomas replied.

"Well hitch up your horses and put plenty of blankets in the back," he added. "We'll have Tom lie down in the back and we will take him into town as fast as we can."

Thomas made quick work of getting the wagon ready and was back before Mrs. McGarrigle had finished packing clothes for young Tom. James and Thomas carried the boy, who groaned with each jostle, downstairs and out to the wagon. Soon they were off to the city. Mrs. McGarrigle sat in the back of the wagon with Tom, stroking his head which rested on her lap.

Tom howled in pain with each bump on the road. "Can't you give him anything, Doctor?" Mrs. McGarrigle implored.

"I wish I could, Mrs. McGarrigle, but I need him awake to tell me of any changes in his condition," James explained. He wished he *could* give Tom something for the pain; the constant jostling of the wagon was tormenting the young lad. He cringed with each cry from the boy.

As they neared the outskirts of St. John, James had Thomas stop the wagon so he could check young Tom. If need be, he would operate in the wagon, but he hoped it would not come to that. However, Tom would die if the appendix burst now. He needed to keep a close eye on it. He did not want to think he'd made a dreadful mistake by not removing the appendix at the McGarrigle home. If Tom died, some in the medical community would condemn his decision to bring the boy to the hospital as cowardice—and Dr. Peters would certainly be contemptuous—but to James, Tom's life was all what mattered. He was taking a chance by bringing him into St. John and not operating immediately, but surgery performed by a man more skilled than he, in sterile conditions, was what was called for here.

He carefully palpated Tom's abdomen and concluded that the appendix was still intact—there were no signs of peritonitis or inflammation of the abdominal cavity, but the area was very irritable to the slightest of pressure. He feared it might perforate soon.

Hold on, Tom," he said quietly. Tom was a brave boy and he was not going to let him die. He touched him on the cheek and bade his father drive on with haste.

When they arrived at the St. John Public Hospital, the sun was just rising. He and Thomas carried young

Tom into the out-patient area and laid him on a small bed. He had a nurse call Dr. Bentley at home. James explained the situation to Dr. Bentley, and he came to the hospital immediately from his home that was mere doors away. He agreed with James' diagnosis.

"We have no time to lose," he said.

Quickly they rushed Tom into the operating room, sedated him, and carefully cleaned and sterilized his abdomen. Then Dr. Bentley deftly made the first cut with a sterilized scalpel, separating layers of muscle as he opened the boy's abdomen. James helped, using retractors to hold the wound open while the nurse wiped blood. James admired Dr. Bentley's skill and confidence as he made the incision. He *could* have done this, but not with the dexterity Dr. Bentley displayed. He was relieved to know he'd made the right choice for young Tom and he was not embarrassed about getting help for this boy. This is the way it needed to be done—*and to hell with what Peters thinks about being a hero!*

He retracted the wound, opening it a bit wider so Dr. Bentley could see better. "Jeez!" Dr. Bentley exclaimed. "Will you look at that appendix! It's about to pop. Don't let the retractor touch it, James!"

James looked down to see the largest appendix he had ever seen—grossly distended and reddish-purple. He forced the retractors as far away from the appendix as he could, and the more he did so, the more the appendage seemed to fill the opening. Tom would probably die if it burst now; there would be no way to stop the infection. Months of compresses and drainage might help, but he had seen patients suffer through this ordeal for weeks and not survive. He wanted to spare young Tom this fate.

"Don't even breathe, James," Dr. Bentley said as he carefully reached around the appendix with some catgut in his hand. Then without seeing what he was doing, he tied a suture around the base of the appendix where it joined the large colon, trying to seal the poison inside the inflamed organ. Carefully removing his fingers from the incision, he obtained another catgut and repeated the procedure, tying a knot in the appendix stalk just above the previous one. Watching him, James was even more convinced he had made the right decision by calling Dr. Bentley in to do the appendectomy. Bentley *was* good.

"James," Bentley said, "I can't grab the appendix with the forceps, or it might burst, so I'll have to keep my hand here supporting it and stretching the stalk. Scissors," he commanded to the nurse.

James watched Dr. Bentley lower the scissors carefully into the wound beside the swollen appendix. He knew Bentley was blindly guiding the scissor tips into place between the two sutures while holding the appendix with his fingers. Sweat was glistening on his face and the neck of his surgical gown was wet. Dr. Bentley raised his head and asked the nurse to wipe his forehead. James made no comment.

Then Dr. Bentley huffed, "I'm there." James heard a snip and Bentley slowly lifted the appendix out of the cavity. Bentley's hand trembled as moved it safely away from the open wound in Tom's abdomen. The appendix burst open like a swollen fruit just as he laid it on the operating apron.

Chapter 9

The Call

TOM RECOVERED NICELY AND THE McGarrigles became good friends with James over the next few months. He came to know them as Anna and Tom, and he often found baked ham, pies, hay for Sadie and the odd bushel of corn, among other things, left at his door by these hard-working people.

He continued to see patients with the usual ailments; colds, sprains and one fractured arm. There were no more local pregnancies for him to tend to, but he had not forgotten about Bessie, nor had he yet forged a plan about what to do about Wilfred—though it wasn't for lack of trying. During idle moments, ideas consumed his thoughts, but every plan seemed foolish when revisited the next day. Finally, he resolved to confront Wilfred and inform him that he knew about the rape, and to tell him that Bessie's suicide was the result of a pregnancy caused by his terrible actions. However, so far he had not had the opportunity to be alone with the man. Wilfred's wife had given birth only a month ago, which was probably why he hadn't been seen at church— still James wondered if Wilfred had been intentionally avoiding him.

Conversely, Mary had *not* been avoiding him; in fact, Mrs. O'Sullivan seemed to make sure Mary was around whenever James came to check on how she was doing with her pregnancy. He hadn't taken the opportunity to ask Mary's parents if he could come calling more formally on Mary, though. Bessie's death had taken energy from his body and dampened his enthusiasm, making him feel a bit empty. However, he felt a jab of anticipation about seeing the young woman whenever he went to the O'Sullivans.

In September, he had a telephone installed. Not many in Rothesay had one except the well-to-do, but Tom McGarrigle's emergency made him realise that a phone was necessary in his profession if he wanted to save lives. His parents had one as well, and he used his newly installed phone to speak to his mother and stay updated about his father's condition. Other than that, because many people did not have phones, the phone had not rung once—so it was surprising when it *did* ring one morning in October.

He was in his office examining a boy who was complaining of a sore throat when it rang. He left the room to answer it. The caller turner out to be Dr. Peters, which was very surprising. "So nice to hear from you," James said. "You are the first to call me on my new telephone, other than my parents. To what do I owe the pleasure?"

"Dr. Wilson ..."

"Call me James."

"Quite," Dr. Peters said dourly. "Dr. Wilson," he continued, and James acknowledged the rebuke, "one of my duties as a board member of the St. John Public Hospital is to oversee the financial health of this institution. In doing so, I routinely look over the expenditures. I see a bill going out to a Mr. Thomas McGarrigle of Rothesay for expenses incurred from an appendectomy to a Thomas McGarrigle."

"His son," James volunteered.

"Yes. Well, I was wondering if you will be adding any expenses to this account."

"No. In addition, if I do so, it will be private. Is the bill very much?"

"It depends on who's paying, I suppose. Can they pay?"

"The McGarrigles are very fine people and if they don't have the money now, I know they will pay up eventually."

"Yes. I'm sure they will. Still … It's a shame."

"What do you mean?"

"That the appendectomy was done here."

He knew what Dr. Peters was inferring; he was letting James know that by bringing Thomas into town for the operation, he was making himself look weak and ineffectual as a doctor. "I weighed my options that night," he said firmly to Peters, "and I felt I had enough time to get young Tom to hospital."

"But I understand you nearly *didn't* have enough time."

"True. The appendix burst as soon as it was extracted."

There was no response from Dr. Peters.

"You're not saying," James finally said, "that I should have performed the appendectomy at home instead of in the hospital? Surely you know that operations have less post-surgical infection when done in the hospital setting? The latest studies have all shown that, and—"

"Young man," Dr. Peters interrupted. "I am quite aware of all the studies, but as I told you when you first came here, this is the *real* world. You chose to set up practise in Rothesay—no one told you to—and by doing so, you put yourself in a position where you sometimes will have to make hard choices to save your patients' lives. You got away with it *this* time, but you jeopardized the young fellow's life by dragging him all the way into the city with an appendix that was ready to rupture!"

James tried to calm his voice before he spoke. "Dr. Peters," he said. "That was *my* clinical decision at *that* critical time. I stand by that decision and I would do the same thing if I was confronted with the same scenario tomorrow."

Dr. Peters said nothing, until finally conceding, "And it turned out just fine. But I'm making a point you'd do well to take." He paused before continuing, "And I want to make you aware of another problem."

"What's that?" James asked. He was having a hard time keeping the anger out of his voice.

"I've heard some grumbling around town. Some of your fellow doctors are saying you're interfering with their patients."

"If you're talking about physicians who tend to the people of Rothesay, I'll have you know that I always recommend to patients who come to me that they should seek council from their own physicians. However, many don't want to make the journey into St. John, and so they plead for my attention. What am I to do in such cases? I have never attempted to steal patients nor will I ever do so, but I won't turn them away. And I insist that they inform their physician of my intervention and follow up with him as need be."

"You are treating some very prominent citizens in Rothesay, people who used to be served by very able physicians in St. John. It's raising a few feathers among your colleagues. I'm just warning you, Dr. Wilson."

He detected malice in Peters' voice, not concern. "Well thank you for your concern," he said begrudgingly. "I'll take it under advisement, Dr. Peters."

"Certainly," said Dr. Peters. "And please don't feel shy about asking your more experienced colleagues for advice. We understand. We were young once too and have probably been through similar situations to that of the young MacKenzie girl."

James felt the blood drain from his face. His legs went weak as he realized that no one except Officer Kimball and he knew about Bessie's situation. He'd been warned that Peters had power and eventually got to know everything that went on in St. John, but did the police not have a code of confidentiality?

Sensing his discomfort, Peters prodded, "You know, the young girl that drowned herself this summer. My understanding is that you saw her the same day she killed herself."

James said nothing, but he was furious.

"You probably wish you had asked one of us for advice now," Peters continued. "But we all make mistakes—that's how we learn."

"I don't know what you heard, or who said anything to you of this," James said coldly. "But what was said that day between Bessie and me is confidential. I will not lower myself to speak to innuendos—"

"I'm not implying anything," Dr. Peters interrupted. "I'm merely saying—"

"YOU'RE NOT SAYING ANYTHING *ELSE*," shouted James. "And you're *not* repeating this story around town." He struggled to gain control, adding, "But I will say this … I'm not sorry I didn't call you or anyone else that day. DO YOU UNDERSTAND?" He slammed the earpiece back onto the cradle of the phone.

He lowered his head and closed his eyes. He was shaking. He had forgotten about the young lad in his office, who must have heard the shouting. He had to compose himself before he went back in.

That damn Peters. Now everyone would know about Bessie coming to him that day. *God knows what they will think!* Probably that whatever he said or did drove her to suicide. That he was uncaring, or incompetent. Was he uncaring? *No.* But he deserved whatever moniker they decided to give him. He *did* fail. He failed a little girl, and now she was dead.

"I'll be back in a moment," he called into his young patient. Then he walked down the hall, opened the door, went outside and rammed his fist into the side of the house.

Chapter 10
Influenza

JAMES' FATHER PASSED AWAY TWO days after Christmas. James was surprised to see Dr. Peters sitting in the crowd at the funeral. They had not spoken to each other since the telephone call. He imagined Dr. Peter's presence was more out respect for his father, or for pretence of respect, than to give sympathy and support. After all, his father had been an important man in St. John.

In the days following Matthew's death, James regretted not having discussed the Bessie MacKenzie incident with him; his father would have given good advice. But Matthew had been so sick that James had felt it selfish to discuss *his* problems with his ill father. In retrospect, he bet his father, despite feeling wretched, would have welcomed solicitation of advice from his only son, and James had no doubt the advice would have been sensible, comforting, and wise.

But now he had to quit dwelling in the past, and that included stopping thinking about Bessie MacKenzie too. He needed to stop torturing himself. But he couldn't. Bessie haunted him like a ghost. The vision of her rocking back and forth on his examination table, her head bowed while she quietly cried, appeared to him throughout the day. He needed to confront Wilfred and resolve these obsessive thoughts to find peace. As yet, however, he hadn't had the opportunity.

James attended many church functions during the Christmas season—even though his father's deteriorating health and subsequent death made him feel less than festive. He hoped for an opportunity to speak to Wilfred alone, but Wilfred stayed near his wife at all times.

Finally, one evening after the children's Christmas nativity play, he bucked up the courage to ask Wilfred if he could have a word with him in private. Wilfred agreed— but later that evening he managed to slip away and James never saw him again.

During the first week of January, he had no time to dwell on his father's death or even on Wilfred, because an influenza epidemic broke out in the community and he was busy tending to the sick. He was called out to many home visits in the middle of the night, and the stress of it all made him weary and dull as the weeks went by. He slept when, and wherever, he could. The days seemed surreal.

In a way, he was grateful for the epidemic. The mind-numbing work and fatigue made the vision and memory of Bessie less frequent as the weeks went by.

He remembered his father at odd times, like when he was sounding a chest or examining a throat, or during the cold rides from house to house. The townsfolk acknowledged his loss and were most appreciative of his attention to their flu-stricken family members in his time of sorrow. Many seemed embarrassed that they had to ask him for care while he was grieving, and many more told him how glad they were to have a doctor in Rothesay now.

He felt guilty for not spending more time with his mother and asked her to move in with him. She told him his duty was to his patients and that she wished to remain in her home.

He did what he could to help his patients fight against influenza. He routinely advised a hot bath, followed by a hot drink of lemonade for the aches and pains, and strict bed rest until the fever broke. He also often prescribed the application of a mustard poultice to a congested chest. He was sometimes tempted to relieve suffering from the high fever of influenza by prescribing antipyrine, but he'd been taught not to intervene unless a patient's temperature caused delirium, and medical texts supported this. Fever and sweating were the best and quickest routes to beat influenza. He had no way of knowing that within a few years this would prove to be a false, and doctors would no longer hesitate to treat fever. He sometimes prescribed Dover Powder, which contained tincture of opium, for a severe cough. He listened carefully for pneumonia, an often-fatal diagnosis.

An elderly lady died three weeks into the epidemic, but no other deaths occurred in the Rothesay district though many infants and elderly people succumbed to the influenza epidemic in the city. He felt it was just luck and not his skill that more people didn't die around Rothesay, but the townspeople seemed to think otherwise—they embarrassed him by showering him with praise for his ability, attention, and care during the influenza epidemic.

By the second week of February, the epidemic was almost over in Rothesay. However, at that time the weather turned frightfully cold. James felt a quietness descend upon the community. It was as if the cold snap provided a deep breath of relief for the town as the people of Rothesay got back on their feet.

James spent this welcome down-time time splitting wood, resting, reading, and visiting the odd patient. He had neglected his accounts during the hectic last month, so he spent time updating his books. He couldn't remember exactly who he saw and when, but it didn't matter—he had received more money in the past month than he had in the previous three combined. He was satisfied and didn't care if he hadn't been paid for all of the visits. He *did* wish people would stop sending food—he couldn't eat it all.

Overall, James was content; he felt needed during the influenza epidemic, which was a good feeling. This feeling was why he became a doctor and why he chose Rothesay to work—he'd seen it as the place where he could do the greatest good. The feeling of satisfaction tempered his lingering guilt about Bessie a bit. Her memories came more frequently in the lull, but held less sting. They were more like a weight, a dull ache, than the stab to his heart they used to be. He imagined he would have to live with this dull pain forever, and felt he deserved to do so. He began to think that even confronting Wilfred—which he still planned to do—wouldn't ease the guilt. He resigned himself to this.

On February 15, James received a note inviting him to a party at the O'Sullivan's on the last day of the month. He was pleased but also wary. Nothing would make him happier than this opportunity to see Mary in her home and perhaps get to know her … but he wasn't sure that the ghost of Bessie was ready to let him.

Chapter 11
The Party

ON THE DAY OF THE party, James arrived right on time. He hitched Sadie up to a post in the yard of the O'Sullivan home and climbed the stairs to the front door. It was dark still in the evening, so late in February, and so the house was lit up like a Christmas tree, candles in almost every window. He admired the deck that wrapped around the front of the house and down the sides.

A young lady he didn't know met him at the front door and took his hat and coat when he entered the house. "Dr. Wilson!" he heard, and before he knew it Mrs. Mawhinney had grabbed his arm. "How nice to see you here! It's quite the affair."

It didn't surprise him that Mrs. Mawhinney had met him at the door instead of Mrs. O'Sullivan; Mrs. Mawhinney was such a busybody she probably knew in advance who was coming and had been waiting for him. "I've never seen so many people at one party," she continued. "They've invited everyone—even the Catholics!"

She locked her arm in his and led him into the great room. Then she pointed to the far wall and said, "There is punch over there … and pastries, meats, and sweets on the table besides. I'm sure Mr. O'Sullivan can get you liquor if *that's* what you want—God knows he has enough of it," she added with obvious disapproval. "Of course, *I* never drink. Liquor has never passed these lips, and never will." With that, she turned up her nose and went back to her post by the front door.

The great room was full. James saw Clancy O'Sullivan work his way through the crowd towards him. "Dr. Wilson," he said. "So glad you could come."

"*James*, Clancy," James told him. "Please call me James. And thank you for inviting me—and for holding this party for the community."

"I thought we could all use a pick-me-up after that dreadful month with all the sickness. Speaking of pick-me-ups, can I get you a drink?"

"That would be fine," James replied. "A glass of red wine, please."

Clancy left to fetch the drink and James searched the room for Mary while he waited, but there was no sign of her. Clancy returned with the wine and then excused himself as another guest arrived. James glanced at Mrs. Mawhinney, still at her spot by the front door. She huffed and looked away, obviously disapproving of his glass of wine. He found this immensely satisfying.

After just two sips of the stuff, he felt the warmth of the wine course through his body and flush his face. He was not much of a drinker and decided to take it slow. He walked about and mingled with the other guests, chatting about the turmoil of the past month and the news from Europe. England was alarmed about how Germany was building up its military force and feared invasion. Talk of what Germany was up to dominated most of the conversation in the room.

"Dr. Wilson!" Mrs. O'Sullivan called to him as she emerged from the kitchen. "How great it is to have you here." She rubbed her pregnant belly and smiled. "It won't be too long now ..." she said.

James kissed her hand. "How good to see you, Mrs. O'Sullivan," he said.

"Oh, please call me Rebecca," she told him. He smiled. It was amazing how open Rebecca was; she was unafraid to show off her condition and she didn't care what people thought of her. James loved that she was a woman who spoke her mind.

"It's so good of you and your husband to hold this party for the townspeople," James told her. "I'm so pleased to be here." Mrs. O'Sullivan smiled her thanks and James decided now was a good time to ask her what, to him, was a rather pressing question. "Mrs. O'Sullivan," he asked a bit timidly, "I know your husband convinced you to have a doctor present at the time of your delivery—and I agree this is a very good idea—but I'm wondering if you mentioned this to Dr. Peters, as I requested. He is your family doctor, is he not?"

"Yes, he's our family doctor. And no, I haven't mentioned it because I haven't seen him. I've always had a midwife attend me, you know, and he's never been to one of my children's births yet. I don't think he even knows I'm pregnant, unless Clancy's told him. Why?" She looked at him, puzzled, as she had every time that he brought the subject of Peters up.

"It's professional courtesy, ma'am. As his patient, he should be the attending physician—or at least he should be notified that you have selected someone else to attend you."

"Well, if it will make you feel better, I will pay him a visit and let him know my thoughts … but I can't see what business it is of his who helps me deliver this baby. Anyway, he'd never come out here to Rothesay in the middle of a night. His *majesty…*" She laughed and covered her mouth with the back of her hand. "Forget I said that, Dr. Wilson." She smiled like a naughty schoolgirl and turned away.

"Mrs. O'Sullivan," he called after her. "Remember, I told you not to be on your feet too much today!"

"Yes, Doctor," she said. She rolled her eyes and walked away, shaking her head.

James hoped she would keep her promise and inform Dr. Peters that she'd been allowing him to monitor her pregnancy. He imagined Peters would be *very* irritated when he found out James was looking after Mrs. O'Sullivan, even if it *was* at her request. But it would certainly be best if Peters heard about it now rather than after the delivery. He wanted Peters to know it was something the O'Sullivans requested so that he wasn't accused of stealing patients again. He was certainly surprised to find out that Rebecca didn't think Peters knew she was pregnant—and if he did know, why had he not called on the woman? After all, from what he knew, Rebecca had nearly died during her last delivery. If he *did* know she was pregnant, then what kind of medical care was that?

A few minutes after his discussion with Rebecca, James accepted a second glass of wine from Clancy and began mingling again. He was laughing with Arnold Freeman, a master carpenter, when he saw Mary coming down the stairs outside the great room. He mumbled something to Arnold, but he wasn't sure what he said because words failed when she entered the room.

She looked at him and his heart jumped. She was beautiful. Delicate. Graceful. Energy seemed to follow her and her presence swallowed the souls around him until he saw only her.

He gawked like a lovesick schoolboy—he *felt* like a lovesick schoolboy. He tried to wipe the foolish expression from his face. He hoped she hadn't noticed.

Then suddenly Mary was coming towards him. His heart began pounding like a galloping horse. His knees felt like rubber and his hands broke into a sweat. He took a gulp of wine.

"Dr. Wilson," Mary said, extending her hand, "so nice of you to come."

"It's an honour to be here, Mary," he stammered. He took her hand in his and kissed it. His lips tingled from the softness of her skin. He felt he had to say something more, but words failed him. Rebecca O'Sullivan saved him by suddenly appearing.

"Are the children in bed, Mary?" she asked.

"Yes, mother. They're all fast asleep except for Timothy and Samuel—they're reading."

"Thank you, Mary," said Rebecca.

"I was just saying that it was nice of Dr. Wilson to come to our party, mother," Mary commented gracefully.

"Yes, indeed. Very nice," Mrs. O'Sullivan responded.

James was almost too nervous to speak. "I'm glad to be here," he managed to say once more. *I've already said that,* he thought. *I'm such an imbecile.*

"It's been awfully cold lately, hasn't it?" Mary asked.

"Quite," he said, appalled at how high-handed that sounded. He needed to add something more intelligent and he desperately searched his mind for topics related to the weather … snow… cold… frostbite—*anything!*

"I'll leave you two to talk about the weather," Mrs. O'Sullivan said. "I must go and see about the food." She started to walk away and then turned to say, "And *then* I'll get off my feet, Dr. Wilson." She smiled and left.

"She had better take it easy," James said to Mary.

"Mother can be pretty stubborn," Mary replied.

He had never seen such green eyes. Her skin was as smooth and translucent as fine china. He felt energized in her presence. It had been awhile since he'd felt anything but remorse. Bessie MacKenzie and his father's deteriorating health had dragged him down so much that he forgot how nice some things could feel. *Now, if only I could talk!*

"Good crowd," Mary commented, breaking the silence that was growing between them.

"It certainly is," he responded. "It is awfully nice of your parents to have this party and invite the whole community."

"Father loves a party."

He was thinking furiously about what to say next, when Clancy called out, "There's my princess!" and came over to give Mary a big hug. James had never seen such outward display of emotion from a man before. The O'Sullivans seemed to have no reservations about hugging and kissing in public. It was strangely refreshing.

"You're monopolizing my daughter, James," Clancy said. "Wonderful girl ... wonderful. She'll make someone a fine wife someday. I just got her out of Boston *just* in time. She was catching the attention of more young men then molasses does flies."

"Father!"

"Well it's true. You are a beauty, my dear." Clancy hugged Mary again and kissed her on the cheek. James had never touched anyone like that, not even his own mother.

"Father, you've had too much to drink. I think I'll leave and let you two gentlemen talk." Mary rewarded James with a smile and walked away.

"She *is* a beauty—isn't she, James?" Clancy said, watching her walk away. "There *were* many fine prospects for her in Boston—fine young men from good families. I'll probably take her back to Boston in a year or two, but right now, she's too valuable to her mother to be married off."

James felt annoyed with Clancy for interfering with the chat he was having with Mary and now his comment about taking her to Boston for a husband added to the irritation. It would seem that Clancy didn't consider him a potential husband for Mary; that he wasn't up to their standards. He swallowed his pride, though, and instead agreed, "She *is* splendid. You have a lovely daughter, Clancy."

Clancy nodded and took a swig of beer. By now, James had almost finished his second glass of wine and his head felt light. He hadn't felt like this for some time. The night he obtained his medical doctorate was probably the last time he'd drunk spirits. He had gone out afterwards with his colleagues, to downtown Montreal, to celebrate. He ended up walking home with Joseph Thompson, stumbling down sidewalks and singing songs into the wee hours. And as wonderful as the evening had been, it was a night he regretted dreadfully the next day. He knew he should stop after this glass.

At that moment, Reverend Philpotts walked by. Clancy and James greeted him, James noting that the good reverend was also enjoying a glass of wine. When the reverend moved on, James said, with a slight slur, "Clancy, if you don't mind me asking, how did an O'Sullivan become a member of the Church of England? No offence, but most O'Sullivans are Catholic."

Clancy placed a hand on his shoulder. "James, me boy," he said. "There's only one God, isn't there? And I don't think he gives a rat's ass where you pray."

"So, what do you think of the unrest that's in Ireland? Protestants and Catholics at each other …"

"I think the English should get the hell out of Ireland, and then you'll see the Catholics and Protestants live in harmony," Clancy replied.

"But wouldn't the Catholic majority swallow the Protestants? The English are only trying to defend their rights—"

"Defend!" Clancy barked. "They're only trying to defend Englishmen and the land they stole from Ireland."

James hadn't meant to anger Clancy, so he coolly said, "I don't know about such things, Clancy. I was just asking. But tell me, why *do* you worship at the Church of England?" Clancy seemed to have no love for the English—so why was this Irishman a practising Anglican?

Clancy looked long and hard at James and then his countenance changed from agitation to calm. "Love, me boy," he said. "My father fell in love with this English girl—my mother, God rest her soul. There was not a chance in hell they could marry in Ireland at *either* church. So they fled Ireland without telling anyone and got married here in Canada by an Anglican priest. The priest was a drunkard and didn't care that 'O'Sullivan' was not your normal, Anglo-Saxon, Church of England name. So, there you have it. My parents raised me in the Church of England and I'm comfortable there. Except when I hear narrow-minded Anglicans belittle Catholics."

James wondered why Clancy acted and sounded so Irish if he was Canadian-born but, deciding he'd asked enough questions for one day, he remained silent. Instead, against his better judgement, he took another glass of wine from the same young lady who'd taken his coat at the front door.

"Excellent wine, Clancy," he remarked, his head floating. "And I appreciate your attitude—it irks me also how people judge others based on their different ways and beliefs. Oh, and by the way. I didn't mean to offend you with my questions."

Clancy laughed and clapped his shoulder again. "No offense taken, my fine fellow. You should know us Irishmen get riled up easily when we talk of the homeland."

Clancy was slurring his words and James thought he probably was too. The thought made him laugh. He felt so relaxed; God, it felt good. It had been a hard six months.

His laugh abruptly died when he saw Wilfred standing on the other side of the room. James felt a jolt run through his body, as if lightening had struck him. Where did *he* come from? Why hadn't he seen him before now?

Wilfred didn't seem to be aware of James. James watched him clap Richard McGovern on the back and break into a laugh that carried above the general din of the crowd. James finished his glass of wine in one draw, excused himself from Clancy's company, and headed towards Wilfred, face flushed, and not just from the wine.

He stopped mid-stride when he saw Mary glide toward Wilfred and stop to make conversation. Wilfred bowed and kissed Mary's hand, speaking to her with all the self-assurance James wished he had. Wilfred seemed so prim and proper, like the perfect country gentleman. James tightened his hands into fists, spun around, and left the room.

He spent the rest of the evening in the library, but came out to spy on Wilfred from time to time. He wasn't going to let him get away this time, but he didn't want to make a scene, either. He sipped his fourth glass of wine; he knew it had to be the last. Occasionally one of his patients or a friend wandered into the room and struck up a conversation. He feigned delight at seeing them, but his mind was elsewhere.

Three fellows, one on banjo, one on accordion, and another on harmonica, started to play in the great room, and in no time people were dancing. James was careful to remain hidden from Wilfred, but managed to watch Mary laughing and dancing in the arms of several young men, which made him jealous. They were holding *his* Mary. They were making her laugh. Wilfred's presence was ruining his chance to be with Mary, to show her he was more than solid, reliable Dr. Wilson. *Would she ever consider me as a husband?* Probably not—he had to talk first. That would be a good first step. He chastised himself for his cowardice He resolved to forget about Wilfred this night; he wanted to be with Mary.

He just was entering the great room when he saw Wilfred place his filthy mitts on Mary's small waist and take her delicate hand in his. They moved to a waltz across the floor. Mary laughed at something Wilfred said and looked up at him as they twirled. She had no concern about this man, and why should she? No one knew about what he had done to Bessie except him. James felt nauseous. This was difficult to watch.

His impulse was to walk away, but he willed himself to stand his ground. He stood ramrod straight on the edge of the dance floor and finished his wine despite the sickness growing in his belly.

When the dance finished, Wilfred spoke briefly to Mary, kissed her hand, and then bowed. He left her and went over to speak to his wife. James was surprised Wilfred's wife was here; it had only been a few months since she'd had the baby. She looked at her husband with an expression he couldn't quite recognize … perhaps with admiration. *Perhaps she is thinking what a lucky woman she is for having such a wonderful husband. If she only knew!*

Then Wilfred headed out the front door. James was afraid Wilfred had seen him and was leaving. He followed him outside.

Chapter 12
Wilfred

It was below freezing outside in the night air. James wrapped his woollen jacket tighter around his body. He hadn't seen Wilfred get his coat—was he making a fast get-a-way?

James scanned the deck and the stairs. He saw no one. He heard nothing. No horse moved. He could only hear his own breathing, breath that turned to vapour in front of his eyes. Then he heard it. A faint sigh. From the yard.

He walked as quietly as he could down the stairs. Shapes formed as he gained his night vision, trees, bushes … until finally he spied Wilfred by a snow bank. He was urinating.

He walked over. "Hello, Wilfred," he said. "Mind if I join you?" He fell in beside him and unzipped his pants.

"Oh … Hi, Doc," Wilfred said. "Were you at the party? I didn't see you there."

James detected nervousness in his voice. He said nothing.

"We better watch it, Doc," Wilfred said. "We better do our jobs quick or get frostbite on our dicks." He laughed at his own wit, but it rang false. James hummed a tuneless song but didn't respond. After a moment of silence, Wilfred said, "Great party, Doc. See you later." He zipped up his fly and started to leave.

"I know what you did," James said, watching his urine disappear into the snow bank.

Wilfred stopped. "Pardon me?"

James said nothing. He finished urinating and zipped up his fly. He was relishing this moment. He had rehearsed it repeatedly in his head for months. He was going to enjoy this and take his time. He turned around slowly to face Wilfred. "You heard me," he said. "I know what you did."

"What did I do?"

"What you did to Bessie … your own niece."

"What are you talking about?"

James advanced closer, so he could see Wilfred's face when he realised James knew the secret. He didn't want to miss this. "You think I drowned Bessie?" Wilfred stammered. "She was my niece … you … you … sick bastard! Bessie took her own life. What reason do you have to accuse me of such a terrible thing?"

"I didn't say you killed Bessie. She committed suicide because she was pregnant. She was ashamed," James said bluntly. "She was a confused little girl. She didn't want to hurt her father by telling him," James said. He wanted Wilfred to squirm. He wanted to see the anxiety build, as Wilfred asked the question that James knew the answer to.

The question came like he knew it would. "So, *what* then?" Wilfred finally asked. "What are you accusing me of?"

"You *raped* Bessie," James said slowly. It felt good to say it, a relief.

"She told you that?" Wilfred hissed.

"No. I just know. Let's leave it at that. It doesn't matter how I know, does it? I *know*."

"Well it's not true! What a filthy, dirty, rotten thing to say." James could hear the strain in Wilfred's voice as he restrained himself from yelling. "She was my dear, sweet niece," he hissed. "How dare you accuse me of such a thing!"

"I know—it sickens me too."

"You have *got* to be drunk!" Wilfred jeered.

"I've had a few, but I know the truth. I have no *proof* that you molested Bessie. The proof died with her. So relax, you're going to get away with it. I won't tell Amos because he'd probably kill you. I tried to tell the police, but as they pointed out there is no proof. So congratulations, Wilfred. You committed the perfect crime. But I pity you, because for the rest of your life you will know your niece killed herself because of you. You will have to deal with your own guilt, and I believe God will make you pay for your actions—if not in this world, then the next."

"I did *not* do this." Wilfred declared forcefully, moving closer to James. Wilfred looked around before returning his gaze to him, probably for witnesses should he choose to hit him. "And I am not standing out here in the cold," he continued, "listening to anymore of this rubbish. If you choose to speak of this to anyone—if you spread sick rumours around the village—I will deny this as garbage, which it is. You are new to this community, and I was born and raised here. Who do you think they'll believe?"

"I don't intend to say anything to anybody, as I said. But don't you ever cross my path ..."

"Don't *you* ever threaten or tell *me* what do to!" Wilfred warned, bringing his face so close to James' face that he smelt the stink of his breath.

James stood his ground and glared back at him, their faces almost touching. "Or what?" he asked. "You sick bastard."

Wilfred surprised him with a shove that sent him backwards into the snow bank. James immediately felt cold and wetness penetrate his wool jacket. He squirmed, rolled over, and then knelt in the snow to get his breath, shocked by the sudden violence. He grimaced when he put his bare hand into the snow to push himself up. "YOU BLOODY, IGNORANT, SICK BASTARD," he yelled at Wilfred, when he got to his feet.

"Shut up!" Wilfred grunted. He hit James with a blow to the abdomen that doubled him over. James couldn't breathe. Wilfred then hit him with an uppercut to his face that dropped him again into the snow bank. Then Wilfred stood over him and warned, "Don't you ever accuse me of such a thing again—or tell *me* what to do!"

Wilfred's voice sounded like he was talking from far away. James saw dark spots on the snow before him. Was he bleeding? Or were his eyes playing tricks? Wilfred's voice turned into gibberish as a ringing noise swelled and drowned out all other sounds. He felt weak. He struggled to a sitting position, hung his head between his knees, and breathed deeply. He struggled to remain alert; he might freeze to death if he passed out in this cold.

Slowly the spots in front of his eyes receded and the ringing sound diminished. A splotch of darkness on the snow between his knees appeared. He *was* bleeding, a steady stream of blood falling from his face onto the ground before him. His nose and jaw throbbed with pain. He spat out a clot of blood. Searing pain flashed along his right jaw to his ear. His vision wavered like ripples on water. Nausea. *I have to remain conscious*, he thought. He closed his eyes again, dropped his head even lower between his knees and breathed deeply. After a few minutes, he slowly opened his eyes; his vision was better. The bleeding had slowed to a drip, but now bloody drool was hanging down from his mouth to the snow. He carefully wiped his mouth with his sleeve and rose to his knees. He remained kneeling until he was sure he could stand up.

Wilfred wasn't around. He heard laughter and music coming from the O'Sullivan home—no one had seen what had just happened. But he couldn't go back inside like this. He staggered over to Sadie and grabbed the saddle for support. Sadie snorted a welcome. He rested his head on the leather saddle until he gained some strength and then untied an extra blanket he kept rolled up behind the saddle. His hands shook as he struggled with the ties. His body trembled violently as he wrapped the blanket around him. He had never felt so cold.

His head throbbed painfully as he opened his mouth to stop his teeth from clattering and jolts of white-hot pain seared the side of his face. His mouth trembled uncontrollably and it hurt to open it but he had to, as the pain created by the violent gnashing of his teeth hurt even worse.

He grabbed the saddle horn with trembling hands, braced his foot in the stirrups, and tried to swing up onto the saddle. He could barely raise his other foot. He tried a few more times before he conceded that he didn't have enough strength to mount his horse. He needed help.

Reluctantly, he stumbled back through the yard and up the stairs of the O'Sullivan home. He pulled himself hand-over-hand along the railing to the front door. He opened the door, staggered in, and collapsed against a wall. The young girl who'd opened the door for him earlier in the evening screamed.

Clancy happened to be coming into the entrance hall from the great room at that moment. At the sight of James, he yelled, "WHAT IN GOD'S NAME HAPPENED TO YOU?" He ran over, grabbed him, and lowered him into a chair by the door. The hallway quickly filled up with people.

"Slipped on the ice," James mumbled, "and fell against a wagon. Right on my face! Nearly knocked myself out."

"My poor man!" Rebecca O'Sullivan said, running over. "Let's get him into the kitchen and Mary—you get a face cloth and a basin of water."

"I'll be alright, Mrs. O'Sullivan. I'll just rest a minute and then go home."

"Nonsense!" she said. "We're going to clean you up and see to your wounds. No fuss! Now the doctor has to listen to *me*."

Rebecca told Clancy and another man to help him into the kitchen. He told them he was fine, but they ignored him, each grabbing him under one shoulder as they carried him into the kitchen.

"Sit him down here," Rebecca commanded. "Now you men, *get*. I've looked after my share of bloody noses around here."

Mary arrived with the basin of water and Rebecca began wiping the blood from his face. When she'd cleaned his face, she surveyed the damage and said, "You'll live." Then she looked at Mary and said, "Mary, will you look after the good doctor for a minute? Our guests will probably want to know what happened to Dr. Wilson and I will go and tell them." She turned back to him and said, "You're in good hands. Mary has wiped almost as many bloody noses as I have."

"I'm fine," he reassured Mrs. O'Sullivan.

Rebecca left and Mary sat in front of him. "You poor man!" she said. She gently wiped the blood from his face. He flinched when she touched his jaw. "Does it hurt?" she asked.

"Just a bit. I think my jaw may be broken. Is it swollen?"

"Quite a bit. I'll be careful."

He closed his eyes. Her touch was so gentle. She was so close.

"Are you okay?" Mary asked.

"Fine. I'm just resting. You are very good."

"I've had lots of practise with all the brothers I have."

"Did I break my nose?"

"It looks straight to me … swollen … hard to tell, but I think it's alright."

It hurt to talk, but it was worth the pain. He was finally talking to Mary. He watched her as she wiped his face. For a moment, their eyes met and she smiled.

"Your lip is split, Dr. Wilson," she said.

"James. Please call me James."

She smiled, threw the cloth in the basin and said, "There. That's the best we can do for now. That was quite a fall."

He was sorry she was finished. "You are very kind, Mary," he said. "You didn't hurt me at all. You're the best nurse I've ever had the pleasure to meet."

"Thank you, Dr. Wilson … ah … James."

He and Mary left the kitchen and headed out the hallway for the front door. His legs felt stronger now. Many townspeople expressed their concern, and he mumbled reassurances to them that he was okay. Rebecca took control, told everyone to leave him alone, and led him to the door. "You can stay here tonight if you wish," she said.

"No. I'm fine. I want to get home but thank you very much—and thank *you*, Mary." As he turned to look at Mary, behind her he saw Wilfred leaning against the doorframe of the great room, looking at him with contempt. He seemed to be daring him to say something. He didn't because he knew he couldn't. The only witness to the crime was dead. There was nothing to go on to arrest the scoundrel, and even if he was tried, a court of law would deem his word speculative at best. *Let Wilfred think he has gotten away with this foul act for now,* thought James. *He will slip sometime, and I intend to watch him very closely for the rest of his life.* At the very least, he vowed to haunt Wilfred and make him uncomfortable by reminding him at every opportunity that he knew the truth. He promised that to Bessie every night before he went to sleep. He owed her that much.

He smiled at Mary, thanked Clancy and Rebecca, and then opened the front door. He started to leave but stopped halfway out the door and turned around to look directly at Wilfred. He stared into his eyes until Wilfred blinked and looked down. James slowly smiled and left.

The frozen air stung his face and nose, and grabbed his chest, making him gasp. It was impossible to breathe through his swollen nose, so he waited until his lungs acclimatized to the temperature before heading down the stairs into the front yard. On the way home, he couldn't help but smile, despite his pain. He had finally confronted Wilfred. Everything had gone as expected, though he hadn't foreseen the violence. He hadn't expected a confession. Why would anyone confess to a rape? But James had felt Wilfred's guilt in his denial. It was a poor, pathetic, desperate denial. Knowing how uncomfortable Wilfred now felt made him smile, even though it also made him wince with pain.

Sadie moved along the snow-covered road at a steady pace. A billion stars shone down on them, sparkling on the snow. A crack from the frozen river broke the silence of the cold night as the ice shifted in response to the frigid temperatures. It sounded like a gunshot, echoing into the surrounding hills, but James hardly heard it. His mind wandered and he thought of himself alone with Mary, reaching out and touching her hair, gently letting his hand fall down along the length to her bare shoulder. He slowly leaned forward to kiss her …

Sadie snorted.

"You can read my mind and you think that's funny, old girl," he chuckled. "You think old James is dreaming. I am. But you never know. Sometimes dreams do come true." He patted her neck and laughed.

All in all, it *had* been a good night.

Chapter 13
An Unexpected Visit

JAMES SPENT A RESTLESS NIGHT. His nose and jaw throbbed with pain. He applied a cold compress to his face before bed to stop the swelling, but it did little to ease the pain. He was tempted to take a little morphine so he could get some sleep but decided against it—someone might need him during the night. Besides, he'd heard horrid stories of physicians becoming opium addicts from self-medicating and he didn't want to chance that. He wondered if he was being overcautious, but decided to tough out the night.

The St. John Public Hospital had recently purchased an X-Ray machine and as he climbed into bed, he thought about getting a picture of his jaw the next day, but then decided it would do no good. He knew his jaw was probably broken, though luckily it didn't seem displaced. He knew X-rays were used at the hospitals in

Montreal, but other than for curiosity and confirmation of a diagnosis, an X-ray wasn't going to help him to heal. There was not much a person could do for a cracked jaw. He'd just have to eat carefully for the next month.

The next morning, he awoke, threw back the sheets and swung his feet to the floor. It was very cold in his house. He had been too sore and tired to light the wood stove in the bedroom before bed. He took a step and immediately noticed his head was pounding. *Too much wine,* he thought … and the uppercut didn't help. He chuckled and then immediately winced in pain and grabbed his jaw. *I guess I know how to take a punch*, he thought, groaning as he held fast to his jaw. *No more laughing—it hurts too much.*

He picked up the pitcher on his night stand and shook it to break up a thin film of ice and then poured it into a basin. He was tempted to start the stove to warm up the water before he cleaned up, but decided the coldness would do his jaw good. As a child in St. John, he'd grown up with indoor plumbing. The city had a municipal water system. Today, most of the finer homes in Rothesay also had indoor plumbing and toilets, but he had chosen an older home with neither. *Maybe I'm taking this country doctor role a bit too far*, he thought. He grunted and braced himself for the shock before plunging his hands into the freezing water.

After he'd washed his face and tended to his injuries as well as he could, he went downstairs and started the living room and kitchen wood stoves. While he was waiting for the house to warm up, he went to the barn to give Sadie some water and hay. In the barn, he remembered his enthusiasm about Mary on the way home last night. He must have been drunk. The previous night hadn't been *that* great. He remembered what Clancy had said, "*There are many fine prospects for her in Boston—fine young men from good families. I'll probably take her back in a year or two; right now, she's too valuable to her mother to be married off.*"

He threw hay into Sadie's stall, replaying the words. '*Many fine prospects … fine young men … good families …*' It appeared a country doctor wasn't Clancy's idea of a fine prospect. A banking family, the old money of Boston, political influences—those were the '*fine prospects*' Clancy had in mind for his Mary. James was 26 and would always be a country doctor. Mary was 19 and her future was wide open. James knew he would inherit a lot of money someday, and he wondered if that fact would make a difference to Clancy, or to Mary for that matter. But he didn't want that to be part of the equation. If he was to be in the running for Mary's hand, he hoped that being a country doctor was good enough. He wondered, did they think him odd for living in a house without running water, using an outhouse and rejecting automobiles? Did they laugh at him behind his back?

He hoped not. But it occurred to him that maybe he *was* odd. He leaned the pitchfork against the wall and headed back to the house.

A fellow named Charlie MacPherson was on his veranda, peering into the windows. His cheeks were blazing red and his mouth was surrounded by ice that was clinging to his beard. Red hair peaked out from under a filthy toque.

"Can I help you?" James called to him.

Charlie jumped. "GOOD GOD," he yelled. "I thought you weren't home. You didn't answer my knock."

"I was in the barn," James said, walking over to Charlie. "I didn't hear you." He knew Charlie lived across the river and didn't come into town very often, so he was surprised by the visit. Charlie made his living in the woods by logging, trapping, and hunting. Most considered him amusing, jovial and polite; a friendly—if somewhat eccentric—Scotsman. "What can I do for you?" James asked when he had reached the veranda.

"Sorry to bother you, Dr. Wilson," Charlie said. "I'm Charlie McPherson. There's been an accident. I fear Frank O'Leary's busted his leg. We were working up at Reed Point, putting logs on a sled to haul to the St. John sawmill. The logs were piled up on this bank and we had taken a few of them and loaded 'em on the sled —I guess that's what made the pile unstable—when all of a sudden, the pile of logs gave way.

"The rest of us jumped out of the way, but Frank didn't make it. The logs fell against him and the sled, pinning him there like a mouse in a trap. He started howling and I guess between him hollering and the crash of the logs, the horses spooked and took off as if they heard demons, which caused Frank to bang his head something fierce against the sled and twist his leg until, honest-to-Jesus, I heard a snap like I'd broke an old tree branch over my knee. It made me want to bring up my breakfast and the rum right then and there.

"I knew what that sound was, but that was the least of my worries. I feared old Frank was dead. The sled damned near took his head off when the horses spooked and then, to make matters worse, the logs moved over him as he fell. He was pretty much covered in 'em. There wasn't a sound coming from him. The rest of us was cussing like crazy, but not a word was coming from Frank under the logs.

"I told the boys to start getting the logs off him and we did. And then, all of a sudden, Frankie starts swearing at us saying we were killing him. I knew then Frankie was all right.

"He kept up the cussing, blaming us for everything from the cost of rum to the unstable log pile. I couldn't help but laugh and tell him to shut up, but once I saw his leg, I shut my trap pretty quick. The leg was twisted and his foot was going where it shouldn't be going. We were afraid to touch it. We stood there gawking until Percy suggested we get you."

Charlie looked like he was about to apologise for bothering him. "You did right by not touching the leg, Charlie," James said. Charlie seemed relieved. "Come into the house," James said. "You look frozen. Come in and warm up while I get dressed warmer and get my things. Then we'll be off."

James went upstairs and put on more layers of clothing, then downstairs to his office where he loaded extra bottles of morphine and bandages into his bag. When he was done, he found Charlie warming his hands over the stove in the living room.

"Come into the kitchen, Charlie," he said, "while I grab some grub—I haven't had breakfast yet." Charlie followed him into the kitchen. James cut off a slice of bread and covered it with jam. "Have a slice, Charlie," he said. Then he cut a piece for himself. He groaned when he tried to open his mouth to eat and after a few attempts he gave up and put the slice of bread down on the table.

"Noticed your face," Charlie said, "but I didn't like to ask. What happened?"

"Fell on some ice last night," James said. "I think I broke my jaw."

"Looks like someone hauled off and gave you a smack."

James ignored the comment. "Looks like I'm on liquids for a while," he said. He went to his icebox and removed a bottle of milk. "I'll have a glass and we'll be off." He gingerly sipped from the glass to prevent his jaw from moving, but it proved difficult. Milk dribbled down his chin. He felt foolish.

"Nice place you have here," Charlie said, looking away.

"It's old. It was built by a Mr. Humphrey for a Mr. Almon. Did you know Mr. Almon?"

"Everybody knew him. Rich bugger. Kept to himself. Those types tend to. Owned lots of land. Sold a bunch of it and took off to Toronto. Probably nowhere to spend his money around these parts. Don't blame him. I'd bugger off too, if I had that money. You'd see ol' Charlie boy dining with those fancy women up in Toronto."

"You're not married, Charlie?"

Charlie looked a little sheepish. "Yes, I'm married," he said. "I guess I'd take Polly and give her a fine house, servants, chocolates—you know, keep her happy while I go bugger off with the fancy ladies." He laughed and winked as if he was sharing a secret.

"You're Scottish," James commented. "Are you born here, or did you come from the old country?"

"I was born and raised in Canada. You're not the first to ask, though. My folks were from Scotland and I suppose I grew up with the accent. There were no kids around us on the other side of the Peninsula where I grew up. I grew up out in the woods and had all my schooling at home, so I never had the influence of others."

James wondered if a similar story explained Mr. O'Sullivan's Irish accent. He took another sip of milk and realized it was impossible to drink anymore; he was losing half of it down his chin.

"Would you finish this for me, Charlie?" he asked, offering him the glass. "Guess we better get going. You thawed out now? We better go before Frank freezes."

"I don't think anything can kill that man," Charlie offered. James wasn't so sure about that; the fracture sounded severe.

He put on his hooded fur coat and mitts and he and Charlie headed outside. His face stung as a gust of wind whipped across it. He gasped and buried it in his coat.

"Bugger! It's gotten colder," Charlie exclaimed.

"How's the ice?" James asked. He had noticed Charlie had come up from the river.

"The ice is fine. Still strong."

"Strong enough for a sleigh? I should take my sleigh to transport Frank—we could lay him out on the back seat to take him home."

"God, yes. The ice is thick enough to drive a wagon loaded with logs over it. No need for your sleigh, though—we'll load him onto the sled we have."

James wasn't sure he'd want to ride on the ice, but he'd have to trust Charlie—the river would be the quickest way to Frank. They hustled over to the barn to saddle Sadie and get some supplies.

James fumbled with the saddle. His hands were stinging and stiff from the cold. Charlie moved with ease, and if he noticed James' discomfort he didn't mention it. "My hands are near frozen already," James complained.

"My hands are so thick and stupid," Charlie chuckled, "they don't know enough to be cold."

James laughed; he liked Charlie. Some fellows would have taken the opportunity to act superior to him—the green, tender doctor. Many men had the past year. But Charlie was respectful, good-natured and patient.

When he finished cinching the saddle on Sadie, he tied two planks of wood together and secured them with rope to it. Then he tied a blanket to the back of the saddle and added the morphine, chloroform, a syringe, and bandages from his medical kit to the saddle bag. He always kept emergency medical supplies in his saddlebag. When he was done, he said, "Ready to go, Charlie," and mounted Sadie.

They followed a trail that led to the river. Ice sheets formed a small wall along the water's edge. He and Charlie dismounted to lead their horses over a small break in the ice wall and onto the frozen river. A hard-packed crust of snow swept smooth by the winds covered the ice, making their way more sure-footed than James expected. The snow crunched under their horses' hooves as they headed up-river.

James heard the ice crack. "Are you sure the ice can take this weight, Charlie?" he asked nervously. He unconsciously gripped the reins and squeezed his knees tighter against Sadie.

"No problem, Doc. This ice is thicker than the mayor's head … and that's pretty thick!" Charlie slapped his knee and rocked in his saddle. "Actually, Doc, the ice *is* pretty tricky. It gets thin around that point sometimes." He nodded to a rocky point on the riverbank. "You have to be careful. I knew a man that fell through right about there a few years ago. Drowned. Found him in the springtime, down by Indiantown. The fish had …"

Then Charlie proceeded to describe to him in detail what fish do when they're hungry. He seemed unconcerned about the ice and gradually James relaxed too, and started trying to keep abreast of Charlie so he could listen to his amusing banter as they rode along. He had to stay close, as Charlie's voice was barely audible in the fierce, freezing wind that blew against them. James tried to protect his face by bowing his head and breathing into his coat. His nose felt like it was freezing; he rubbed it to increase the circulation. How did Charlie keep talking? He could barely breathe.

They rode along for about 30 minutes, until Charlie finally announced, "Here we are!" James looked up with relief at Reed Point. His face felt like it had been slashed with whips and the cold penetrated through his fur coat to his bones. It sure didn't feel like early March. It was far too cold.

They climbed a path from the river's bank into the forest. James was grateful for the shelter of trees, which protected them from the stinging wind. "Glory, I'm cold, Charlie," he said. "My feet are like ice cubes and I feel the cold clear into my bones. And if my face wasn't sore enough from my fall, the wind has now lashed it into raw meat."

Charlie laughed. "Bet you thought I was a chatterbox, eh Doc? I learned if you keep talking in the cold your face won't freeze and it seems to help keep your body warm. Don't believe me? Proof's in the pudding, Doc. Don't feel too cold at all. Wait 'til we get to Frank—we had a pint of rum and what you need is a good shot … that'll warm you up. Set your innards aglow with warmth and comfort."

James was surprised to hear singing coming from the road just ahead. Charlie smiled at James' puzzled expression. "That would be Frankie," Charlie said. "Told you we had nothing to worry about—Frankie's a tough old bird. Take more than a busted leg and freezing to do him in."

James could hear the words as they approached, "*In Dublin's fair city, where girls are so pretty …*"

Chapter 14
Frankie

FRANKIE WAS LYING ON THE snow with a blanket under his head when they arrived. A fire was crackling beside him while he waved a cup in the air in rhythm to his song. Two men sat by him, leaning on a sled that looked like a wagon with runners instead of wheels. Two horses, who James supposed pulled this sled, were unhitched and tied to a tree nearby.

The two fellows stood and welcomed him and Charlie with hoots of joy, and one yelled, "THANK THE GOOD LORD!"

Frank ignored all of them and cursed his companions: "AHHH, SWEET MARY AND JOSEPH. YOU SONS-A-BITCHES MOVE THAT LEG ONE MORE TIME AND I'LL KILL YOU. I SWEAR TO GOD I WILL."

"Sorry, Frankie," one said, trying to suppress a giggle.

"What in God's name are you idiots doing?" Charlie asked as they dismounted from their horses.

"We're just cheering up Frankie-boy," one said. "We needed more than this fire to keep us warm." The man who answered swung his arms open and nearly fell into the fire. He staggered, fought for his balance, and then smiled like an idiot.

"Doc, this sorry-excuse-for-a-man is Percy," Charlie grumbled, sweeping his arm towards the fellow who had just stumbled. "It was Percy's bright idea to fetch you. Now I see why he didn't object too strenuously when I volunteered to go—he and Robert knew they were going to stay here and DRINK ALL THE RUM!"

"Easy, Charlie," Percy pleaded. "We had to do something to ease poor Frankie's pain and warm him up." He hunched his shoulders and extended both his arms toward where Frank lay, as if producing self-explanatory evidence.

"That was very thoughtful of you and Robert," Charlie sneered, "but you fellows didn't have to drink too!"

"We couldn't have him drink alone …" Robert chimed in, in an equally inebriated voice. "That would not …" Robert paused and looked to the sky as if he was searching for divine inspiration, "... be nice," he finally pronounced.

While they were arguing, James took Frank's pulse. Frank didn't say a word to him, even when he asked how he was doing. Instead he just looked at him with suspicion, as if James was neither expected nor wanted.

Charlie knelt down beside James. "How are ya', Frankie?" he asked.

"Fine," Frank said. "Fine, Charlie. Just lying here on a fine day in the snow, drinking rum and getting drunk with a busted leg. Say, how's the wife and kids?"

Charlie laughed and pounded Frank on his shoulder.

Frank yelled, "JESUS, DON'T TOUCH ME!"

"Sorry, Frankie, sorry," Charlie pleaded, holding his hands in the air. "Frankie," he said, nodding towards James, "this here's Dr. Wilson."

"I know," Frank said quietly. "I've heard about you."

"Don't believe everything you hear," James joked.

Frank didn't laugh. He looked serious. "I hope not," he said.

James tried to ignore the comment. "Let's have a look at your head and then your leg," he said. He felt a large, swollen, bruised area behind Frank's head, at the base his skull. It appeared to be only soft tissue damage—there could be a small skull fracture under swelling, but there were no neurological signs to indicate serious intracranial damage. Bruises and abrasions marked his face, not to mention a swollen right eye. Satisfied that Frank had sustained no serious brain or neck damage, he turned his attention to the leg.

Frank's right leg was obviously broken; his toes were pointing unnaturally sideways. James saw a bulge under Frank's blood-soaked pants above the inside of his knee. He left Frank to obtain a pair of scissors and bandages from his saddlebag.

When he returned, Frank took a swallow of rum and said, "What are you planning to do with those scissors? You're not using them on me."

"No, they're not being used on you," James reassured him. "I have to cut your trousers to get a good look at the leg. Don't worry." He smiled at Frank, but Frank didn't return the smile; instead, he continued to look at him with suspicion. James wanted to ask him just what it was he had heard about him, but it wasn't the time. Whether Frank knew it or not, his life was at stake.

He cut the trousers from the bottom up to his groin and gently pulled the material away from the fracture. Frank howled in pain, his jaw clenched.

"I can't believe you're feeling any pain," Charlie said, "with all the rum you've drank." He laughed. "You'd think—oh, sweet Jesus," he exclaimed, when he saw the blood and a huge bone sticking out of Frank's inner thigh.

"Shut up!" Frank growled.

James didn't see any active bleeding coming from the wound, but the broken, blood-covered femur, surrounded by a mass of coagulated jelled blood, obscured a full view. He worried Frank might still be bleeding under the clot.

Untying Frank's boot, he pulled down his sock and felt for a pulse at the ankle. "Good," he said when he felt the familiar thrum of blood under his fingers. "I can feel a pulse. That's good, Frank. That means you haven't hurt the main artery down your leg."

Percy knelt down beside James and in a serious, hushed tone said, "Doc … he busted his leg up here … not his foot down there." He and Robert sputtered and then broke into laughter.

"All right, you clowns," Charlie scolded them, "show the Doc here some respect. He didn't come all this way, in this freezing cold, to hear you idiots acting like fools. How in the name of God did you fools get so drunk off a pint of rum?" They smiled but didn't answer him. "Percy, you only had a pint ... right?" Charlie asked.

"Yeah, I only had one," Percy said. "But so did Robert … and Frankie."

"Could you spare some for Dr. Wilson here? He's pretty cold and could use some to warm up."

Percy looked up at Robert, but he was searching the heavens again for some divine inspiration.

"You idiots didn't go and drink the whole three pints?" Charlie implored, glaring at both of them. Percy stood up and went to stand beside Robert.

"You was gone a long time, Charlie," Percy pleaded. "You probably don't realize that. And Frankie here was in a lot of powerful pain—"

"Sweet Mary and Joseph!" Charlie exclaimed. "Sorry Doc." He turned to Frankie. "Did they give you some rum, Frankie, or did they hog all of it for themselves?"

"Oh yes," Frank slurred. "The boys are very generous. Aren't you, boys?" Frank looked up at Robert and Percy, who were smiling like choirboys.

As James thought about how best to treat Frank's wound, Robert suddenly lurched forward, off-balance. He had to grab the side of the sled to remain upright. He smiled and tried to arrange one end of a scarf that had escaped his coat to hang below his crotch and James noticed his oily, long, black hair framed a pockmarked face as it spilled out from under his lopsided toque. He reminded James of a drunken Mr. Fagan from *Oliver Twist*. Percy was his opposite; rotund, with fat red cheeks, a thin, spotty, brown beard growing high on his cheeks and a brown toque that threatened to pop off his head. His brown, soiled coat hung open, despite the cold, showing his ample frame. James would have found these two comical at another time; but right now, he had to concentrate on Frank.

"Did the rum help the pain?" James asked Frank.

"It eased it some," he said. "There's no doubt. But it still throbs something fierce. I know it's going to be God-awful when we try to move."

Frank was a large man with huge hands. His face was clean-shaven, his features coarse and mean. Even in his fragile state, he was intimidating.

"We've got to get you out of here," James said to him, "and to the hospital."

"No hospital!" Frank barked.

"You can't go home like this, Frank," James replied.

"I got a good woman to keep care of me, Doc. And I ain't got the money for hospital."

"The church could raise …"

"I ain't a church-going man. Besides, I don't think too many people come out of the hospital alive. I'll take my chances at home, thank you. I ain't going!" Frank looked at him as if he was daring him to say another word.

"All right, Frank," James said. "You win. Where does he live, fellows? We have to get going, before Frank gets too cold." He looked up at Charlie, who had joined Percy and Robert beside the sled. As the three of them looked at Frank's wound, and the severity of it sank in, they were silent. Percy looked noticeably paler.

"You got it, Doc," said Charlie. Then he commanded Percy and Robert to come with him to hitch the horses up to the sled. The sight of blood and wounds seemed to have sobered them up significantly and they sprang into action, albeit a bit clumsily.

"Now I have to move the leg a bit, Frank," James said. "I have to twist it and get that bone back in place. It will hurt something awful, but there's no way around it." Frank started to protest, but James held up his hand. "But … I'm going to give you some chloroform," he said. "It will make you sleep a bit, so you won't feel a thing."

As Charlie and the other fellows finished hitching the horses to the sled, he left Frank to get the chloroform and a mask from his saddlebag. "I'm going to need a hand in a few minutes," he said to the men. "Almost done?"

"Give us five minutes," Charlie said.

The wind had calmed down a fair bit; James couldn't hear it moan anymore and the trees were only gently swaying instead of bowing in distress. However, high above, the clouds were still gliding by quite quickly. *It must be near noon,* thought James. *Damn, I'm cold.*

He moved to the fire, knelt down, and warmed his hands over the heat.

"Cold, Doc?" Frank asked, sipping more rum.

James looked over at Frank who was watching him curiously. "Damn near frozen to the bone," he replied. "How are you?"

"My back is cold. I feel the freeze from the ground. But I'm not too bad." He held out his cup of rum. "Here. Have a swig of this—that'll help."

James accepted the cup and took a gulp. The rum burned, but he felt a surge of warmth spreading in his belly. "Thank you, Frank", he said, handing back the rum. Frank didn't seem so gruff now. "Frank," he said. "Just what did you hear about me, anyways?"

Frank looked troubled. He mumbled, sighed, and finally said, "Nothing. Gossip is all. I shouldn't have said anything. I'm a drunken fool—pay me no attention."

"I'm just curious, Frank. I won't hold it against you, whatever you say. Tell me."

Frank wiped his mouth. "Thirsty," he said. "I never told this to a soul … maybe my wife … but not another soul. I don't gossip."

"You're a good man," James said.

"I heard Bessie MacKenzie saw you the day she died; she was looking for help and …" Frank paused; he seemed at a loss for words.

"Who told you this?" James finally asked.

"Same fella' who told me that you nearly lost young Tom McGarrigle. He said he heard you should have taken the lad's appendix out at home."

James growled. "Dr. Peters," he grumbled, shaking his head.

"No, but Dr. Peters told Wilfred MacKenzie, and it was him that told me."

James took a minute to respond. "Frank," he said carefully. "There's a lot more going on here than you know. First, that's just not right—Dr. Peters talking and spreading false statements about another doctor. I did the right thing for young Tom. Evidence shows much better results when a serious operation like an appendectomy is done in a hospital instead of at home. Peters knows that. He doesn't like me and the reason why is childish. Leave it at that. But it's true that Bessie MacKenzie came to see me the day she drowned. I can't tell you about what, but I did see her. However, I didn't see her suicide coming. I've wracked my brain since then to see if I could have prevented it ..." He sighed in frustration, clearly distraught. Then he lowered his head, embarrassed by his emotional outburst. He had never spoken to anyone about this.

"You can't help everyone, Dr. Wilson," Frank said quietly. James felt the sincerity in Frank's voice.

Just then Charlie called over, "We're ready, Doc. What can we do to help get him in the wagon?" he asked as he and the others walked over.

"You're going to have to help me set the fracture," James replied. Then to Frank he said, "I'm going to give you some chloroform that's going to make you sleep. Are you ready?"

"Ready," Frank replied.

James put a hard rubber mask, that opened to a gauze surface underneath, over Frank's mouth and nose. He dropped chloroform onto the gauze surface. "Just breathe nice and slow," he commanded.

Frank gasped. He seemed to be panicking. His eyes looked wild.

"Easy," James said, holding the mask firmly in place. "Slow breaths."

After a minute, Frank began to settle down. His breathing slowed down, his eyes dulled and then finally they closed.

"Christ, I thought you were killing him," Robert said.

"It's never easy to go under," James replied. "It feels like you're smothering for a moment or two."

"Will you look at that now," Charlie said, leaning over Frank. "Frankie? Frankie can you hear me?"

"No, he's out cold, Charlie," James said. "But we've got to hurry. I didn't give him much chloroform, just enough to keep him out while we get that leg set."

James ran his hands down to Frank's upper thigh. "I want you to grab his leg about here, Charlie," he said, grabbing Charlie's hands and planting them firmly in place above the fracture site. "I'm going to pull his leg back into place and you will have to hold very firmly as I pull his leg down below.

"Robert, you hold him under the left arm—that's right—more under the armpit. And Percy, you take his right shoulder." James watched them take their places. When he was satisfied that they were in position, he said. "When I say, 'pull', "you guys pull hard—got it?"

"Me too?" Charlie asked.

"No. You just hold the upper leg as steady as you can."

As the men assumed their positions, James poured carbolic acid over the exposed bone and wound. Then he moved down to grab hold of the ankle of Frank's wounded legs with both hands. He steadied himself in the snow and called out. "Okay, ready guys?" They affirmed they were, and he could feel the increased tension as they tensed and prepared to pull on Frank's inert body.

"PULL!" he yelled.

At that, the three of them pulled with all their might. James kept his eye on the wound. He could see the exposed end of the bone slip deeper into it. "KEEP PULLING!" he yelled. Frank groaned.

"Jesus, he's waking up!" Percy grunted.

"Not quite," James called. "PULL! HARDER!"

"We're going to pull off his bloody leg!" Percy yelled.

"There's bleeding coming from the hole!" Charlie warned.

James ignored their comments. "Not there—yet," he growled. He pulled harder. He felt Frank's muscles contract and work against them. Then he finally felt a slight relaxing of the muscles.

"We're nearly there …" James groaned. Given last night's events, it was almost too much for him. But he couldn't stop now. He summoned the strength for a final pull.

"Hang in there with me, gents!" he yelled and as they all heaved together for the final time, he twisted the leg clockwise and felt a pop. "There!" he yelled. "Let go!"

Then he fell back into the snow, exhausted.

"And …" Percy gasped, leaning against the wagon. "I thought… doctoring … was easy work."

Wearily James got up and went to assess the bleeding Charlie had mentioned. Using a bandage he had stashed in his coat, he put pressure on the wound and after a few minutes, the bleeding abated. Then he wrapped a roll of gauze tightly around the leg and fastened it firmly over the wound. He checked Frank's ankle for a pulse to make sure the artery was still intact. It was, he was relieved to find. He got the fellows to fetch the wood planks he had earlier strapped to Sadie, then, after protecting Frank's broken leg with strips of blanket, he placed them on each side from his hip to ankle. As the men held the planks tight to Frank, he lashed them in place with rope. The leg was firmly splinted in a straight position to prevent the fracture from moving too much. "Okay, fellows, it's time to lift him onto the wagon," James said.

Frank started to groan as they lifted him up and placed him in the wagon with a blanket under his head. James wished he had more blankets to keep Frank warm. He knew he would lose body heat fast being unconscious.

The wagon was securely hitched to Robert's horses, and so Robert tied Sadie and Charlie's horse to the back. Then, as Charlie took the reins and Percy jumped into the front with him, he clambered into the back of the wagon with James and Frank. They headed down the trail and were soon on the river, taking Frank home.

Chapter 15
Home Care

THE COLD AIR STUNG JAMES' face as they travelled over the ice. He tucked his chin as far into his coat as he could and held his hands firmly on Frank's splint to prevent movement. The sled runners made a swishing sound as they rode over the hard-packed snow. The ride was much smoother than he had anticipated.

James wiggled his numb fingers, trying to feel something in them. They were freezing, even under his thick mittens. "Where does Frank live?" he asked Robert.

"Upriver," Robert replied, "towards Hampton. We should be there in less than thirty minutes." James shivered and groaned. "Bloody cold for early March, Dr. Wilson." Robert commented.

"I think I dropped a toe," James joked. "Froze plum off. If you see it around will you let me know? I'm awfully attached to it."

Robert laughed and then looked over the side of the wagon. "Sorry we drank all the rum," he said.

"That's quite okay, Robert. I'm not much of a drinker. I had a hard time swallowing the mouthful Frank gave me."

"It was good of you to come," Robert said. He rubbed his nose, cupped his mittens over his face and breathed into them. "Think Frankie will do alright?" he asked, his voice muffled.

"It will be a long haul," James replied, "even if things go right. A couple of months in bed and then he can slowly get back to walking. He'll need crutches for a long time."

Frank was moaning more and more; he was coming out of the anaesthesia. James looked down at him. "And that's if everything goes *fine*," he continued. "I have to watch for wound infection, pneumonia ... lots of things. He'll be lucky to ..." He was going to say, 'survive', but realized quickly that he really should talk to Frank's wife first.

Robert didn't notice his near-gaffe. "I'm glad you're around, Dr. Wilson," he said. Then he asked, "You like being a doctor?" Before James could answer, he added, "Why'd you become a doctor?"

James smiled. "I want to help people," he said. "I want to do things like this. I've always been interested in how the human body works, and right now there is some exciting progress in medicine. Germ theory has revolutionized the way doctors treat disease and there are many recently developed tools to treat the sick that I find fascinating, like antitoxin injections, anaesthesia, and some wonderful new surgical techniques. Further, for the treating mentally afflicted, there some new and interesting theories developing in the field of psychiatry…"

He was talking too much; Robert's eyes were losing focus. "Anyway…" James said, "Yeah, I'm happy."

"Married?" Robert asked.

Frank's eyes began flicking open and he started moving his arms. James heightened his focus on him; he had to be wary of Frank vomiting. He wasn't fully awake and would be in danger of choking. He answered Robert, "No," he said. "No wife."

"You gotta' get a woman, Doc. Nothing like sliding against a warm body on a cold night and maybe cozying into that warmth … cozying and sliding … and you get cozying so much that soon she's cozying too … and sliding … soon you're both cozying, sliding so much … well a body can't take that much cozying and sliding … soon as you know it, you're sliding into something else. Know what I mean, Doc?" He smiled and winked.

This sort of talk always made James feel uneasy. He was supposed to say something clever and equally naughty, but he had no experience in this talk. At a loss for words, he didn't respond; instead, he pretended to be busy and began searching his saddlebag for a 'lost' item. "Can't find the darn thing," he murmured.

"Need something?" Robert asked.

"I guess it's not important," James replied, glad the subject of sex had been dropped. Frank's hand began wandering up to his face and James grabbed it. In his semiconscious state, Frank could poke and damage his own eye. After this pause in the direction of the conversation, James felt more comfortable and decided to be polite and ask Robert about his life. "Been married long, Robert?" he asked, holding Frank's arm.

"Eighteen years. She's a good woman, my Isobel. Maybe a bit fat, but I'm not complaining, Doc. No siree. Not one bit."

James smiled and looked at the man, only to be hit by a glare of bright winter white light. The sun on the ice and snow was blinding, making his eyes water and sting as if someone had thrown salt in them. He blinked and rubbed them, then finally shut them. With his eyes closed, it felt like they were floating through space with only the grinding of the runners orienting him to earth.

"I'm glad Charlie and Percy know where we are," he said to Robert, wiping the tears from his eyes.

"They probably don't," Robert snickered.

Just then, Frank started to shiver and mumble something about being cold. "He's coming around,"

James said. "We have to give him heat. I'll cover his chest and you cover his abdomen, Robert." Quickly, they covered Frank lightly with their bodies.

"What the goddamnjesuschris' is going on!" Frank suddenly mumbled.

"We're trying to keep you warm, Frank," James answered. "You're okay. We got your bone set and you're in the wagon heading home. We're nearly there."

Frank mumbled, "That's nice," and started to snore again.

Robert laughed. "Don't ever tell him I was laying on him or I'll be killed, Doc."

Frank suddenly woke up and yelled, "HOLY MARY AND JOSEPH. MY LEG!"

"Sounds like our sleeping beauty's awake," Charlie yelled back. "Almost there."

"I'll give you something when we get to your house," James reassured Frank.

"Here we are!" Charlie declared.

James looked up to see a log cabin all by itself on the riverbank. He knew this area of the river—he and his father had often come up here to fish. The river narrowed dramatically at this point, creating marsh banks rather than rock or sandy sides.

As they jostled over the snow bank on the edge of the river onto land, the sled bumped and lifted, making Frank howl. James held Frank's leg as fast as he could to the floor of the sled. Frank's wife must have seen them coming because she was waiting for them outside the cabin as they arrived.

"God sakes almighty!" she cried with concern as she ran towards them. "Is that Frankie? Well, for the love of God! Frankie, what have you gone and done now? Is he drunk?" she asked Charlie.

"Calm down, Marg," Charlie said. "Frank's been hurt. Broke his leg. This here's Dr. Wilson. Dr. Wilson, this is Frank's wife—Margaret O'Leary."

Margaret glanced at him, said 'hello', and ordered them to bring Frank into the house. They did as she asked. Frank howled and cursed as they lifted him off the sled and carried him into the cabin.

James was grateful for the warmth as soon as he entered the small cabin. Under Marg's direction, they carried Frank to a small bedroom in the back of the common room and laid him down. Margaret brushed Frank's hair back from his forehead and kissed him, then jumped back and said, "He *is* drunk! No wonder he got hurt. The old bugger's drunker than a skunk."

"We gave him the rum on purpose," James said, "for the pain. Actually, the fellows gave him the rum before I came. They did well. I would have done the same."

Robert and Percy looked gratefully at him.

"We had no drink while we were working, Marg," Charlie said. "I swear. We had a little nip to keep us warm before we started to work, but that's all—a small nip—as God is my witness."

Margaret tightened her mouth and looked up, weighing the truth of this information.

"I swear too, Marg," Frank said.

At Frank's insistent plea, Margaret smiled, apparently convinced. She wiped his forehead and James saw the love in her eyes and thought, *with her as a nurse, Frank might be alright.*

James liked her immediately. Her obvious affection for her husband and her wide, open smile offset her somewhat rugged, unfeminine features. She was wearing a plain brown dress that fell to her ankles with a white apron tied around her waist, her grey-streaked brown hair swept back in a bun. She reminded him of a fishmonger he had known when he was a young boy. He had loved visiting this woman on the docks; she had been so kind. She always had time for him, turning to give him a wink or making a comment that made him laugh, between calls of "Fresh salmon!" or "Get yer shad here!" It wasn't until he was in university that he realised that that happy, kind lady probably didn't have much in life—but despite her hardships, she had enough love in her heart to show kindness to a spoiled little rich boy who had no awareness of the plight of the poor.

She was no longer there when he returned from university one summer. He never inquired about her, perhaps afraid of what he might find: A poor woman from the tenets, who eked out a living selling fish on the docks, alone in life, unloved, and who died by herself in the poor house.

"What's the fool broken, Dr. Wilson?" Marg asked tenderly, pulling him out of his reverie. She touched Frank's cheek. "Looks like his leg."

"His femur," James said. "That's a big bone right about here." He showed Margaret where the fracture was. "He's lucky to be alive. I'll let the boys tell you what happened."

While Charlie told Margaret the tale—interrupted by Frank's spin on things and grunts of pain—James removed a case containing a glass hypodermic syringe and needle from his saddlebag. He waited for Charlie to finish talking and then said, "I think Frank could do with something for pain." Frank grunted his approval. James asked, "Could you boil some water for me, Mrs. O'Leary?"

Margaret left the bedroom and James followed. She filled a kettle with water from a bucket, placed it on a wood stove, and went back to her husband. When the water was boiled, James sterilized the needle and syringe with it and carbolic acid. He turned around and saw Robert and Percy had left the bedroom and were watching him with interest.

"I'm killing germs," he said to them.

They nodded as if they knew that.

He was warm now. He took off his coat, rolled up his sleeves, and leaned back against the sink while he waited for his instruments to cool. The cabin was very cozy. There was a wood stove, kitchen table, and a sink under a window on one side. On the other side of the room were the front door, a stone fireplace, and a few rocking chairs. Simple, but pleasant. He rather envied the O'Leary's: A simple life in the woods—just the two of them. "Do they have any children?" he asked Robert and Percy.

"Nope," Percy answered without further elaboration.

James twisted the needle back onto the syringe and went back into the bedroom. "How's Frank?" he asked.

"He's in a lot of pain, Dr. Wilson," Margaret said. She sat by his side, holding his hand while Charlie stood at the foot of the bed.

After asking Margaret and Charlie to roll Frank onto his side and pull his pants down to expose a buttock, James drew up the morphine. Frank hollered and cursed as they moved him.

"Frank, there's no need of that," Margaret told him repeatedly, which only caused Frank to increase the expletives. Margaret shook her head. "Forgive him," she said. "He's not usually so crude."

After the morphine injection, Frank settled down. James wearily sat in a wooden chair by the bed and looked around. The room was very small; there was space enough for the bed and a dresser, and not much more. A tiny, curtained window was on the opposite log wall and beside it was a small shelf with a china figurine on it. Pictures of what looked like the Irish countryside hung on the other side of the window. They seemed to have so little.

After a while, Frank started to snore. James took his pulse and then left the room, asking the men if he could speak to Mrs. O'Leary in private. They understood, and after making sure Margaret didn't need them anymore, they reassured her that one of them would return later that night and they left.

"Mrs. O'Leary," James said, when they had gone, "this is a bad fracture and there is a grave danger of infection. And even if he doesn't get an infection, it will be months before he can get up, and then months beyond that before he learns to walk again ..."

Her lip quivered. "What are we going to do?" she mumbled to herself.

"I'm sure your friends will look after you and Frank, Mrs. O'Leary—"

"Marg."

"Marg. Charlie, Robert and Percy seem like nice folk. And I bet others will pitch in too."

He asked Marg if he could stay the rest of the day and night to watch over Frank. She told him she was delighted and relieved. She offered to make him lunch, but he requested only bread and jam.

He asked Marg to sit down with him while he ate. He gingerly chewed the bread.

"Quite a swelling and bruise on the side of your face, Dr. Wilson," Marg commented. "Hurts to chew, I see."

"Fell last night. Probably broke my jaw," he said. She was right; it did hurt to chew, but he was famished, and no amount of pain was going to stop him from woofing down this delicious bread with strawberry preserve. He managed to swallow with very little chewing.

When he'd finished the last of it, he licked his fingers. Marg immediately brought him a napkin. She looked at him with curiosity and he decided it was best to take the bull by the horns. Someone was out to ruin his reputation, and he was pretty sure who.

"Frank told me," he said, putting down his napkin, "about things he heard about me. I want you to know most of what you may have heard is not true. No matter what others think, I know I did the right thing by taking the boy with the appendix to hospital. He's fine today and the result may not have been as good if I had performed the operation at home. And I feel awful bad about Bessie MacKenzie. It's true I did see her the day she died, but she gave me no warning that she might do harm to herself. Believe me, I feel terrible about her." He did not add how terrible he felt about his indecision and hesitation to inform her father, but the full explanation was impossible to convey without exposing Bessie's pregnancy. He honoured Bessie's confidence even more in death. She had desperately wanted to protect her father from the awful truth.

"Dr. Wilson, I never took stock in what Frank told me and I know he didn't either. Who are we to judge? Besides I also heard about the good care you gave to people during the past two months. I heard you came to people at all hours of the night and day. I've only heard good things about you." She wiped the table with her cloth.

"That's nice to hear, Marg. I just try to do my best."

The rest of the day was uneventful. He gave Frank morphine throughout the day, but was able to decrease the amount as the day wore on. Marg made a fine soup for supper and even with his sore jaw he could eat the soft vegetables and meat she'd cooked to perfection all day. He enjoyed their conversation throughout the day and at bedtime, Marg fussed over making him a place to sleep on a rug by the fireplace and apologised many times for her lack of better accommodations. He knew it didn't matter where he slept; he was so tired. She also gave some hay and vegetable scraps to Sadie and made sure she was protected from the cold in the small stall out back.

After saying goodnight to Marg, he wearily climbed into the blankets and was asleep before a thought crossed his mind.

Chapter 16
Rebecca

JAMES SAT IN HIS CUSTOMARY seat beside Mrs. Mawhinney at church the following Sunday morning. He had stayed with the O'Leary's on Friday night and most of Saturday, returning home just before nightfall on Saturday evening. Frank had done better than expected after such a terrible fracture. In fact, he was in relatively good spirits and good shape, considering how grave his situation was. James intended to go back to check on him after church.

"Goodness gracious, look at you!" Mrs. Mawhinney exclaimed. "I hope you put a bread poultice on your face! I shouldn't be telling a doctor what to do, but I've always found a bread poultice to be just the thing for swellings. Other people use rice bags, apple peelings, lotions of all kinds, and lord-knows-what-all, but I stick to my bread poultice. I swear by it. I soak ..."

"Yes, Mrs. Mawhinney," James interjected. "I did put on a poultice." That was a lie, but he didn't feel like being told how to make a bread poultice at the moment.

"You slipped?" she asked.

"Foolish of me, really. I should have been more careful. But it gets very slippery when the snow gets packed down like that."

"Didn't Mr. MacKenzie hear you or see you fall?"

"Wilfred?"

"Yes. I saw him come in from the outside just before you came in. It's a wonder he didn't hear you fall—you must have cried out in pain. He was out there at the same time."

"It was very dark … we must have missed each other."

"I suppose," she said slowly. She examined him like she knew he was lying. "There was a period of time," she finally said, measuring each word, "between when he came in and you did. You must have fallen after he came in."

He could feel himself blush as he fought for something to say. Thankfully, she opened her prayer book and ended the conversation.

What was he doing? In effect, he was covering up for Wilfred. How ironic was that? Was he protecting Amos and honouring Bessie's last wish, or was he just protecting his own reputation? He had known her uncle raped her and done nothing. Instead of telling her father his suspicions he'd gone to a stupid meeting, agreeing to let Bessie—a mere child—handle this on her own. He had let a minor decide the course of action, rather than take charge himself. He was weak. Some doctor!

He rubbed his forehead. Emptiness washed over him. He felt as if he was falling and could do nothing about it. He had tried to set things right by informing the authorities. Was it his fault that the police chose not to do anything? He was still angry at the way they brushed him off. But if they weren't going to bring Wilfred to task, could *he* find a way to expose him? Should he?

He closed his eyes and prayed for forgiveness, the wisdom to know what to do, and the strength to find a way to expose the truth.

He opened his eyes in time to see Wilfred and Amos walk down the aisle with their families. Wilfred never glanced his way as he entered his regular pew, rows ahead and to the left of where James sat.

He wanted Wilfred to look at him. He wanted Wilfred to see him again and again and remember Bessie each time and feel the shame of his actions and the fear of discovery. He was angry Wilfred hadn't even sent a wary glance his way, that he'd ignored him. Maybe Wilfred was incapable of feeling remorse and guilt like a normal person. Clearly he didn't fear James. His anger turned to frustration. James knew then that he *had* to find a way to expose Wilfred, with or without the help of the law.

The organ struck up the notes of the opening hymn and the choir emerged from the doors beside the sanctuary. He noticed the O'Sullivans weren't present in church. Mrs. O'Sullivan was due any day now. He hoped he hadn't missed her delivery yesterday. He must call her as soon as he got home.

A few hours later at home, the phone rang while James was eating lunch in the kitchen. He rushed to the hallway and picked it up, bringing the hearing piece to his ear.

"Dr. Wilson? Clancy here. I think Rebecca's going to have her baby!"

"I'll be there in less than thirty minutes," he said.

He rode Sadie hard and arrived at the O'Sullivan house twenty minutes later. "Come in," Clancy said. "Come in, my good man. We're glad to see you. Contractions are about every five minutes. Shouldn't be long now." Clancy seemed so calm—nothing seemed to bother this man.

The O'Leary children ventured into the hallway as James took off his coat. "Hello, children," he said.

"Away with you all now," Clancy ordered, "before I take the stick to ya!"

The children squealed, pretending to be scared and scampered away in different directions, stumbling over one another. Clancy smiled.

Clancy lead him upstairs to the bedroom where Rebecca was. "Dr. Wilson!" Rebecca grunted when he entered. "Join the fun!"

"Mother!" Mary cried. "This isn't the time for frivolity." She was sitting beside the bed, holding Rebecca's hand and wiping her forehead.

"Mary," Rebecca said. "You take things too seriously. I'm the one in pain!" She patted Mary's cheek and smiled. "Thank you for coming, James," she said.

She blew strands of her dishevelled hair from her red, puffy face, as if she was totally exasperated by the whole situation. James almost smiled. "Let's have a look at you," he said.

He asked Clancy to leave and then determined the position of the baby and the cervical dilatation. "It won't be long," he said to Rebecca. "You're fully dilated."

Rebecca groaned and grabbed Mary's hand as another contraction came.

"How can I help?" Mary asked him after her mother relaxed.

"Help me bring her down on the bed, Mary," he requested, grateful for her assistance. After they lifted her down, he asked Mary for more sheets, hot water, and cloths. Mary scurried off to do as he asked.

Less than thirty minutes later, with a minimum of grunting and pushing, Mrs. O'Sullivan delivered a baby girl, with no complications—unlike the last time she gave birth. Given the past few days of excitement, James was grateful to the Lord for this gift of an easy birth. He was still exhausted.

"I guess I didn't have to be here after all," James said as he placed the baby on Rebecca's abdomen while he tied and cut the umbilical cord. "You did all the work."

"Thank you, James," Rebecca said weakly. She struggled to catch her breath, her face flushed and at the same time, triumphant. She laughed. "Thank you. I should have had you here for all my babies—that was the best delivery yet. A girl! Won't you have fun, Mary." She cooed in awe as she held the baby steady on her abdomen.

Mary, who had held her mother's hand throughout the delivery, kissed her, took the baby and wrapped the infant in a blanket. James watched Mary's face glow as she looked down at her new sister.

"That is *my* child, Mary," Rebecca said with a smirk on her face.

"She is beautiful, Mother," Mary said. She passed the baby back to her mother.

"Could I please have another basin and cloth, Mary?" James asked. He was awaiting the delivery of the placenta.

When Mary handed him a cloth their hands touched. He felt a surge of energy course through his body as if a spirit had entered. He looked up at Mary and knew she had felt it too. "Thank you, Mary," he managed to say.

Mary smiled.

James coaxed Rebecca to give a final push and safely delivered the placenta. Then he and Mary set about cleaning up the room. When they were done, Rebecca asked Mary to fetch Clancy.

"Before I get Father," Mary said. "Promise me that this is the last child! Father is not to do this to you again! You're too old to be having children. Promise me!"

"I'm too old?" Rebecca replied. She smiled and looked at James.

"Yes! You know I'm right, mother. Promise me before I get him."

Rebecca smiled and patted Mary's hand. "I promise, Mary," she said. "Your father and I love each other."

"But mother, that doesn't mean—"

"Of course not, dear." Rebecca hugged her baby tighter and kissed the small forehead. "My hope is that one day, you too will find someone to love—then you'll understand." Mary said nothing and left the room to get her father.

James, surprised that Mary had even brought this up to her mother in his presence, felt uncomfortable. It was a private family conversation. However, Mary was right and he took the opportunity to say so. "She's right, you know," he said, as he wiped away the last of the blood and fluids from the bed where Rebecca lay.

"I know. I shouldn't have more children." She touched her baby's cheek. "Are you almost finished down there, James?"

"I'm just cleaning up and checking the placenta. Everything looks fine."

He straightened up and placed the basin with the placenta behind him on a dresser. When he turned around, Rebecca was still looking at her baby. He was amazed at how quickly women recovered from the trauma of labour. She looked peaceful.

"James," she said, without looking up. "Have you ever had a serious relationship with a girl? I hope you don't mind me asking—you're single and … you must have had relationships. A broken heart perhaps? A traumatic secret?"

Clancy was taking his time coming in, he thought. He was uncomfortable discussing personal matters with other people, let alone one he barely knew. He pulled the bloody sheet out from under Rebecca's bottom and pulled her nightgown down to make her presentable for Clancy. "No secrets or broken-hearts, Rebecca. I never had the time, or perhaps the good fortune, to meet the girl who could become my wife."

"Are you sure?"

Was she hinting about Mary? His heart sped up and he felt his face flush. He didn't want to appear foolish and make that presumption. "We'll lift you back up in bed," he said, "when your husband comes in."

"Fiddlesticks," she said. "I don't need help." She handed the baby to James and shifted her body higher in the bed with only a small grunt. *She is one tough lady,* he thought.

"Mary is a lovely girl, don't you think?" she said to him as he gave her back the baby.

"Yes … she was a great help."

"I don't mean today." She looked annoyed. "I mean a man … some man … someday will be thankful to have her for his wife."

Where was Clancy! "Any man," he said carefully, "would most definitely be thankful to God to have Mary as his wife. At least he *should* be … she is very beautiful … and most delicate in spirit."

Rebecca smiled. "James, all the man has to do is to ask Clancy for permission to visit and sit with Mary. That's usually how these things start."

"I thought—"

At that moment, Clancy stormed into the room. "REBECCA MY LOVE," he yelled. "YOU'VE BROUGHT US ANOTHER PRECIOUS BABY."

James was left open-mouthed at how easily she'd seen through him.

Chapter 17
Dr. Peters

AFTER SUPPER THAT EVENING, JAMES rode out to see Frank O'Leary. Frank was lying in bed, hair plastered to his forehead with sweat. He grunted a greeting to James through clenched teeth.

"How're doing, Frank?" James asked. He knew Frank must be in a terrible amount of pain and before Frank could respond to the question, he added, "I didn't *think* the pain pills would do the trick. You'd be better off in hospital—the nurses would give you injections for pain."

"I know," Frank muttered through his discomfort. He looked at his wife and smiled. "But she'd miss me too much."

"It'd give me a break, I tell you," Marg responded, pretending to be serious. "You're not as needed as you think, Frank O'Leary."

James wasn't fooled by their loving banter. While the love these two had for each other was apparent from the first time he met them, he understood that their financial situation was the real reason Frank didn't want to be hospitalized. He also surmised the O'Leary's were the type of people who wouldn't accept charity from him or anyone, so there was nothing he could do to sway them and he wasn't going to try.

He drew up morphine and, after rolling him onto his side, injected it into Frank's buttock. While he waited for the morphine to take effect, he placed a thermometer in Frank's mouth and then listened to his chest. Blessedly, his temperature was normal and his chest clear. Then he removed the old dressing, which was saturated with serous fluid and pulled off easily, to expose the thigh wound. The wound seemed clean enough, but he knew it was too early for signs of infection to develop. He cleaned the tissues with freshly boiled water and carbolic acid. He thought about loosely suturing the ragged edges of the wound together to promote healing, but abandoned the idea—closing a dirty wound promoted infection and he needed a conduit for the pus to drain anyway. He cleaned the area one more time and finished by applying a new dressing.

He instructed Marg that Frank was to remain strictly in bed. Unfortunately, it would be some time before the danger of infection was over and he could immobilise the leg in a plaster cast. Until then, Frank had to remain still.

Marg took over the task of cleaning up, while James washed his instruments in a basin of water. "Are you sure the ice is still okay for travelling on?" he asked Frank as he worked. "When I was riding up, Sadie's hooves were breaking through the top crust. The weather has changed drastically from a few days ago; it was mild today and the sun was strong. Do you think the ice will still be safe?"

"This weather is typical of March," Frank said. "It changes so fast. One day it's freezing, or we're having a blizzard, and the next day you're taking off your winter coat and getting a tan!" He scratched his two days' growth of beard. "The ice shouldn't break up 'til early April," he said. "She starts to rot on top first, but under that she'll be strong for a while. You should have another two weeks of safe travel on it yet."

The 'should' bothered him but he didn't say anything.

He finished cleaning his instruments with carbolic acid and wiped them dry. "I'll be back in a few days, Frank," he said, while he packed away his tools. "No getting up. You're to pee and use the bathroom in bed."

"You mean shit … in *bed*?"

"I'm afraid so. You can't put any weight on that leg, and we can't bring the outhouse in here …" He chuckled and snapped up his medical bag. "Since we have no potty around, we'll have to get the boys to rig you up a chair with a hole in the seat so you can defecate into a bowl, but until then ..."

"*Defecate*? You mean *shit*!"

"Yes."

"How is a man to shit in bed?" Frank was beside himself with concern.

"I'll tell Marg the best way to manage that. And I'll leave you more pain pills," James told him. "It won't be that bad."

He nodded to Frank and left the bedroom. Marg was cleaning cloths in the kitchen sink. He explained to her how to manage Frank's toilet needs in bed, and suggested she ask one of the men to rig up a potty chair. Then he bade her farewell and left just as the sun was setting.

He looked down river as he and Sadie stepped onto the ice; he wasn't planning on riding on this ice any more than he could help it, despite Frank's reassurances. He headed directly across the river to meet a road that would take him home—a longer, slower, but safer way home. He heard and felt Sadie's hooves break through the top layer of ice and her body drop under him with each step as they crossed. With every jolt he anticipated he and Sadie breaking through the ice and sinking into the freezing water. He knew Frank was probably right—that they were only breaking through an ice crust that had melted and reformed and that the ice underneath was still very thick—but that didn't stop his imagination from running wild. He was grateful when they reached the opposite shore and climbed a currently unused boat landing to dry land.

It was completely dark by the time he and Sadie met the road, though it was not far from shore. Luckily, the snow on the road was packed down hard and so the two of them made good time getting home. Once there, James immediately fed and watered Sadie. Then, when he finally entered his house, he went straight to bed without bothering to eat or wash up. He was so tired. He groaned as his body sank into the mattress.

Sleep didn't come right away; he kept thinking of his patients. He had to find time to check on Rebecca tomorrow. And he needed to confront Dr. Peters, he thought, as exhaustion spread over his body. He didn't care how influential Peters was in the city; he had no right to talk behind his back and make accusations about him to people who might someday be patients. And to bad-mouth him to Wilfred, of all people! He didn't understand why Peters seemed to hate him so much; he generally got along with everyone. And while he wasn't usually a confrontational type of fellow, Peters was giving him no alternative. They would have to have it out.

His mind drifted and he woke briefly with a start to realise in his dreams he was talking to Mary O'Sullivan and they were fishing on a river he had never seen before. *I must have dozed off.*

Later this week, he would ask Clancy if he could visit Mary. He smiled and fell asleep, trying to find Mary by the river again.

The next morning, he saw Randall Fillmore, a young lad of ten, who had been suffering from a sore throat for a week. His mother was concerned because he hadn't improved. James examined him and diagnosed a stubborn case of pharyngitis, or sore throat. Luckily for young Randall, there was no evidence of tonsillar involvement, nor any protracted fever. In fact, the tissues in the back of the throat were only mildly inflamed. He suspected Randall of malingering. Being sick was a good excuse for not going to school and avoiding some chores. He tussled his hair and told Mrs. Fillmore that her boy would be better in two days. Then he prescribed saline gargles and potassium iodide drops. In James' experience, it was amazing how quickly children improved once they had to take those horrible tasting drops.

Next, James saw Mr. Murdock for his lumbago. James inserted multiple needles into Murdock's lower back. He had learned this procedure from Dr. Miller in Montreal. He had performed the needle insertions every two weeks for the last three months on Mr. Murdock, who reported the needles relieved the pain for about a week.

It was midmorning before James finally phoned Dr. Peters. "Dr. Peters, I think we need to talk," he said tersely.

"Yes, James," Peters said. "I've been meaning to phone you. I would like that very much. Could I meet you at the Union Club, tonight? Around six? Supper's on me. Good? See you then."

James was confused as he hung up the phone. He had expected an unpleasant conversation with Peters, and instead Peters had been friendly; humble, even. He even used James' first name. He frowned and shook his head. He didn't know what to think of that conversation. Perhaps Peters was setting him up for some unpleasant surprise. Could he possibly be sincere? And if so, why the sudden change?

He spent the rest of the morning cleaning instruments, examining blood and urine samples, and reading a few medical papers. After lunch, he rode over to see Mrs. Perkins, a charming lady in her seventies who, unfortunately, was dying from what seemed to be stomach cancer. He'd originally suspected stomach ulcers after she vomited a small amount of blood four months ago. He prescribed a diet and tonic to remedy that; however, she didn't responded to the diet and he could now palpate a firm mass in her abdomen. It was almost definitely cancer. Further, she had become anorexic—her arms were thin, her face gaunt, and her ribs showed pitifully through her chest wall. But despite her condition, she welcomed him with a smile when her daughter let him into her cozy home.

He examined her in bed. She was barely able to raise her arms when he sounded her chest and fluid bubbled throughout the lower zones of her lungs. *It won't be long now,* thought James. He patted her shoulder and asked about her breathing and the pain. She told him she was comfortable and that she thought the medication was helping. He felt like such a fraud—all he was doing was watching her die. He left her daughter some morphine to administer for pain and then left to visit Rebecca O'Sullivan.

As he and Sadie rode to the O'Sullivan's, he noticed that patches of wet ground were appearing on the road as the snow melted. He felt the strength of the sun when the wind abated; otherwise, it was chilly despite the bright day. He eyed the Kennebecasis River, thinking about calling on Frank. It was still frozen, but the top layer of snow looked even slushier. River riding days were over, as far as he was concerned.

Sadie seemed to have an extra little bounce today. He imagined she was grateful for less snow on the road and that she sensed the coming of spring—fresh grass to graze on, the freedom of a gallop in the pasture, and the feel of the warm sun on her back. He patted her neck.

When he arrived at the O'Sullivan's home, Mary met him at the door. "You haven't been knocking long, I hope?" she asked. "I was in the kitchen helping Eva with the dinner meal."

James told her he had just arrived, and she ushered him in. Mary took his overcoat. She looked so pretty. Her cheeks were flushed, making her look delicate and exciting at the same time. Naughty, even. He was tempted to ask her if he could call on her, but he knew that wasn't the proper protocol; he would ask Clancy for permission later this week.

After Mary hung up his coat, she led the way to Rebecca's upstairs bedroom. He tried to ignore her swivelling bottom as she ascended the stairs in front of him by keeping his head down and eyes focused on the steps. He blushed and coughed when she turned and smiled after she reached the top of the stairs.

She led him down the hall and opened the bedroom door. He thanked her as he walked by her to enter Rebecca's room. He could smell her perfume. She wasn't giving him much room to get by—was this on purpose?

"Why, Dr. Wilson, how nice of you to come," Rebecca said.

"I'll leave you two alone," Mary informed them and closed the door.

The baby was sleeping in a bassinette by the window. "How is she?" James asked.

"Fine," Rebecca answered. "Feeding well. Urinating. And she had a small bowel movement."

"I'll let her sleep and examine you first," he said.

"Is it warm out? You look a bit flushed." She smiled impishly like she knew exactly what he was flushed about. Were they both teasing him?

The examination didn't take long. Rebecca and the baby were both doing very well. He began packing his things, preparing to leave, when Rebecca asked him, "Dr. Wilson, would you like to stay for dinner?"

"As delightful as that sounds, I can't," he told her wistfully, not liking that he was giving up a fine opportunity to spend time with Mary. "I have a meeting in St. John."

"Well that *is* a shame," said Rebecca kindly.

He breathed deeply with regret as he walked down the stairs. As Eva was still busy preparing dinner, Mary met him at the foot of the stairs, fetched his jacket and showed him out.

"Good bye," Mary, he said wistfully. She gave him a half-smile. Was she disappointed that he was not staying? His stomach flipped at the thought—*I'm nervous like a boy,* he thought. He was going to have to do better if he was to court Mary. He was a grown man. A doctor. He couldn't be nervous like a lovesick schoolboy. *You would think I'd have enough confidence to talk to the girl!* He chuckled at his own foolishness and mounted Sadie.

The sun was staying higher in the sky now as the days got longer. It was still light when he reached Marsh Creek. Long, yellow, dead strands of grass waved in the gentle breeze now, having escaped their winter blanket of snow since the last time he had passed through. Spring was coming fast.

He passed through the marsh and then through city streets, reaching the Union Club a little after six. The attendant at the front desk told him that Dr. Peters was waiting for him in the meeting room. *This doesn't look good,* he thought, as he walked down the hallway to the meeting room. *Peters wants us to be alone.*

Dr. Peters was sitting at a table near the entrance of the meeting room when James walked in. He surprised him by standing up, shaking his hand, offering him a chair, and pouring him a glass of wine. What the devil was going on?

"You wanted to talk to me?" Peters asked. Then he noted James' bruised jaw. "Whatever happened to your face, James?"

James coughed and drank some wine. "Long story," he said, "And yes … yes, I do want to talk to you, Dr. Peters—"

"George," Peters interrupted, smiling. "Call me, George."

This was becoming more confusing. James took another swallow of wine and got right to it. "I recently found out that you discussed my medical care of young Thomas McGarrigle with a patient of yours," he said evenly, "and that you also spoke to this same person about my involvement with Bessie MacKenzie."

"Quite so," Peters acknowledged. "And my apologizes for doing so. I was angry at you after our little spat, and Wilfred told me you saw Bessie on the day she died—"

"I thought the *police* told you!"

"No, it was Wilfred MacKenzie who mentioned it—that's who we are talking about, isn't it?"

"Yes."

"Wilfred came to me shortly after Bessie died, to express his concerns about Amos. He wanted me to look in on him."

James couldn't stop his eyes from rolling upward in disbelief.

"While he was there, he asked me what I thought Bessie might have said to you that fateful day. He then said something like, 'it must be hard to be a doctor and to have to make life and death decisions', and I—like a stupid fool—blurted out how I thought you should have made a different decision about the McGarrigle case. I am so sorry. I have no excuse for my bad judgement."

He seemed really sincere, which surprised James. He had never seen this side of Dr. Peters before.

"How did you find out I had foolishly spoken about these matters to Wilfred?" Peters asked.

James told him about Frank O'Leary's accident, and how Frank had had recounted what he heard from Wilfred.

"Ah, yes," said Peters. "That makes sense. By the way, I heard about the fine work you did on Frank O'Leary. You saved his life."

"For now," James said.

"I never liked that man."

"Frank O'Leary?" James asked.

"No. Frank is a salt of the earth type of man. No, I mean Wilfred MacKenzie. There is something insincere about him. And he has a lot of nerve to spread such gossip."

James tapped the table and wondered if he should talk about what he suspected. Dr. Peters must have read his indecision. He asked, "Is there something you want to tell me?"

It would feel great to share this secret, James thought, *but I don't know if I should.* After all, what he surmised about

Wilfred raping Bessie was really only a suspicion—he had no proof.

Peters noted his hesitation. "Is it about a patient of yours?" Peters asked.

"No. Wilfred is not my patient."

"Well you wouldn't be breaking any doctor-patient confidence if you talked to me about him, would you?"

The transformation from the gruff Dr. Peters to this fatherly figure who wanted to help and offer advice was remarkable, but it seemed a sudden change and he was still not sure of it. "I may have been mistaken about you, Dr. Peters," he ventured. He saw Peters wince.

"Call me George," said Peters.

"Alright, George, then … Frankly, I thought you were a gruff, condescending fellow—at least to *me*." He watched George's face for a sign of anger, but George only chuckled. "Why the sudden change in attitude?" James asked. "I've been functioning on the assumption that, for reasons of your own, you don't like me much."

George poured him some more wine and said, "Because I've seen that you're a fine physician and I admire you." George noted James' surprised expression. "Surprised, are you? You shouldn't be, because I understand now that you're a dedicated, compassionate doctor. I heard about the tireless, selfless way you worked to help the people of Rothesay during the recent flu epidemic. I heard about the home visits in the middle of the night, how you helped Frank O'Leary and Rebecca O'Sullivan—Clancy sings your praises—and I could go on."

James didn't know what to say.

"I'll admit I was wary of you at first," Peters continued. "You arrived, and before we even got to know you, you started spouting off about how we needed a surgeon. I'm rather protective of our hospital and my colleagues—probably too much so—and I didn't want them to think I thought their surgical work was shoddy, so I made sure to put you in your place."

"I didn't mean to infer that!"

"I know. I know *now.* But at that time, I thought you might be a bit of a know-it-all and some others were hinting to me that they thought so too."

"So, when you called me, you were protecting me telling me I was putting people's noses out of joint?"

"Yes. And I'm afraid I let that conversation deteriorate." He laughed and shook his head. "The truth is, doctors *were* talking about you stealing their patients and I was trying to warn you, but I let my smouldering animosity towards you get a hold of me and I took the opportunity to berate you. Forgive me."

"I'm sorry, too," James said. "I was probably looking for a fight. It never occurred to me that you were being sincere."

"You have proven yourself to be a fine physician and valuable to your community, and I know you have gained the respect of all your colleagues, so I won't be hearing anymore of that rubbish."

James was floored at the words, but when he thought about it he realized that during the last few months other doctors who had never been friendly to him before had started being quite chummy at medical meetings.

George said, "I'm afraid I was being a little too territorial. The funny thing is that I agree with you. I think a surgeon would be a wonderful addition to our medical community and just last week a Dr. Arnold Smith, who trained at McGill, applied for surgical privileges at our hospital. Do you know him?"

"Yes," James said. "He was in residency while I was a student there. As I recall, he's a very good fellow and an excellent surgeon."

"That is wonderful news," said George, as James finished his glass of wine.

Then James looked evenly at George. *I might as well get everything out in the open*, he thought. "So, about Thomas McGarrigle …" James began.

"That was a clinical decision you made, and it turned out to be a good one. I probably would have done the surgery in the home, but I'm old school. I wouldn't have wanted to take the chance of a perforated appendix. But I wasn't there and I didn't examine the boy. If I had, it's possible I *would* have made the same decision, though I doubt it. Nevertheless, I can't fault a successful outcome."

James nodded acknowledgement.

"As I said," continued Peters, "I have a great deal of respect for you, and when I called you that day I was probably just looking for something to fault you on so I could bring you down from your high horse."

"My high horse? That's funny," James mused. "Is that how people see me? I think I need *more* confidence."

"Well, you *should* be confident, James, because you're a fine doctor."

James mumbled a thank you and scratched his chin. *I guess it's true that you never really know people until you spend some time with them,* he thought. He was as guilty as Dr. Peters when it came to being judgemental; he should have taken the time to sit down with him and discuss the conflict they were having, instead of misinterpreting the intent and character of the man. After all, his father had seemed to like Dr. Peters. He should have taken heart from that alone.

"So, what's this concern you have about Wilfred?" George asked as the waiter refilled their glasses. He looked sympathetic, the way James' father used to look when James was troubled. Despite a bit of hesitation about doctor/patient confidentiality, he decided to tell

Dr. Peters the whole story—about Bessie's visit; his suspicion about Wilfred raping her; the visit to the police; and, the fight with Wilfred. He hoped that Bessie in her home up above would not mind him confiding in a fellow doctor.

"I never have liked that fellow," George reiterated. "I don't know why, but I just can't feel friendly toward him." He stared down at his lap and sighed. He seemed to be deep in thought. "If what you say is true, then what a rotten, disgusting bastard he is," he finally mumbled, more to himself than to James.

"Perhaps," James said, "I shouldn't have said anything."

George looked up at him. "Oh no, James. I'm glad you did. I'm just thinking about what we can do. He never confessed to the crime during the fight?"

"Not in words, but his actions and manner convinced me of his guilt."

George leaned forward and put his arms on the table. "I'm afraid the police are right, though. You can't charge and convict a man based upon suspicion, no matter how convincing those suspicions are. I see no way to bring him to justice without proof."

"I know," James said. "I've thought and thought about it for all these months and I concluded long ago that there is no way to prove Wilfred's guilt. I resolved then to make his life miserable by never letting him forget that I know the truth."

George folded his arms and sat upright. "James," he said, "Some things you can't change. Miserable injustices happen every day in this world. I applaud you for trying to right these wrongs, but don't make your life miserable by becoming obsessed with this."

"I won't," James said, trying to stop his voice from shaking, "but I owe Bessie, and I vowed to her in my prayers that I wouldn't let her down."

"You sound like you feel guilty over Bessie MacKenzie's death." It was a statement and George was expecting him to respond.

James didn't know what to say. He felt responsible because of his indecision on that fateful day. He was afraid if he told Dr. Peters about his pact with Bessie, he would sound like he was excusing his part in her death.

"James, you aren't guilty of that girl's demise," George said when James didn't answer. "You can't tell if someone is going to take their life if they haven't expressed suicidal ideas. She didn't, right?"

"No. She was distraught over the news of her pregnancy, but she never once mentioned being so desperate that she would take her own life. But I wonder if maybe I missed a sign. Perhaps I should have—"

"There are no 'should haves'," George interrupted. "You should know better than that! All doctors on occasion question their judgement and wonder if this or that might have unfolded differently if we had done things differently. But we're not perfect. I'm sure you did all you could."

James wished that were true, but he knew better. He should have told Amos about the pregnancy that very evening. Bessie was too young to be left alone with that terrible secret. He should never have complied with her request to let her handle it by herself.

"Did you ever consider the possibility," George suddenly asked, "that Wilfred might have killed Bessie and made it look like a suicide?"

James eyed Dr. Peters. "Yes …" he responded slowly, staring cannily at him. "Actually, I discussed that possibility with the police, and it was pointed out to me that we have even *less* proof of that. Wilfred is a creep, but he wouldn't murder his own niece … would he?"

"You never know what a man will do if his life or reputation is threatened," Dr. Peters said direly. There was a moment of silence as James and Dr. Peters contemplated this. Then Peters said, "Let's adjoin to the dining room and order dinner, James. As promised, the meal's on me."

They went to the dining hall and were seated promptly. James ordered soup and custard because of his sore jaw. He endured a round of good-natured jesting from some other doctors in the hall when they saw the condition his face was in.

Dr. Peters didn't speak of Bessie MacKenzie over supper. He talked only of hospital and city affairs, and James mumbled comments to keep the conversation going—but his mind was on Wilfred MacKenzie. He was dumbfounded by the renewed idea that Wilfred may have not only raped, but murdered Bessie. Officer Kimball had inferred that the police did not want to engage in speculation, and nor should James, but it was thought-provoking to have an uninvolved observer suddenly raise the question again.

At the end of the evening, he shook Dr. Peters hand and thanked him for his kindness and for listening to his troubles as they parted.

"My pleasure, James," Dr. Peters said. "It's good for us to start over again." James was grateful for the words.

As he and Sadie headed home, a strong north wind blew directly into his face just when he entered the marsh on the outskirts of the city. Frank O'Leary was right; the weather could sure change fast in March. He pressed his face into his coat. Sadie snorted and lowered her head as if she too was complaining. He patted her neck and they continued. It was quite dark in the marsh field, away from the city lights. He could hear the dead grass stalks rustling beside him and the wind moaning in the trees on the other side of Marsh Creek.

This has been quite the evening, he thought. His impression of Dr. Peters had been transformed almost magically and the idea of Wilfred murdering Bessie was a renewed revelation of almost biblical proportions. *Could a man be so desperate he would kill his own niece?*

He was lost in his thoughts when halfway through the marsh, he heard a noise behind him. Sadie whickered at the sound and he turned around in his saddle to see if something was following them, but couldn't see much beyond Sadie's rump in the darkness. The grass beside him swished with a gust of wind. *Probably that.*

Further along, he heard a noise again, like dirt being scuffed. "Hello?" he called, as he reined Sadie to a stop and turned around in the saddle again. No one answered. "Hello!" he yelled more loudly. Nothing.

I'm just spooked over the thought of murder, that's all, he thought. *Of course there are sounds—it's blowing hard.* He urged Sadie to resume their journey with a nudge of his heel and a giddy-up.

He rode along but still he heard scuffles and creaks coming from behind him. He had an eerie feeling that he was being followed. He listened as intently as he could. *A scuff. Closer.*

He turned once more. "Hello!" he yelled again. Nothing. A moan arose from the tree line and wind whistled by his ears. "Is anyone there?" he asked.

As before, no one answered. He decided to wait on the other side and listen for a horse clip-clopping over in the darkness. He rode over the wooden bridge spanning Marsh Creek as it met the Rothesay Road. He waited.

A good ten minutes passed and still he heard nothing. Feeling foolish, he finally commanded Sadie to go on. As they rode, all he could hear was the wind howling over the river to his left.

Soon, the first homes of Rothesay appeared on the hill to his right making the night seem less frightening. There were no more eerie tree moans and rustling grass sounds. *You're such a child*, he thought.

He passed by Mary's house and felt excited, anxious and happy. A wave of joy swept over him. Sometime this week, he was going to ask Clancy if he could visit Mary. He nudged Sadie to speed up.

As he rode into his yard, he thought he heard a horse snort. He turned Sadie around and sat quietly listening. Again, he could hear nothing. Suddenly there was a laugh in the darkness. It seemed to come from the meadow across the road. "Wilfred!" he cried. A horse galloped away. "I know it's you!" he yelled. The sounds faded. "You don't scare me!" he yelled after the noise.

He waited for a moment to see if he would get a response, but when the sounds of the retreating horseman vanished, he turned and led Sadie into the barn.

Was it Wilfred, he wondered? *Who else would it be? What does he want?*

After he settled Sadie for the night, he slowly reopened the barn door to go to his house. He expected a blow to his head at any moment. The door creaked. He slid out the opening and latched the door quickly behind him. He crept across the yard until he was at the stairs and then he flew up them and into his house as quickly as he could.

He had lied to Wilfred, or whoever it was—he *was* scared.

Chapter 18
The Request

JAMES WAS IN THAT DROWSY middle state between sleep and wakefulness when he ran his hand over his jaw. He froze as a bolt of white-hot pain raced from his ear to sear the whole side of his face. He moaned, cradled his jaw, and curled up into the fetal position.

It had been difficult to sleep; he must have turned onto his bad jaw half a dozen times throughout the night. In a few minutes the pain subsided somewhat and he wearily swung his legs over the side of the bed, shuffled to his nightstand, and poured water into a bowl to wash his face. He inspected his face in the mirror—the jaw was swollen and turning darker. "Good wooking fewwow," he said to the mirror, laughing.

This isn't a good time to go a-courting, he thought. Then he remembered the feeling of brushing by Mary at her mother's bedroom door. He splashed cold water on his face. No matter if he was battered and bruised—he had to see her this week. He shaved, dressed, and went downstairs for breakfast.

The day passed slowly. He did chores around the house, split wood outside, and saw a few patients in the office. Mrs. Perkins' daughter called to tell him her mother's breathing was becoming more laboured. He agreed to visit her after supper and instructed the daughter to increase the dose of morphine. Finally, after supper that evening, he telephoned the O'Sullivan home and was embarrassed and shocked when Mary answered the phone. Why hadn't he anticipated this possibility? And why was he so nervous? He was such an idiot. He wondered if Mary could read the anxiety in his voice when, through his battered jaw, he managed to say, "Good evening, Mary. I wonder if I could speak to Clancy, please?"

"Of course, Dr. Wilson," she said in her beautiful voice. James smiled in spite of himself.

In a few minutes, Clancy was on the line. "James, nice to hear from you," Clancy said, when he came to the phone. "Is there anything the matter?"

"No. Nothing's wrong … How's Rebecca?"

"Fine. Thanks for coming over yesterday to see her."

"My pleasure. You have a beautiful, healthy, baby girl."

"Yes."

The pause seemed to last forever as James screwed up his courage to ask the next question. Finally he managed to blurt out, "May I speak to you tonight, Clancy?"

"Why of course," Clancy answered. "What about?"

"I'd rather not talk about it over the phone," James told him. He was afraid the operator might be listening, as she was prone to do. If so, the news would be all over the village by tomorrow morning—*Dr. Wilson is calling on Mary O'Sullivan!*

"I'm very curious now," Clancy said.

"I have to see a patient first and then I'll be along … about eight. Is that okay?"

"Of course, my good fellow," Clancy assured him.

They hung up and James collapsed against the wall with relief. He wondered if Clancy had any suspicion about his intention. Would Rebecca have discussed this possibility with her husband? Certainly *she* seemed aware of his interest in Mary. But his request might come as a great shock to Clancy. *Mary has many fine prospects for a husband in Boston*, he had said. *Young men of good standing.* Would Clancy laugh at his audacity? Would he make uncomfortable excuses about Mary's unavailability or be rendered speechless at James' request?

He hoped not; there was nothing he could do but try.

He went upstairs to change and freshen up, and then an hour later, he saw the almost comatose Mrs. Perkins and concluded that she would probably not make it through the night. He instructed her daughter about how to care for her over the next few hours and sat with her awhile before leaving.

He headed to the O'Sullivan home with an odd mix of sadness and anxiety in his heart. He was experiencing the heaviness that always preceded the death of one of his patients and at the same time, he was anxious about the conversation he was about to have with Clancy. He tried to relax his grip on Sadie's reins and he swung the stirrups to ease the tension in his legs. He took several deep breaths and then exhaled, but it was to no avail. His anxiety mounted as he travelled closer to the O'Sullivan home. He blew out one last deep breath when he turned into their yard.

Eva met him at the door. "Mr. O'Sullivan is waiting for you in the study," she said. She hung up his coat and led James to the room. James was grateful Mary hadn't met him at the door—that would have been very awkward.

Clancy sat in a big leather chair, smoking a pipe and reading a paper. A kerosene lamp burned on a table beside him and the fireplace was lit in front of him, spreading an inviting heat throughout the room.

"Dr. Wilson is here to see you now, Mr. O'Sullivan," Eva announced.

"James! Have a seat. Can I have Eva get you a drink?"

"A scotch and water, please." He thought he might need this.

Clancy offered James a chair across from him and folded the paper he was reading upon his lap. He asked James about his mother while Eva was preparing the drink. Then he said, "I suppose you've been reading about how the German's are building up their army."

James nodded, indicating he had.

"I don't know why the Brits are getting so upset over this," Clancy went on. "It's not like they're going to declare war."

"I hope you're right," James said. "But I think they fear the Germans might have a hidden agenda."

"Paranoid rubbish!"

Eva placed James' drink on the table beside him and asked Mr. O'Sullivan if there was anything else she could do. When he said 'no', she left the room and closed the door.

James took a gulp of the scotch and nearly coughed. He struggled but finally managed to swallow the liquor without spraying it all over himself and the floor. He looked up to see Clancy sipping his wine with an amused look on his face.

"So," Clancy said, "what did you want to see me about?" He rubbed his face as if he was trying to hide a smile.

If Clancy was trying to disguise his amusement at his obvious discomfort, James thought, he was doing a poor job of it. He put his drink down and faced Clancy. "Mr. O'Sullivan—"

"Mr. O'Sullivan, it is now? This must be serious!"

"Clancy …" James said. He wiped his palms on his pants. "I would like to ask you your permission to visit Mary … sometimes."

Clancy burst out laughing. James panicked. It was worse than he thought. *Clancy thinks this is hilarious.*

"I *am* sorry, James," Clancy said, trying to compose himself. He took out his handkerchief from his vest pocket, dabbed his eyes, and then blew his nose. "Forgive me, my dear fellow, but … but … you will call on her more than *sometimes*, won't you?" He broke out laughing again.

James finally realised that Clancy wasn't laughing at his *request*; he was laughing at his awkwardness. He took another drink to gain his composure. "So, you don't mind if I see Mary?" he asked to confirm, glancing up at Clancy.

"James, nothing would make me happier. Rebecca told me you were interested in Mary, and Mary in you. I knew, or at least I guessed, why you were coming here tonight. Actually, Rebecca and I hoped this would happen *months* ago. You don't take hints very well, do you?" He added, "I shouldn't have laughed at you. I'm sorry, but you were so nervous I thought you were going to spill the scotch before it touched your lips." Then Clancy bent over in laughter once again.

James allowed himself a small chuckle. "So, you *don't* mind if I see Mary?" he repeated.

"Not at all! You have our blessings and … we'll just see what happens." Clancy took a sip of his wine and got up from the chair. He walked over to James and, shaking his hand, said, "We are very, very pleased. I'll call Mary in and then I'll go up to tell Rebecca. Would that all right? Fine."

Clancy went to study door, opened it, and called for Mary. James felt panic rise in his belly again. He had been numb with relief at Clancy's reaction, but now things were now happening *too* fast—he was about to see Mary. Would she be shocked at the news? Disappointed? Clancy said she was interested in him *months* ago. Had anything changed?

Mary appeared suddenly at the door before he could think further. She mustn't have been far away.

"Mary," Clancy exclaimed, grabbing both her arms. "Dr. Wilson has just asked my permission to visit you. I have given him my blessing. I must go and tell Rebecca; she'll be pleased."

Clancy left, leaving Mary standing at the door. James felt uncomfortable, and noted that Mary did too. He remembered his manners and stood up. "Won't you come over and have a seat?"

She smiled and walked over with her head down. She seemed so different. He had always found her to be quietly confident. He had never seen this vulnerable side of her. He relaxed.

She sat in a chair to his side. He guessed the chair opposite him was her father's chair and only he sat in it. "Mary, you don't have to welcome my visits," he said, sitting down. "I can just make up some excuse to your parents."

Mary smiled at him and said, "Dr. Wilson, I am honoured that you would consider me worthy of your attention. I most certainly welcome your visits." She blushed and looked into his eyes.

He imagined his own face was scarlet by now, too. He searched for something more to say and felt the familiar onset of panic. "That's fine then," he finally blurted out. "Just fine … Maybe I can come over Sunday afternoon before I go to my mother's for supper?"

"I will look forward to your visit," she said.

He talked with her about the new baby, the weather, her siblings. She asked about Mrs. Perkins. He was amazed at how easy it was to talk to Mary. They endured no embarrassing lags in conversation. He already knew Sunday couldn't come fast enough. *This is only Tuesday; why didn't I suggest Thursday, or Friday?*

His excitement and joy were at an all-time high when Clancy came into the room and dampened things by declaring, "Rebecca has informed me it isn't proper to leave you two alone."

He walked over to a table that held a variety of spirits and poured another glass of wine. James caught Mary smiling when her father turned his back.

"Have another scotch, James?" Clancy asked.

"No thank you, I'm fine," James said. "I should go. It may be a long night … Mrs. Perkins is not well …" He didn't know how much to say about the dying woman.

"Yes," Clancy said. "I heard about the poor dear. Dreadful. Well, I understand," he said. When James stood, Clancy walked over and shook his hand. "I'll say good night to you now," he said. "Mary would you please see James out?" He picked up his paper, cleared his throat, and sat down.

James followed Mary out of the room to the front door. She took his coat from the closet, handed it to him and smiled, shy again.

"I look forward to Sunday," James said as he put on his coat.

"And I," Mary responded.

He was unsure if he should kiss her hand, or of what to say. Surely, a kiss would be too bold? In the end, he elected to do nothing and simply bade her goodnight. She smiled. He smile back as best his battered jaw would allow.

As he rode home, he felt a pang of guilt—poor Mrs. Perkins was dying, and he was happier than he'd ever been. *Is that wrong?* He felt like singing like a fool and riding with speed through the night, laughing and shouting with glee into the silence; but he contained himself with little grunts of suppressed joy as he rode along.

He decided to visit Mrs. Perkins again before he went home. After all, he was first and foremost a physician, and his patients came first. Besides he needed a good dose of sobriety right now. He chuckled and turned off the river road to go see Mrs. Perkins.

Chapter 19
Another Decision

JAMES AWOKE THE NEXT MORNING to the unfamiliar sound of rain lashing wildly against the window of his bedroom—a full spring gale. Frank was right; weather was sure changeable in March. He'd long since ceased traveling over the river ice. No matter what Charlie, Robert, or Percy might say, he was certain it was not safe.

His face throbbed. He had stayed with Mrs. Perkins through the night until she passed away early in the morning and hadn't got to bed until a little after six; then he'd tossed and turned, battering his poor face in the process.

He checked the clock on his bedside table. It was after nine. His head felt heavy and dull. He rubbed his eyes and tried to orient himself to the new day. *I have an appointment at ten,* he suddenly realized. *Damn!*

James sprang out of bed and hustled to the bureau to wash and shave. The windows rattled with a surge of wind and rain. *The trip to the outhouse will be memorable this morning,* he thought. He grinned and turned back to the mirror. There was no one to blame but himself. It had been his choice to buy a house with no indoor plumbing.

He touched his swollen blue-purple jaw and winced. It would be porridge for breakfast *again.*

A few days later, on Sunday morning in church, Mrs. Mawhinney shook her head and clucked like a hen when she saw his face. The swelling had regressed, but a patch of wrinkled, dry, purple-black skin remained.

"I think you've lost weight, Dr. Wilson," she said.

"I think so," he replied. "I've been living on thin porridge."

"Look," she commanded, glancing behind him. "There are the O'Sullivans. Doesn't Mary look stunning?"

He resisted the order to turn around. He saw Mary pass by, herding one of her young siblings along in front of her with a touch of her hand. She wasn't looking at him. Was she ignoring him on purpose? Was she embarrassed?

He suddenly lurched forward as a strong hand pounded on his upper back. Clancy chuckled, pounded him a few more times, and then walked by without saying a word.

"Humph," Mrs. Mawhinney muttered. "What did he do that for? This is the Lord's place. It's not the time for backslapping and laughing. I don't approve of such frivolity in church. No, sir. No need for it." She sniffed and opened her prayer book.

He gazed at Mary as she settled in the pew with her family. He had never seen her look so pretty. Her red hair was tied back in a bun and her cheeks were flushed, a condition he'd lately become quite familiar with. The glow on her face enhanced her delicate features. She wore an emerald green dress with a lacy collar and sleeves. He'd never seen it before. Did she wear it for him? Was she flushed because of him?

His reverie was broken as Wilfred walked past. This time, instead of ignoring him, Wilfred turned to glare back at him as his children filed into their regular pew. His wife was nowhere to be seen.

Isn't he just the epitome of a fine, upstanding churchman, James thought. *He's left his wife at home with the baby but is making a show of attending to his children's religious education.* James scowled.

When the service commenced, he tried to drive all thoughts of Wilfred, and even his beloved Mary, from his mind. He needed divine inspiration and didn't want his mind to be closed to what the reverend was saying.

After the service, he met the O'Sullivans in the churchyard. "So, we'll be seeing you later?" Clancy asked with a grin.

"Yes," James answered. He glanced at Mary. She was looking down, her cheeks still flushed. The morning was grey with a biting wind and wisps of her hair swept past her face, making her look prettier than ever.

"Great!" Clancy exclaimed. "We'll look forward to it. Won't we, Mary?"

Mary didn't say a word. She turned and started to walk toward their automobile. Clancy followed, chuckling to himself.

Wilfred walked by. "Mind if I have a word with you, Wilfred?" James called. "In private," he added, when Wilfred turned around, glaring at him.

James led him to a large horse chestnut tree that grew on the edge of the churchyard.

"What do you want?" Wilfred growled.

"Wilfred," James responded, "I will not put up with you following me around in the dead of night. If you—"

"You're daft! I did no such thing. I've got better things to do than sneak around following the likes of you."

"Like molesting young girls."

"I swear to God, you'll get more than a swollen face if you keep up that filthy talk."

"I want you to know that people in authority have been informed about you and if anything happens to me, you're going to be the first suspect."

"You're spreading these false accusations, these lies about me, around the community… behind my back … to my friends and *neighbours*!" His face puffed up and turned red like a tomato about to burst. He sputtered out the last words so harshly that James could barely make out what he said.

"Relax," James scoffed. "I'm not that type … even though you deserve it. I didn't gossip or tell anyone else but the police so as to protect the other young girls in this community. If any girl around here is harmed, you will be suspect number one."

"Damn you to *hell*! You'll be sorry," Wilfred hissed. Then he turned and stalked towards his carriage, yelling, "Come on, children! Come on!"

James saw people turning around to look at Wilfred, surprised by his sudden outburst. He walked over to Sadie, untied her from the hitching post in front of the church, and left the churchyard, unnoticed by the congregation.

When he crested the pasture hill, he was surprised to see a horse hitched up in front of his house, the rider sitting on a porch chair. As he got closer, he could see the fellow was Robert.

"Robert, good to see you," James called out as he entered his yard. He rode up to the front porch, dismounted, climbed the front porch stairs and grasped Robert's hand. "To what do I owe the pleasure?" he added.

"It's Frankie, Doc. He's burning up and Marg says the leg ain't looking too good."

He had been afraid of this—infection. He been hopeful that infection wouldn't set in, that maybe they had avoided it by some miracle; but he also knew it was a dirty wound and despite the carbolic acid, most likely he would have to deal with infection sooner or later.

"I was afraid this would happen, Robert. I'll come right away. Like to come in while I change?" he asked.

"Naw, I'll just stay out here, if you don't mind."

James unlocked the door and went upstairs to change. It wasn't until he started back down the stairs that he remembered: *Mary!* He was supposed to call on Mary in a few hours! He had to telephone them. He went to the hallway outside his office to use the phone. No one answered. Rebecca was still in bed—she couldn't answer—and Clancy, Mary and the other children must have stopped at someone's home on the way home from church. *They probably went to the Perkins house to see if they could be of any assistance.* He had to tell Mary that he couldn't visit today.

He dialled '0' for Bernice, the telephone operator. "Hello, Bernice," he said.

"Hello, Dr. Wilson. What can I do for you? I see the O'Sullivans didn't answer you."

It surprised him how much Bernice knew, but of course she was the one who put the calls through—*and she probably would have listened to the conversation if he had gotten through*, thought James. He wished there was some way to protect privacy on telephone calls.

"Yes, I know they are out today. I saw them at church," James told Bernice. "They must have stopped to visit someone on the way home." Then he asked, "Bernice, could you do me a favour? The O'Sullivans are expecting me to visit them this afternoon, but an emergency has come up and I can't make it. Would you be so kind as to call them later and explain the situation?"

"Where will you be?" she asked.

He knew she was dying to find out what the emergency was, but he ignored her question. "Where I'll be, they don't have a phone, Bernice."

"Were you going to see Mrs. O'Sullivan? She's okay, I hope?"

He knew asking Bernice for a favour was going to be a mistake, but he had no other choice. "Mrs. O'Sullivan is doing well. I was invited to their home for conversation and tea."

"How nice," she said with a hint of disbelief in her voice. "I'll tell them, Dr. Wilson, when I get a chance."

He wondered how busy she could be—the local phone exchange had what ... five phones? He thanked her, grabbed a few supplies from his office, and joined Robert on the porch.

They were soon on their way up the river road. James was glad Robert had no intention of riding on the frozen river. When they arrived on the shore opposite the O'Learys, a canoe was waiting. "Got to leave your horse here, Doc," Robert said. "We're crossing the ice by that canoe."

James tied Sadie to a tree, removed the saddlebag with his medical supplies, swung it over his shoulder, and walked down to the canoe.

Robert had already hauled the canoe up and over a small bank of ice on the shoreline. "The ice is pretty good here," he said from beside the canoe, "but it's kinda soft in places out there." He swept his arm out to the middle of the river. "Hold onto the canoe with both hands and run along beside it." He turned and grabbed each side of the canoe and ran a few steps, bent over. He stopped, turned, and looked back at James standing on the shore. "When the ice gets too soft," he called, "jump in the canoe. Sometimes we have to propel ourselves along by pushing with one leg out and one in. You ever done this before?"

He hadn't. It seemed awkward at first, but he followed Robert's lead and soon they were gliding over the ice. His back ached before they got halfway across the river. His feet randomly sank and then found firm ice as they travelled across. He watched Robert's legs, ready to jump in the canoe when Robert did.

James was sweating and breathing heavily when they finally reached the opposite shore. He gingerly straightened his back. Robert heaved the canoe up the riverbank without taking a break.

"Let me give you a hand," James called out.

"I'm fine," Robert answered. "You okay, Doc?"

It took great effort to raise his legs out of the deep, rain-heavy snow with each step. He fought his way up the bank, grabbing branches and shrubbery until he crested the incline onto the O'Leary's front property with a final hand from Robert. His first impression of Robert as a weak, cunning, Mr. Fagan from *Oliver Twist* was quickly changing.

"Thank you for coming, Dr. Wilson," Margaret O'Leary called from the front door. They walked across the front yard and up the stairs to Margaret. "The leg looks bad," she whispered to James. "I think it's infected like you warned me. He's feverish and the wound is swollen and red. He's babbling nonsense sometimes."

It sounded like the infection had spread into his system. This was bad—very bad. James stepped into the kitchen.

"It's bad, isn't it, Dr. Wilson," Margaret said, as if she had read his mind.

"Infection is never good, Marg," he answered.

When James entered the bedroom, Frank was huffing and puffing, his lips flapping like a spent horse. He didn't seem aware that James had arrived. "Frank," James said, placing his hand on Frank's forehead. "Frank."

Frank opened his eyes. "Hi, James," he mumbled. "Not feeling so good."

His forehead was hot and dry. His lips were cracked. James grabbed Frank's wrist and felt his pulse—fast and thin. James took his stethoscope out of the bag and listened to Frank's heart and lungs. Thankfully, there was no signs of heart failure or fluid in his lungs. He drew the blankets down. The leg was swollen above the knee like a bloated fish. The dressing was soaked. It was a big change from a few days ago.

James took forceps and scissors out of his saddlebag, cut the bandages, and peeled the dressing off the wound. He had to suppress an involuntary retch when the putrid smell hit him.

Margaret covered her nose. "It didn't smell like that yesterday," she said. "I cleaned it like you told me. I saw the swelling and the redness and there was a bit of pus yesterday. But I thought it'd be okay until today." She was clearly worried. "I didn't mention it to Charlie, who was here yesterday. Maybe I should have! I knew I needed you this morning when I woke up and found Frank burning up and shaking. I just prayed Robert would show up like he said he would."

"You did everything just fine, Marg," James reassured her. "You couldn't have done anything better." He could see pus oozing out from between the muscles overlying the fractured bone. "I'll need fresh boiled water, Marg, and some clean rags."

Margaret left the room. "Still with me, Frank?" James asked.

"Yeah," Frank groaned.

"I've got to clean your wound. I'm going to give you some chloroform to put you to sleep."

This time, Frank didn't resist. James put the mask on his face and Frank was snoring within five minutes. Margaret came back with the boiled water and rags. James soaked the rags in the water, squeezed one dry, added carbolic acid to it and began wiping pus from the open wound. After cleaning it as best he could, he tried to get a look at the fracture by gently parting the overlying muscles with two retractors. The muscles contracted quickly with the manipulation and then involuntarily closed. He pulled on the retractors, but the spastic muscles would not budge.

"Margaret, I'm going to need your help," he said. Then he asked Margaret to hold the retractors while he worked a carbolic-saturated rag between the muscles to where he imagined the fracture was. This rag, he hoped, would act as a conduit for pus to discharge to the outside, instead of spreading throughout Frank's body. Finally, he applied a fresh bandage around the wound, leaving the 'wick' of the rag free to hang out.

Robert went home early in the afternoon, but James stayed the rest of the afternoon and had supper with Margaret. Robert came back after supper to help James across the river. Before he left, James gave Margaret antipyrine for Frank's fever and general instructions for his care. She already knew about giving cool sponge baths and was adept at most other nursing duties. She also knew Frank's condition was extremely dangerous; her father had died from an infected cut.

This side of the river the O'Learys lived on was in shadows by the time he left, but the opposite shore was in sunshine and the clouds had disappeared. James looked forward to being in the sun.

As he prepared the canoe, Robert asked, "It's bad, ain't it, Doc?"

"Yes it is, Robert. It will be a miracle if he survives an infection like that. The only hope to save him is amputation, and Frank won't entertain that thought. I'll give them the night to think about it. Can you meet me back here tomorrow morning, at about eight? With a wagon in case we need to take him to hospital?"

"I'll be here with Charlie and Percy Doc, but the snow's still too deep for a wagon up this way... I'll bring a sleigh instead, and then we'll transfer him over to a wagon at your place."

James was frustrated as he rode home. He was pretty sure he would have to amputate Franks leg and wondered if he had made a mistake that might have cost another life. Should he have taken Frank's leg while he had him asleep? That way, there would have been no consulting, no awkward discussion with Frank or Margaret about the choices. *Maybe I should have just made a medical decision,* he fumed. *No need for sleighs, wagons, or hospitals.* This was a dirty wound. He could amputate a leg in ten seconds. And yet, upon awakening, Frank had refused amputation, saying he would rather be dead than be without a leg. Was he being cowardly or compassionate to let Frank and Margaret have a say in the medical decision? He couldn't give them much more time to think about it—the earlier the amputation, the better the results.

He arrived at the outskirts of the village and could just make out St. Paul's Church on his left in the dwindling light. *You tell me, God,* he thought as he gazed at the church. *Am I being indecisive again? Or am I letting your will be done?*

Chapter 20
A Few Visits

JAMES TELEPHONED THE O'SULLIVANS AS soon as he arrived home. Mary answered the phone, again to his surprise. "I'm sorry I couldn't come today to see … everyone," he stuttered. "I had an emergency. I'm sorry."

"That's quite all right," Mary replied. "No need to apologize. Bernice phoned and explained the situation. These things happen."

He loved the sound of her voice. "I'm afraid I may be busy over the next few days with this gentleman. It may be a while before I have a chance to see … you." There, he had said it—he was visiting, seeing, and courting Mary.

"I'll look forward to it," she said.

He went to bed replaying that statement over and over in his head. The tone of *"I'll look forward to it,"* was warm and sincere; the cadence exciting; the infliction teasing. He curled up on his side and felt a wave of exhaustion wash over his body despite the exhilaration. He managed to stumble through and complete his prayers before falling asleep.

He was at the riverbank across from the O'Leary home by seven-thirty the next morning and Charlie, Percy, and Robert were waiting for him, sitting on the back of a sleigh having a smoke.

"Thanks for coming, guys," he said, dismounting from Sadie. "Any news about Frank?"

Charlie picked a piece of tobacco off his tongue and said, "I stayed with them most of night. I heard Marg coming and going to the sink during the night and I heard Frankie mumbling and yelling something, but Marg never called me for help. As far as I know everything's about the same. Which isn't too good, I guess. Marg looked like she was ready to keel over this morning."

James tied up Sadie while the boys finished their cigarettes. He faced the sun, but could feel no warmth even though it was glowing in the sky just above the tree line.

"Sun's up earlier now-a-days, Doc," Percy commented.

"Ice'll be breaking up soon," Robert added.

They finished their smokes and walked down to the river. There were two canoes now. "I brought another canoe," Robert said. James was grateful they'd thought of that. They might have to get Frank to the hospital as soon as possible.

They were soon across the river and lumbering up the bank. Percy was wheezing, his lips blue and puckered like a fish. "It's the bronchioles," he explained.

James smiled and nodded as if he understood and agreed, but he knew Percy's weight was a major contributing factor to the wheezing. However, this wasn't the time or place to be giving unsolicited medical advice.

When they arrived at the front door, Marg met them before they had a chance to knock. She *did* look tired. "Thank you for coming, Dr. Wilson" she said. "He's not good." She led him into the bedroom without saying more.

Frank was awake. "Don't even think about it!" he growled.

"About what?" James asked.

"The leg. My mind hasn't changed—you're not taking my leg!"

"He told me countless times," Marg spoke up, "through the night and just a few minutes ago. I'm not to let you amputate." She placed her hand on Frank's face. "And I promised him I would not."

"The chances of surviving without amputation are pretty slim, Frank," James said.

"I'll take my chances," Frank relied. "I appreciate everything you're doing James. I mean no disrespect to you, but I don't want to live without a leg. I know about the wooden legs and I've seen a fella' or two with 'em, but that won't be me. Marg and I have already talked it over. If I don't make it, she's to go live with her sister and her husband in Ireland. I made her write the letter last night to explain the situation to her sister so she's aware."

Marg was caressing Frank's face. "You see? I have my orders." She straightened up with her back to James and said, "I'll get some clean rags," and quickly left the bedroom.

James cleaned the wound without putting Frank to sleep this time. The redness and swelling were about the same as yesterday, but he knew this didn't mean too much—the infection could be silently advancing inside his body like fog rolling over the countryside.

He returned to see Frank every second day for two weeks and was astonished to find the redness and swelling retreating by the end of the second week. He had no fever after four days. The wound began drying up and he was able to start drawing the wick out of it for the first time. This could be a good sign—or it could mean the wick wasn't draining the pus properly—or worse, than an abscess was forming deep inside the leg. But it didn't seem that way.

Over past two weeks, as word of his care of Frank spread, he received many complementary comments from colleagues and others. Dr. Peters even called him with an offer of assistance, and he could feel and hear admiration and respect in the voices of the townspeople when they asked him about Frank. But he felt like a fraud. True, he was giving Frank good care, but his recovery was just plain old good luck and he wasn't out of danger yet. The bone may not heal, creating a useless, inconvenient appendage better removed than kept; a blood clot in the lungs could result from the prolonged bed rest; or, abscesses may be lurking inside the man like a foul secret.

A secret! He'd been so busy with Frank that he'd spared little thought for Bessie and Wilfred and the secret he carried that could destroy a life—maybe *many* lives. He hadn't seen Wilfred these last two weeks and hadn't had time to dwell on the affair. *Just as well,* he thought.

It was Saturday. He had finished breakfast and was relaxing in the living room. He had nothing to do today and no patients to see. He had seen Frank yesterday and wasn't planning to see him again until Monday. He had slept *so* well; now he was sorry his thoughts had resurrected Wilfred. It had been a relief to be relatively free of the obsession.

He took a sip of coffee, closed the newspaper he was reading, and let his head sink back onto the wingback chair. He should have supper with his mother tomorrow; before that, perhaps he could *finally* see Mary.

He waited with Clancy in the parlour. "You're going to visit your mother later this afternoon, I understand," Clancy commented.

"Yes, I'll have supper with her," James responded as he fidgeted with a doily on the armrest of the chair he sat on.

"Give her my regards."

"I will." He wished Mary would get here; this was uncomfortable. Clancy was usually so easy to talk to, but not today.

"She shouldn't be long," Clancy said. Mary opened the door as Clancy said this and entered the room. She said 'hello' and Clancy bade her to sit in a chair beside him.

"James tells me it's still nice out, Mary," Clancy said.

She nodded and smiled and then the three of them had tea and made light conversation for over an hour, with the reason for James' visit never discussed or approached.

James felt uneasy. Mary was a delight, but the situation seemed awkward. He was almost relieved when it was finally time to leave.

"I'm afraid I have to go," he said when the clock struck four. "It was a pleasant afternoon. Thank you."

"Would you see James out, Mary?" Clancy asked. "And please come again, James. It *was* pleasant."

Clancy stood, shook hands with him and sat down again. Mary led James to the front door and handed him his coat.

"It was nice to talk to you, Mary," he said, after putting on his coat. "I had a great time. Perhaps I could come again?"

She looked up at him. "I would like that very much."

"Next week?" he asked hopefully.

"I'll look forward to it." She offered him her hand to kiss which he did with barely disguised delight.

He had to force himself to walk and not jump down the stairs as he left the O'Sullivan home. The uneasy feeling he had had in the parlour melted away.

Chapter 21
Intrusion

REBECCA O'SULLIVAN SAT WITH JAMES and Mary the next week. The week after that Rebecca left them alone for a short time. The following week, Rebecca, Mary, and James went for a walk together one evening.

The month of April had been wet, but May was warmer than usual. The trees were full by midmonth and the river had started to rise with spring runoff. The first warm spring wind had arrived that morning, surprising James as it did every year. Tonight was still warm.

The three crossed the road in the early darkness and followed a path down to a stretch of sandy beach. Mary and James walked along the riverside at a leisurely pace talking about his experiences of Montreal, when James realized Rebecca wasn't there. He turned around but couldn't see her. "Where's your mother?" he asked Mary.

"She told me before we came out that she didn't want to walk far tonight. She must have turned around."

"Should we go back?"

"No, let's walk a bit further. It's such a beautiful night."

It was. The moon was full. The river was calm, reflecting an undulating cone of moonlight across the surface. She placed her hand in his. He was surprised how small and dainty her hand felt. He forced his hand to relax. She said nothing and they walked on.

Unnerved, he began rambling on about the night air, her family—random thoughts to fill the silence. Silence heightened his anxiety.

They rounded another bend on the river. She laughed and fell against his shoulder to something he said. What had he said? Her laughter was an antidote for his anxiety. He felt instantly calm and he laughed with her. She stopped, looked at the stars, and then looked at him. "It's so beautiful tonight," she whispered.

He followed her gaze to the sky. "Yes, it's spectacular," he agreed. At that moment, he had never seen a moon so big, smelled such fresh air, or heard water lapping water on the shore so crisply He looked down at Mary and she looked up at him expectantly. Without thinking about it, he kissed her.

A thousand sensations exploded within him when their lips met. He drew back, both pleasantly surprised and shocked. He looked at Mary and she looked at him with shining eyes, and then looked down. It was his first kiss, and he was both relieved and triumphant that it had gone quite well (he thought). He touched her chin and raised her face to kiss her again. Her lips met his willingly.

Not wanting to be too obvious, after a few minutes they turned back and met Rebecca, who was waiting by the beginning of the path to the beach.

"Nice walk?" she asked.

"Lovely," Mary replied.

James was excited and charged all the next day. He chatted with each patient with such exuberance and enthusiasm, that a few noticed and remarked upon his good mood. The day passed quickly.

When he went to bed that night, he was not sure he'd be able to sleep, despite spending hours that evening repairing the fence around Sadie's pasture. But he must have dozed off, because he awoke in the middle of the night from a dream that left him unsure of where he was. He searched the darkness for a clue. He was in bed, in his bedroom.

Then he heard a sound—a squeak as if the door had been opened. *Downstairs.* He silently waited for another sound, wondering it was just his imagination. He held his breath to hear better. *There!* A shuffling sound. A creak. He imagined a person creeping up the stairway.

He got up and silently left the bedroom. Then he stood in the hall and waited for his eyes to adjust to the darkness, watching the stairway. Nothing. No one was ascending the stairs. He could see all the way down to the main floor. *I'm probably overreacting to the simple creaks and groans of an old home* … but his body told him different. House noises had never awoken him before, not even during stormy nights. Why tonight?

He continued to stand in the hallway, listening for any sound. He felt his body relax and was about to go back to bed when he heard a definite scraping sound. His office? Was someone in his medical dispensary? Were they looking for morphine?

He descended the stairs as quietly as he could and grabbed a walking stick he knew was in the hallway by the front door. He fingered the knob. The front door was still locked; they had come in from the back. He crept down the hallway to his office, thinking of calling the police as he passed the phone, but decided that would only alert the robber. He wished he had grabbed the rifle from the hallway closet instead of the stupid walking stick!

Slowly, he opened the office door. The door to his right, the one that led to the waiting room, was open. He was sure he'd shut it before shutting the office for the night. He looked around the dark room. No one was there. On the opposite wall, the dispensary door was still closed. *I need to check my drug supply.*

Wary that the intruder might be in the room, he slowly advanced—and then the door suddenly swung shut behind him. A thud and flash of sparkling light were the last things he remembered as something struck his head … and then, nothing.

Chapter 22
Officer Kimball

JAMES FELT A THROBBING PAIN in the back of his head. *Dark.* Where was he? He lifted his head and rolled onto his side, one elbow on the floor. *My home.* It was night and he was at home. Someone had broken in and knocked him unconscious. They had been hiding behind the door.

He slowly arose and then sat down in the chair in front of his desk. He gingerly felt the back of his head. *The assailant might still be here*, he realized. He listened for any sounds and when none were heard, he lit a kerosene lamp that sat on his desk. He grabbed the lamp and looked around the room. Nothing seemed out of place.

He cautiously left the room carrying the lamp. He went into the waiting room. *Empty.* But the office door was ajar and a broken pane of glass explained how his assailant had entered. *What was he after?*

James returned to his office and went into the dispensary to check the drugs he had stored there. Nothing appeared to be out of place. The morphine supply was intact and none of the other medications had been taken. Had he interrupted a burglary before they could take anything? *No, they would have finished the job while I was unconscious.* Why? Who?

Wilfred! But what would he want besides the opportunity to terrify me? Perhaps he is looking for any proof I might have that he assaulted Bessie. He went to the filing cabinet and checked Bessie's patient chart. It was not altered or out of place, but that didn't prove he hadn't looked. But all he would have seen is that James had written 'pregnancy' and nothing more.

He went to the kitchen and wet a cloth with cold water for his head. Pressing it to his injury, he then went into the hallway to telephone the police and report the burglary.

Officer Kimball answered. "I'll be out tomorrow, first thing," Kimball told James.

James wearily went back to his bedroom, and wondered if it was a coincidence that the same police officer who'd showed him Bessie's body and had listened to his suspicions about Wilfred was the one who was coming to investigate the break-in.

"And he didn't take anything?" Officer Kimball asked the next morning. "You're sure?"

"I'm sure," James said. "I checked everything thoroughly again this morning."

"You must have surprised him. It would seem he fled after he hit you."

"But as I stated, he could have taken *anything* then—I was unconscious."

"He didn't know that. It was dark. He probably hit you and ran like hell."

"Maybe …"

"What other explanation could there possibly be?"

"Maybe Wilfred wanted to make sure I had no concrete evidence that he molested Bessie?"

"Do you?"

"No," said James.

"But you think Wilfred thinks you do?"

"Yes," James said. Then he told Officer Kimball about the fight with Wilfred, the night someone followed him, and the confrontation he'd had with Wilfred after church.

"I'd sock you in the kisser too if you ever accused me of such a thing and I was innocent," Officer Kimball admonished him. "I suggest you lay off harassing the man. He has every right to lay an official complaint about you."

"Officer Kimball, Wilfred is getting away with rape and the destruction of a young, sweet girl—his own kin! I will *never* let him live in peace. As long as I live I will make sure he never forgets what he has done. I swore that to Bessie."

Officer Kimball stared at him and then said slowly, measuring his words, "Maybe *you* molested Bessie."

James was too shocked to respond.

"I'm just pointing out to you," Kimball went on, "that you have no *proof* that Wilfred did this. Just as I have no proof that *you* molested Bessie. Heck, you could have been the one who *drowned* Bessie for all I know. You're going to get yourself in a mess of trouble if you keep harassing Wilfred. Law is based on fact, not hearsay and that's all you have. I suggest … no, I *demand* that you end this vendetta right now!"

James felt his face burning. He was being lectured to, as if he was a schoolboy. For an instant he felt indignant and he nearly voiced a pompous, "How dare you!" But this was not his nature. Instead he muttered, "If you so advise."

"I do," Officer Kimball said firmly. He stood and looked at James, as if to make sure he'd made his point. Then he said, "Well, there's nothing more I can do here," and walked to the door. Before leaving, he turned around to say apologetically, "I really don't think you molested or murdered Bessie, you know. I was just making a point."

James nodded. "I understand," he said.

"And you better get this window fixed," Kimball added as he opened the door.

James looked at the broken window and back at Kimball. "Officer Kimball," James said, "what about fingerprints? Don't you want to check the door handle?"

Kimball smiled. "This isn't Montreal," he said and left.

James sat down at the kitchen table. How did it come to this? He was innocent of any wrongdoing and yet he was the one being lectured to by the police. Apparently, Wilfred was allowed to harass him, but he wasn't allowed to harass Wilfred! James snickered woefully and shook his head. Kimball had made a good point. He couldn't continue to openly harass Wilfred. He had to change tactics. His treatment of Wilfred had to be subtler. He had no intention of stopping, despite Kimball's warning—he owed at least that much to Bessie.

Chapter 23
Misgivings

"WELL YOU'VE HAD QUITE THE busy month," Frank said.

"You heard about the break-in at my office, I assume?" James replied.

"That and Mary O'Sullivan," he said with a sly smile.

James returned the sly smile. "How do you hear gossip like that way out here? You heard right, though—I've been seeing Mary for over a month now. It's no secret. I sit beside her in church with the rest of the O'Sullivan family, so everybody knows. She's a wonderful girl, Frank."

Frank masked a groan as James lifted his leg slightly to rewrap the splint to his leg. He had just finished cleaning and inspecting the wound and was now applying the splint. The wooden splint, made by Charlie under James' guidance, ran along the outside of his leg with a joint beside the knee that allowed the device to be bent so Frank could ambulate with crutches. James would normally have enclosed a fracture like this in a full leg cast, but you can't enclose an open wound.

"How are you doing getting around now?" James asked. Frank had been walking with crutches, putting only a light amount of weight on his bad leg.

"Fine. The pain in the leg is less now when I walk. The splint is a bloody nuisance in bed, though. When can I get rid of that?"

"Soon. In two weeks if you promise to keep your full weight off the bad leg for a month after that."

Margaret came back into the room with fresh, clean bandages for James to finish wrapping the splint. "I heard that," she said. "He's been threatening to throw the splint in the river, Dr. Wilson."

James laughed, "I don't blame him. I'm sure I'd feel the same. Just a little bit longer, Frank. You've come a long way. I'd hate for you to stumble, refracture the bone, and have to start back at day one."

"In bed for six weeks again! Oh no! I'll keep the splint on for months if you want. You've done so much for me, James. I can't thank you enough."

"Yes, James," said Margaret, "We know his recovery has been a miracle. I've since heard of so many cases where people died from broken bones poking out of their skin. What do you call that?"

"An open fracture. In Frank's case an open *compound* fracture. I can't take the credit. I did my best, but really it was either just luck or God's wish. It also helped that it was winter and a bloody cold day when the logs rolled on you. If you had messed up that fracture with dirt and mud, I know you wouldn't have survived."

"In any case, we're grateful," Margaret said. "So many people with such great sorrows. When I think of Amos MacKenzie and the pain he's had to endure: first his wife and then his young girl … heavy burdens. Isobel, Robert's wife, came for tea this past week and was telling me that Amos is a lost soul. He keeps up appearances for his children, but she can tell. She says he's nothing like he was before his wife's death and he's become even more of a ghost of himself since Bessie died."

James finished wrapping the splint. He turned to recap the carbolic acid sitting on the bedside table. "Amos has my admiration. I'm sure you're right and that he's holding on only for his children's sake. Do Isobel and Robert know Amos well?"

"Isobel is Amos' sister-in-law. His late wife was Isobel's sister," Margaret replied.

"I didn't know that," James said, surprised.

"I wouldn't expect you would. Felicity, Amos' wife, died before you came here. And the Ramseys live on Hammond River."

"Ramsey is Robert's last name?"

"That's right," Margaret murmured fixing the blankets over Frank.

James felt a paralyzing fear grip his body: Robert was *also* a relative of Bessie's. "How many children do the Ramseys have?" James asked trying to sound nonchalant.

"I believe they have six. The oldest is 18, a boy, Arnold, and the youngest is around five."

James breathed a sigh of relief. Isobel wasn't pregnant when Bessie died. Robert was not the relative Bessie spoke of.

"Isobel and Robert have a grandchild, too," Margaret went on. "A baby boy… must be about a year old now."

James felt a cold wave wash over his body. "The 18-year-old had a child?" he managed to ask.

"Yes, Arnold. He married, left home and had a child all within a year. Isobel wasn't too pleased with him, I can tell you … but what can you do? He moved to St. John and got a good job working the port, so you got to give him credit. He supports his family and Isobel says their little boy… Peter, I think they call him … is a joy."

"You sure are curious for a man," Frank remarked grinning up at James. "Gabbing like a lady about families and who's related to who."

"It's the nature of the job," James replied, his heart thumping as he considered for the first time that he may have been mistaken about Wilfred.

He quickly packed up, despite being offered tea by Marg. The idea that Bessie had *another* cousin whose wife was expecting a child at the time Bessie was raped was excruciating. He excused himself, saying "I must be going now, but I plan to return in two weeks. Don't hesitate to get me if anything changes, Marg. Continue cleaning the wound every second day. And Frank, you keep that splint on, okay?"

It was about noon when he left the O'Leary home, his guts churning with the fear that he may have falsely accused a man of a horrible act. He descended the riverbank to a rowboat which, when the ice melted, had replaced the canoe as the way to get across the river. James shoved the boat off and started to row. The sun was high and the wind light. Small waves tickled the side of the boat as he gained speed leaving the shore. He tried to enjoy the experience of rowing, but all he could think about was Arnold, the 18-year-old boy with the pregnant wife, another of Bessie's cousins. Could that Arnold have come all the way from St. John to go to a social in Rothesay?

At the time, the pregnant relative Bessie spoke of seemed so obviously to be Mrs. MacKenzie … *but maybe I was blinded by the most probable answer, to the point where I was unable to consider alternatives.* Was Wilfred an innocent man? Had he seen been short-sighted when it came to Wilfred, they way he had been when he made assumptions about Dr. Peters?

As he rowed, he gripped the oars so tightly and pulled so hard as he forced the boat across the river at maximum speed, that his hands and arms ached. He had to hasten home. He may very well need to correct a terrible error, though Wilfred might still be guilty. And now, after all this time, he couldn't very well ask Amos if Bessie had asked to go home with *Arnold* on that fateful night. It would come across as a very suspicious question and Amos would immediately deduct the implication, which might cause undue anxiety for him. And again, there was still no legal resolution, even if it *was* Arnold who attacked Bessie and not Wilfred. James had no proof of anything, just as Officer Kimball said. He had only added another suspect.

James lifted the boat's oars and pulled them into the boat as he came up to the sandy beach. He climbed out of the boat and onto the beach, and then rolled a log under the boat's bow and pulled it up the shore beyond the high tide mark before tying it to a nearby tree. Then he grabbed his medical bag and walked up to greet Sadie, who was tied to a tree by the road.

He had no right to hassle Wilfred anymore. If he had only told Amos that night about Bessie, the truth might have been revealed and Bessie would still be alive. Instead he went to a stupid meeting. Once again he was left with the disturbing conclusion that it was not the rapist who killed Bessie, but his own indecisiveness.

He mounted Sadie and headed home.

Chapter 24
War

James bought another horse that summer, a male gelding he called Bob. Sadie seemed to like the company, but she made sure Bob knew who was boss. He purchased the horse for Mary, so they could go riding together. Mary had learned to ride as a young girl, so it didn't take her long to became comfortable on a horse again. On the weekends, they rode together all over the countryside, bringing picnics to enjoy beside the river and in neighbouring fields.

Mary laughed when he first told her he was thinking of purchasing another horse so they could ride together. She teased him about his displeasure with the automobile and called him a 'good ol' country boy'. She said things in a light-hearted manner, with a gleam in her eye that let James know she was teasing. He could talk to her now with ease, and she with him. He was in love.

The summer seemed to go by so fast, from weekend to weekend. Mary and he got into a routine of Saturday and Sunday afternoon rides, and Sunday suppers with either his mother or with her family. Of course, weather conditions and medical emergencies arose that altered these outings, but such things did little to dampen his spirits.

He was grateful to have Mary's light and love to distract him, because without her he might have succumbed to negative thoughts. He felt guilty still about the indecision that lead to Bessie's death and now he carried a further burden as he wondered if he'd been too hasty in accusing Wilfred of raping his niece. Since finding out about Alfred, he had stopped the glares, insolent attitude, and disgusted expression he'd been using when he encountered Wilfred, replacing them with feigned indifference. He didn't know if Wilfred was aware of any change; he continued to eye James suspiciously.

James knew his indecision that night was understandable; but he also knew that part of the reason he had decided to attend the Medical Society meeting instead of talking to Amos and Bessie was because he feared Dr. Peters. *And he wasn't my enemy after all,* he mused. While Bessie might have committed suicide even if he'd spoken to Amos, perhaps things might have turned out differently and the truth would have come out. Would confessing the identity of the rapist to her father have changed anything? James had no way of knowing and it made him anxious. Such questions rolled around in his head obsessively, distracting him. Mary was his comfort.

The two of them had been growing closer daily, and had progressed from talking only of inane, safe things to speaking of their core beliefs, thoughts, hopes and dreams. In Mary, James was startled to find a compassionate friend as well as potential lover and wife. But he kept his most secret worries from her until one Sunday afternoon in early August, while they were sitting in the shade of an ash tree at the top of a sandy beach. Without really planning to, in a soft moment of confession, he told her the whole story of Bessie and his thoughts and actions—including how he had accused Wilfred of rape.

"The poor girl," Mary commented sadly. "I'm sure you drew the best conclusion you could about Wilfred. And maybe you were right. But I don't understand why she would take her own life. Indeed, her father said things that must have hurt her, but did it hurt her enough for that? I knew her. She seemed like a very sensible girl. I would think Bessie would understand that her suicide would hurt him far more than learning what had happened to her. Knowing the guilt he'd feel, I don't think she would be so cruel. Besides, she obviously admired and loved her father, from what you told me. So to me, suicide doesn't make sense."

"Well she was young … and she left that note," James remarked. "What else are people to think?"

"From what you've said, the note did not specify that she was going to kill herself, just that she wanted to handle things her own way. Perhaps it was merely a runaway note? Do you remember what it said?"

"Well I don't remember it word for word," James said. "But Amos and I checked the train station the night she disappeared, so I guess at the time we must have entertained the notion that she was running away … I had forgotten about that. Yes, the note wasn't necessarily suicidal. What are you suggesting, Mary? Do you think it was murder?"

"Well it *did* occur to me. If a relative raped her and he felt threatened that she would tell someone …"

"I entertained that thought for awhile as well," said James, "but the police told me it was improvable, and so was the rape."

"I don't know this Arnold Ramsey," Mary said, "but I do know Wilfred MacKenzie, and I must say, I find his guilt hard to believe. He always seemed like such a kind man. But you never know about people …"

"Oh Mary, I feel so guilty about accusing him now. What if he is innocent?"

"James, you are only guilty of being a compassionate man. You care too much. You cared about breaking a promise to Bessie. You cared about hurting Amos. You cared about getting justice … and now you care about a possible *injustice*, to Wilfred. For all you know, he *is* the guilty party. But no one can prove anything. It will take a confession from either him or whoever the rapist is, and if that happens it will be on a deathbed 40 years from now. You can't torment yourself any longer. You did all you could."

James reached out and touched her soft red hair. "You're right, of course," he said. "You are so wise and you are such a dear. I should have shared my thoughts with you long ago. I love you, Mary." He leaned in and kissed her lightly on the lips. He had never kissed her in the daylight or told her he loved her before.

Mary smiled. "I'd kiss you harder, Dr. Wilson, but we are close to a public road—scandalous." She giggled, her hand covering a naughty grin.

The following week, James asked Mary to marry him and the week after that he formally asked Clancy for his blessing. The wedding was planned for the following spring.

James was thrilled. With Mary, he found a sense of peace and happiness that suppressed the negative thoughts he still carried about the Bessie affair. He slowly came to accept the fact that the truth behind her pregnancy and death might never be known, and that circumstances similar to this injustice happened all the time. Rapists got away with rape and killers got away with murder. He prayed there would be justice in the afterlife.

The town seemed to have forgotten Bessie. Their attention was on other matters. The day James asked Clancy if he could marry his daughter, on August 14, unbeknownst to James at that moment, Britain declared war on Germany, and that meant Canada was automatically at war too.

James considered himself to be quite knowledgeable about world affairs and yet he found the events that lead to this war rather mundane by world standards. Germany was invading Belgium and France, who were alliance partners of England, and that was war-provoking. It seemed a duke being assassinated in Serbia lead to a series of accusations that eventually provoked Germany to mount an invasion of nearby neighbours. Surely the whole matter could have been resolved before this call to war? Maybe Clancy was right—he eventually changed his mind and told James long ago that Germany was up to something, and now he said that the assassination of the duke was just an excuse for war.

Canadians were in a fervour to head overseas and fight, which James found surprising, given how far removed the country was from its European roots. However, many seemed to believe that it was an honour to fight and die for their country and that the war would be over quickly. He wasn't sure about the war being over so swiftly, nor if these young men really understood death. While it was true that the Commonwealth wasn't worth much if allies didn't help one another, this all seemed like madness to him. Couldn't a simple chat iron out differences and misunderstandings?

For the most part, he kept his thoughts to himself because it seemed his views put him in a minority of sorts. Around him, patriotism was awash. The newspapers screamed it, and at church on Sunday Reverend Philpotts encouraged young men to enlist. Even Clancy supported the war, and he had a dislike for the English.

James was unaffected by the tide of mass patriotic fever that swept through the country. His mood was mostly peaceful. He was grateful to have met and got to know Mary and was imagining a life of married bliss with her. Even his guilt feelings about Bessie's death had less sting now that a future with Mary by his side seemed set. Life was settling into a routine that he welcomed, and as fall approached he attended to the mundane tasks that would see him through the winter, like chopping and stacking wood, content.

He had just finished eating his lunch and was settling down to read when he was surprised by unexpected visitors.

"Margaret! Frank!" he exclaimed when he answered the door. "Is everything all right?"

James had removed Frank's leg splint about a month ago. Frank was walking with crutches now, and occasionally a cane. James was delighted by Frank's progress but never expected to be greeting him at his door, at least not this early in his recovery.

"We're fine," Frank said. "We rowed the boat down. It felt good. I need to build up some muscle after lying around since my leg broke."

"Come in! What a pleasant surprise."

"We're not interrupting anything?" Margaret asked.

James assured them that they were not. "I put some wood away for winter this morning and I just finished my lunch," he said. "My arms are sore."

Frank chuckled appreciatively. He knew what that was like.

James led them to the sitting room and left to make a pot of tea. When he returned, he poured them all a cup.

"The weather's been good for fall," said Marg.

"It certainly has," said James.

"I heard you are engaged to Clancy's daughter," Marg said. "Congratulations."

"Thanks," said James. "She is a lovely woman and I feel very fortunate." Then he asked Frank, "And your leg? It's okay?"

"Yes, it's fine, Doc," said Frank. "But the reason we came to visit you today was to ask for some information for a friend."

"Oh," said James, instantly on alert.

Frank suddenly seemed nervous. He said, "Our friends, Isobel and Robert, came to see us the other day, quite disturbed. Their son, Arnold, was accused by someone of rape and he's been questioned by the police down in St. John. The police won't tell Isobel or Arnold who the girl is, and Arnold won't tell them either. But the boy seems to be in big trouble."

James flushed. How was this possible? Another girl raped, and the accused was a young man he already had suspicions about. Was this proof that it was indeed Arnold who assaulted Bessie, and not Wilfred? Was it possible that Arnold was a *serial* rapist?

Frank went on, "The Ramseys are nice people. Robert may be a little rough around the edges and I know he looks shifty, but inside he's a good man. Isobel is a sweetheart. This is eating them up. They tried to raise that boy right, but now he's in trouble. And if he goes to jail for it, what will his wife do? They have a son, Isobel and Robert's grandchild! He's not even a year old. I'm here, James, because you've always seemed awful curious about Arnold. Do you know something?"

James tried not to be too obvious about his interest in Arnold after the first time he was mentioned in conversation, but occasionally obsession got the best of him and he'd ask a question that was more pointed than he wanted it to be. "No, I know nothing about this matter," he said, which was true. "I don't know Arnold and I have never treated him or his family."

"Of course," Margaret spoke up. "I guess we were hoping for some advice. It's just that we feel so sorry for Isobel and Robert and we want to help them. You're a doctor; maybe you heard something about the rape from one of your colleagues. Surely the girl is being looked at by someone in St. John? Perhaps word that he is not the only suspect, or that the girl is unreliable, has come your way?"

"I'm sorry," James replied. "I know nothing. This is the first I've heard about the police case and another physician would, or should not, speak to me about this matter if it involves one of their patients. But please tell Isobel and Robert that my door is always open to them if they want to talk."

"Well, that's that," said Frank, disappointed. "Poor Robert."

"Yes, and we do appreciate you giving us the opportunity to ask you, Dr. Wilson," said Margaret.

Frank and Margaret had a second cup of tea and the three of them discussed how well Frank was healing and how Percy, Charlie and Robert were going to see to it that Frank and Marg had wood for winter … but honestly, James couldn't wait for them to leave so he could ride over to see Amos. It was time to talk about Arnold to him.

Chapter 25
Amos

It was late afternoon when James rode up the narrow lane to Amos' home. As he made his way up to the MacKenzie farm, dry leaves rustled from the crisp wind blowing from up the river. He hoped Amos was home.

He could see smoke coming from the chimney of the MacKenzie house as he emerged from the lane. The house stood to the left, bordering the forest. Straight ahead stood the barn, and sloping right and far back was the pasture and ploughed fields. Behind him was a marvelous view of the Kennebecasis River and Long Island.

James tied Sadie up to the railing of the front steps, climbed the stairs, and knocked on the front door. A young fellow he knew as Tommy answered the door, quickly followed by Evelyn, a girl only slightly older.

"Hello Tommy, Evelyn," James said. "Is your father home?"

"Pa! A man wants to speak to you," Tommy cried.

"It's the doctor," Evelyn said looking at her brother with disdain, like he should have added that information.

Amos came to the door with an apron on. "James! Come in. How nice to see you."

James heard Tommy grumble to Evelyn in a low voice, "I knew that," as they went back into the house.

"Looks like you're cooking supper. I can come back later," James offered.

"No. I'm making a stew to have for the next few days. Tonight, we're finishing up the beans and bread … all I have to do for supper is just warm up the pot. You can stay for supper if you'd like."

"Thank you, but no—I just need a few minutes to talk to you about something. Is there somewhere I could speak to you in private?"

Amos showed him to a room facing the lane James had just ridden up. A large window with many panes of glass looked out past the fields to the river. The room was long and narrow with a long sofa and rocking chair on one side of the room, facing the window, and two high-backed chairs and a table holding a kerosene lamp opposite.

"I get a nice view of the river from here," Amos said. "My late wife and Bessie loved to do their knitting here." Amos closed a door behind them. "Have a seat." He indicated the rocking chair looking out the window while he sat in a chair facing James. "What's on your mind?"

"Amos," James said. "It has just come to my attention that your nephew, Arnold Ramsey, has been questioned by the police for a possible rape. Does this have anything to do with Bessie?"

Amos looked to his side, at a view of the woods behind the house. He said nothing for a long time. Finally he said sadly, "Yes, it does." Then, after another pause he faced James and asked, "Who told you? Only the police, Arnold, and I know about this."

James explained how he came to hear of this from the O'Learys, and they from Isobel and Robert.

"I suppose Arnold would tell his parents. I couldn't. I couldn't look Isobel and Robert in the face and tell them I think their son raped and possibly killed my Bessie."

"I don't think they know it was you that made the accusation, nor do they know the name of the girl involved."

"I guess Arnold would be too embarrassed to mention it was his dead cousin he raped," Amos said bitterly. "I don't feel good about this. I feel rotten, but Bessie deserves justice. That miserable little creep can rot in hell! I came pretty close to murdering the little bastard myself. All that stopped me was the thought of my children—they have lost their mother and sister and I couldn't risk them losing their father too. So, I gritted my teeth and went to the police. And why haven't they arrested him by now?"

"How did you figure it might be Arnold who raped Bessie?" James asked.

"Evelyn reminded me Bessie kept a diary. I probably knew that at one time but gave it no thought since. She wrote in it every night before she turned off the lights and she hid it somewhere, for privacy. I forgot all about it after she died. It was her business. Anyway, about a week ago Evelyn said to me, '*Do you suppose it would be all right now if I used Bessie's diary? She made me swear that I'd never read it or tell a soul where it was. She said the devil would haunt me for the rest of my life and probably make me blind if I did … but since Bessie's gone does the curse still count?*' Like I said, I plumb forgot the girl ever had one. I immediately wondered if Bessie had named the father of her baby in that book. I asked Evelyn to show me where it was. She'd hidden it under the right side of her dresser. The opening between the floor and the dresser was so small my hands wouldn't fit in there, so I got Evelyn to fish it out for me.

"I took the diary to my bedroom to read it alone. I couldn't believe it. There it was in black and white. She wrote that Arnold raped her … after I gave her permission to go home from the church social with him! I talked to Arnold that night, I asked him about his wife and how the job was in St. John …" Amos paused, pained, and looked up at James. "I didn't even ask why he was there without his wife. I thought it was odd, but I assumed that she didn't come because she was nearing her time to have the baby. If only I'd questioned the boy! But I had no reason to doubt him; he's kin. And so, when Bessie implored me to let her stay longer and ride home with him when I wanted to leave, it never occurred to me she'd be unsafe with him … her *cousin*." James saw tears in his eyes. "If her mother had been alive right then, Bessie would still be alive today."

"Don't say that," James interjected. "Your wife might have thought the same thing. Why would either of you doubt a family member?"

"My wife had more sense about these things then me," Amos said as he wrung his hands and looked to the floor. "I read about Arnold taking her to the backwoods, pretending he had something to show her. Then I read about the months of anguish after she realised she was probably pregnant. It broke my heart reading about the distress she was going through, all by herself. If she had only told me, James … She was keeping this secret to spare me. Can you imagine?"

Amos started to silently cry, tears rolling down his weathered cheeks. He ran his hands through his long, straight, black hair and hung his head, his shoulders heaving. James went to him and placed his hand on his shoulder.

"You know what, James?" Amos said, wiping his eyes. "She was not angry with me after I called her those vile names that last night. She didn't write anything about me. She had every right to call me a goddamn bastard, a poor excuse of a father. She didn't."

"She loved you very much, Amos, and she was wise beyond her years. She would have understood your anger. She was an amazing girl."

At that moment, Evelyn spoke from behind the closed door, "Pa, are you crying?" she asked innocently.

"Just a bit, darling. Everything's okay," Amos reassured her. "We'll be out in a few minutes. Have you've been snooping in back of the door, young lady?" He smiled.

"You're talking about Bessie, aren't you?" she said. "Do you have to go somewhere now, Pa?"

"No. We'll be right out and I'm not going anywhere. I'm fixing stew and you're helping me. Now you go back and peel the carrots. If we have any news about Bessie, I'll tell you later. Honest. Go on, now."

James sat in the rocking chair again. Amos wiped his eyes and said, "Sorry about that. I get emotional talking about Bessie. And these days Evelyn doesn't like it when I go anywhere. I suppose she's afraid I may not come back, like her mother and big sister. Wilfred and his wife have been awful good, looking after my kids every time I go anywhere."

"And that leads me to a matter I have to confess to you," James said. He tried to summon his courage. He felt guilt for not coming to see Amos that night, and rightly so. Amos would have known there was more than one relative with a pregnant wife. He may have figured out it was Arnold. He took a deep breath and began, relating to Amos what Bessie had told him in confidence in his office that day.

"Amos, I have struggled with this for so long," he said, relieved to get this burden off his chest. "Bessie asked me to let her handle her problems by herself and to tell no one, and I said I would, because she was my patient and I was trying to be respectful. At one point I changed my mind and I was going to come and tell you despite my promise to her, but before I could, she was found dead. For this, I am profoundly sorry."

"Well, Dr. Wilson," said Amos thoughtfully, "It really isn't your fault. My Bessie was going to do whatever it was she intended to do. She ran away and she either killed herself, or that boy killed her. Me knowing *after* the fact who made her pregnant wouldn't have changed things. And you had no way of knowing about Arnold because he doesn't live here. But I can't believe you thought it was Wilfred! What did he say when you accused him?"

"I got a busted jaw and black eye for my troubles, and I deserved it."

"Wilfred did that? I can see why—accusing him of raping Bessie! I suppose you're lucky he didn't kill you. But then again, though Wilfred looks gruff and tough, he wouldn't hurt a flea. He's a big teddy bear. But why didn't you tell me you suspected him?"

"I couldn't ask you to believe that about your own brother. I was afraid you'd either kill him, or me. Besides I had no proof—the police told I needed proof before making such an accusation."

"You told the police?"

"My suspicions were eating me up. I thought it was my duty to share what information I had with the police and they, rightly so, told me my words were hearsay and speculation. But I was so *sure*. And after awhile, I got so angry about it, I decided that if Wilfred couldn't be charged and tried, I was going to make life miserable for him as long as he and I were alive. I'm afraid I've behaved rather badly. I've been saying and doing things to give Wilfred the impression that I find him repulsive. I'm going to apologise to him as soon as I leave here. I wouldn't blame him if he never forgives me. And I don't blame you if you never forgive me for not telling you what I knew."

Amos smiled. "I think you'll find Wilfred to be a forgiving soul, but you're right—you owe him a big apology," he said. James nodded. Amos continued, "And I respect you for keeping Bessie's confidence," he said quietly. "My Bessie was a mature girl for her age and she deserves our respect. If she wanted you to keep a secret, then I thank you for valuing her opinion."

James did not expect this; he'd expected much harsher judgement. *Perhaps*, he thought as Amos sat quietly, *once he's mulled it over, he'll see Bessie's life may have been spared if I'd come to see him that night, and then he will display the anger toward me that I deserve.* But he suspected not. Amos appeared to be at peace with Bessie's death. Justice was going to be served.

James arose from the chair. "I'd best be off and let you get supper on," he said. "Thanks for seeing me." He turned and walked to the door, but as he placed his hand on the door knob, another question occurred to him. "Amos," he asked hesitantly, "You said Arnold probably murdered Bessie. Why did you say that?"

"The last entry in Bessie's diary," he said slowly. "She wrote she was going to meet Arnold that night and tell him about the pregnancy. She was going to ask him for money. She wrote about going to visit the Sisters of Charity in St. John and arranging a stay in a convent in Montreal to have the baby. It sounded like the nuns were going to provide the travel fee and put her up for free, but Bessie wanted to pay them something. She figured Arnold owed her plenty so she asked him to help out. After all, he had a good job in St. John."

"If she had only told us months previously, none of this had to happen," James remarked. Amos looked up at him and they shared a look of regret. As James opened the door to leave, he saw Evelyn busy at the kitchen table peeling carrots and Tommy playing with wooden animals on the floor. They seemed almost too well behaved for children of that age—the silence lay heavy in that house.

It was too close to suppertime to visit Wilfred, even though he lived just behind Amos' home on the other side of the woods. James decided to go home and have something to eat, although he had no appetite.

He mounted Sadie and headed down the lane.

Chapter 26
Wilfred

JAMES LED SADIE TO HER stall, gave her fresh hay and water, and left her saddle on. He'd only be an hour at the most.

His legs felt wooden as he strode across the yard and entered his house. Anxiety, he supposed. His stomach was taught with tension. He had been too proud, too confident, too sure of his deduction of Wilfred's guilt.

He hung his jacket on a peg just inside the front door and went into the kitchen. He relit the wood stove and moved the kettle over the cast iron plate to boil water for tea. He sliced a thick piece of bread he had just baked yesterday and spread molasses over the top. He ate because he knew he had to, not because he was hungry.

James wondered, *how many innocent men are hung because the evidence against them seems so sound? How many men were actually telling the truth as they were led to the gallows, wailing and screaming their innocence?* He had never thought of this before. *Perhaps capital punishment should be abolished.*

Since Bessie's death, James had given up the notion of 'God's plan' as an excuse for atrocities, misfortunes, and untimely death. In fact, he was questioning many of the tenets of his faith. He kept his musings to himself, but he could not be blind anymore. He prayed for understanding and forgiveness from the Lord if his questions went too far, but he couldn't stop asking the questions of his God and of himself.

The water boiled. He made himself a cup of tea and ate another slice of bread and molasses. He stared out the window while he sat at the kitchen table rehearsing the upcoming conversation he needed to have with Wilfred. He had never been so dead wrong in his life. The ironic part of the whole situation was that he considered himself to be a sensitive, non-judgemental person, prone to be reflective thought and not opinionated. Was his rush to judgement a reaction to his guilty feelings about Bessie?

By six o'clock, James knew the MacKenzie family was probably wrapping up supper. By the time he got there, it would be six-thirty and he wanted to catch Wilfred before he got involved with another chore. He grabbed his jacket and headed out the door, leaving the dishes on the table.

The sun was low, hidden behind the trees. The wind had picked up, sending leaves scurrying across his yard. Sadie bent her head low in protest as they started out.

The lane to Wilfred's farm ran off Rothesay Road and was just before the lane to Amos' home. Wilfred's house lay further up the hill above his brother's place, separated by a 50-foot band of woods. James had been told this was once a one-titled property that the MacKenzie brothers subdivided after their father's death, at his request.

Wilfred's home was white-shingled with green trim. It was obviously newer than Amos' house, as it lacked the detailed gables. Kerosene lamps burned inside, shining through a window and onto the porch. James assumed that the brightly-lit room was the kitchen.

James tied Sadie up to the railing of the front steps and knocked on the front door. Wilfred answered immediately, which caught James off-guard. Wilfred said nothing.

"Hello Wilfred" James started. "I'm probably the last person you'd expect to show up at your door," he said with a nervous chuckle. "However, I have to talk to you about something important. Actually, I have to apologise to you … If I could just talk to you privately, I'd most appreciate it."

Wilfred continued to hold the door just slightly ajar and remained silent. James felt very ill at ease, but he continued. "I don't deserve your time, Wilfred, but I wish you would hear me out," James said, his voice trailing off.

"Stay here," Wilfred said gruffly and closed the door. Shortly, he emerged with his coat on, telling his wife as he shut the door behind him, "I'm just going out for a bit to show Dr. Wilson something."

"Well invite him in later, for heaven's sake," she cried as he shut the door firmly behind him.

"Let us talk on the porch, Dr. Wilson. Mavis knows nothing about our conversations." He led James around the front of the porch to a bench on the side facing the river.

"You've never told your wife about my accusations?" James asked.

"How could I tell my wife you're accusing me of having relations with my own little Bessie, my dear niece, whom we both loved?" he said angrily. "She would have scratched someone's eyes out. Probably yours."

"Look, Wilfred," James said, "I was wrong. Amos knows the truth and I do too, now. I'm sick knowing the pain I caused you. You have every right to remain angry. All I can do is offer my sincerest apologies."

Wilfred studied James without expression. Finally he asked, somewhat impatiently, "Why would you think it was *me*?"

James told him about the conversation he had with Bessie that day, and why he jumped to the conclusion he did.

"I've felt guilty about that girl's death all this time," he admitted. "And I've been determined to find justice for her."

James watched Wilfred's face soften, "So you heard about Arnold, then? It's sad. The young fellows often get into alcohol outside the church at these socials and I expect Arnold did that night. That's the only explanation I can come up with because he seemed like such a good young man from the times I met him. Certainly he comes from good people. And believe me, Bessie wasn't the type to lead a boy on. She was a mature, responsible young girl." He looked sadly at James.

"I know she was a mature young girl—even from the one time I talked to her. That's why I tried to respect her wishes." Then he hung his head in shame. "I am so sorry, Wilfred."

Wilfred rubbed his face and glanced down at the river. "Everyone was telling me what a nice guy you were. What a great doctor; so courteous, so caring—so approachable. I thought you were nuts. Looney."

"You must have hated me."

"I was more confused. My experience of you seemed so drastically opposite from everyone else—it just didn't make sense."

"That probably explains the blank expressions I got from you. I thought you were feigning innocence or trying to deny my existence."

"I wanted nothing to do with you. You accused me of raping my niece."

That stung James. He said, "I don't expect your forgiveness … I just want you to know I realise I was wrong."

Wilfred clapped him on the shoulder. "I *do* forgive you," he said. "The good Lord says we should forgive those who sin against us, and I do. Besides, I admire you for trying to find justice for Bessie. You could have let the matter drop like most people would have, but you chose to be involved. And you had no idea who Arnold was or that his wife was pregnant. It would have seemed logical to point the finger at me. I understand."

James felt like hugging this man and bursting into tears. He lowered his head instead and said, "Thank you, Wilfred. I don't deserve it."

"No harm done. I'm sorry I hit you so hard. Did I really break your jaw? Somebody told me you had a broken jaw from a fall; I suspected it was from me."

"I deserved the broken jaw and worse."

"Let's you and me just start afresh and forget about it. I must say, I'm relieved to understand now why you accused me of raping Bessie, but the whole affair still makes me sick. I'd like to kill Arnold, but on the other hand I feel sorry for him too. Like I said, he may have had too much to drink and that momentary loss of judgement will probably ruin his life. Bessie ended her life because of him, and he has to live with that."

It was more than a momentary lapse, James thought, but it was not his place to say so. "I think you should talk to your brother," he said, tight-lipped.

Wilfred studied James before responding. "So, there's more to learn," he said.

"I've talked enough for one night."

"Fine, but before you go you have to come in and say hi to Mavis and the kids or she'd kill me." Wilfred got up and offered his hand to James to shake.

James arose and shook it, then, trying to conclude the whole awful business, he asked one last question. "Wilfred, did you break into my office one night and clobber me over the head?"

Wilfred looked stunned and drew his hand back swiftly. "No. Why would I do that?" he asked

"Someone did, and because you and I were feuding, I thought it was you. I caught the assailant in my office in the middle of the night. When I entered the room, I was struck from behind and knocked out. They didn't take anything—no drugs or money. So, because I was so certain of your guilt, I wondered if *you* had come, possibly to destroy Bessie's medical records or find out if I had evidence against you."

Wilfred suppressed a wry chuckle. "I'm obviously not that bright. It would never occur to me to do that. Though I was mighty curious as to why you were accusing me of molesting Bessie. I couldn't believe Bessie would say that about me to you."

"Well then, it's still a mystery," James remarked, a little unnerved. "Forgive me for asking, but did you ever follow me on a horse?"

"No," said Wilfred. "I did the best I could to avoid you, that's all."

"Well, somebody did—a few times. I'm sure of that. Perhaps it was Arnold."

Wilfred paused and gave it some thought. "It hardly seems worth the risk over rape," he finally said. *Not if murder was involved,* James thought. "It's hard to prove rape, no matter what Bessie told you," Wilfred continued. "But being caught breaking and entering … well, that'll land a person in jail."

James nodded his agreement. Who would be trying to spook him? Who would break into his office, then?

"Come in and say hi to the misses," Wilfred said leading James around the porch to the front door.

Together they went into the warm, safe house. But James couldn't warm up as he wondered about his unknown assailant.

Chapter 27
An Update

OVER THE NEXT FEW WEEKS, James admitted his mistake and shame about falsely accusing Wilfred to all the people he had shared his suspicions with. During this time, Mary was a great support. She listened with sympathy and understanding as he spoke of his guilt and remorse. It was good to have someone share his thoughts and feelings with. He couldn't believe his luck at finding such a wonderful girl; with her at his side, he felt an immediate calmness, no matter what thoughts tormented him.

The first call he made was to Officer Kimball. He admitted his inexcusable mistake about accusing Wilfred and praised Kimball for his correct and wise advice. Kimball listened to all this without much comment and ended the phone call in a rather stand-offish manner. James took this to mean that Kimball thought he should have known better, and he felt chastised after that phone call ended. *I was probably looking for a friendly pardon to ease my own guilt,* he thought. He supposed that expecting reassuring comments from Kimball that his accusations were plausible and forgivable was a bit much. He understood it was official police business and that Kimball took accusations of that nature seriously; however, he had hoped for more empathy. *Oh well,* he thought, *I did what I had to do by admitting my mistake and I can't expect anything more.*

A few weeks after that call, James spoke to Dr. Peters after a medical meeting about his false accusations.

"Well, James," said Dr. Peters, "Let me remind you about my own character assassination of Wilfred at the time. I don't really know the man well enough to be judging. I was too quick to support you, which makes me just as guilty."

November brought the usual cases of colds into his office. He prescribed a few poultices for middle ear infections and once, in a stubborn case where an ear would not drain on its own, he had make an incision through a boy's eardrum to drain it. He sent a case of TB to the sanatorium for isolation. Two people died—one from heart failure and the other from old age. A young lad broke his wrist from a fall and needed a cast. He delivered a baby and assisted in two operations at the hospital in St. John. He was busy, but happy. There was no news of charges being laid against Arnold until one day in late November.

The first snow of the year fell that Saturday morning. It was only a mild dusting and it blew around the yard in random spurts. James was sitting in a rocking chair in the front window of his living room, sipping coffee and reading the newspaper, when he saw two riders on the Rothesay Road approaching his lane. As they turned down the lane, he became aware that it was Amos and Wilfred. He arose and welcomed them from his front door. "Good morning, gentlemen. Is anyone ill?"

They stopped in front of his porch. "This is a social visit, James," Amos said. "Are you busy? Do you mind if we have a word with you?"

"Not busy at all. I was just reading the paper over some coffee. Please come in. I have a full pot of coffee on the stove."

Amos and Wilfred dismounted, tied their horses to the railing, and followed James into the house. James bade them have a seat in his living room while he went into the kitchen to pour coffee for them all. James noticed they were pleasant enough—but something was on their minds.

"It's wonderful to see you both," James said as he put their cups of coffee down in front of them. "But I have a feeling this isn't *just* a social visit." He looked from Wilfred to Amos as he sat once more in his rocking chair.

"We shouldn't need a reason to come for a visit, but we all tend to be busy—you especially," Amos said. "I hate to intrude."

"You both are welcome anytime. If I'm busy, I'll tell you. Honestly. I like company."

Amos attempted a grin but it quickly faded. He swept his long, black hair back and rubbed his chin. There was something bothering him. James looked at Wilfred who averted his gaze and looked at his brother. Amos took a sip of coffee before he spoke, "Officer Kimball came out to see me yesterday. He told me they aren't going to lay charges against Arnold for Bessie's rape."

James heard Amos trying to control the flow of his voice, which was breathless and strained.

"Kimball told me they have no proof," he went on. "Arnold admits to having sexual relations with her, but he said it was consensual and that it was Bessie who made advances to him. Arnold told him she made up an excuse to stay late at the social in order to come home with him, and that it was her idea to go to the woods up by Miller's pasture."

"Oh, for heaven's sake," James exclaimed crossly. "You and I both know that's not true. That's a complete lie."

"Officer Kimball said that Arnold admits he was very weak and that he is guilty of succumbing to temptation," Amos said. "He told Kimball he feels very bad that it happened, and even worse that Bessie chose to end her life because of it." Amos looked wretched.

"Damn it!" exclaimed James. "There must be some way to break him down! You would think the police could handle this by interrogating him and making him sweat until he slips up!"

"Kimball said they did all that. He said Arnold's wife backed up his story. She said Arnold told her what happened that night and that he broke down and cried and asked her forgiveness. She said she had seen Bessie flirting with Arnold before. At the time, she thought it was an innocent young girl's crush and was amused, she told Kimball. Then she said she had no idea the infatuation was so serious, or she would have warned her husband."

"No. No. No." James mumbled, looking down and shaking his head.

"Kimball said it was a typical 'he said, she said' case," Amos remarked, "And that it was impossible to prove either way. The police took what they had to the prosecution and they determined that there was not enough evidence to lay charges."

James looked over to Wilfred, who had not said a thing thus far. He shrugged his shoulders and made a facial expression that said, 'what can you do?'.

Finally James asked, "Did Arnold say anything about the night she died?" James asked. "She went to meet him. That's what you said she wrote in her diary."

"He said the meeting didn't happen," Amos replied. "He said Bessie met him a few days before at his work and asked him to meet her by the wharf in Rothesay on Friday night. He said he told her 'no' and not to bother him again at work. She didn't want to take no for an answer and said he'd want to hear what she had to say. Then, according to Arnold, she left. Arnold told the police he felt it best to stay away from her and never met her on that Friday. He told them he wanted nothing to do with her. Then he told them he was home with his wife and child the night Bessie died, and his wife backed him up."

"His wife is lying," James said. "She probably doesn't want to be left alone with a child if her husband is jailed. I doubt Arnold even told her about Bessie before the police showed up. This is all fabrication."

"James," Amos said. "The police believe Bessie. They believe her diary. But they can't disprove Arnold. Officer Kimball was very apologetic and I think he was very sincere. But he was clear that the words of a girl's diary aren't enough to charge a man."

Wilfred finally spoke, "Amos and I talked late into the night. Our emotions ran from anger to sadness and everything in between. We talked about how we could prove Arnold guilty. We talked about making him pay for what he has done if there is no way to prove his guilt. But we know of nothing we can do to make him pay that won't hurt our own families. We will definitely shun him forever, but that's not much of a punishment. We have no other ideas. We know you felt deeply about Bessie and that you wanted to see justice done … even if it was misguided," he added with a wry smile. "So, we wanted to share this news with you and ask for your opinion. What can we do?"

James took a sip of his coffee and glanced out the window, grateful that Wilfred could laugh about his 'misguided' justice. He wondered if he would be as forgiving if falsely accused in that way. Wilfred *was* a good man.

The skies were still grey, and it had started to lightly snow again. It looked cold. "Well," James said slowly, "I only met Bessie once, and she impressed me as a sensible girl—but it was only *one* meeting. Don't take this wrong, Amos, but for a brief moment, I wondered if she was deliberately blaming a man for her own indiscretions." He watched Amos for his reaction, not wanting to offend, but saw only curiosity, so he cautiously went on. "Is there any possibility that Arnold is telling the truth, Amos?" he asked.

Amos didn't hesitate. "Not a chance," he said marking each word.

"No way," Wilfred added.

"I never doubted her integrity," James said. "I wouldn't have taken such great efforts to make your life miserable, Wilfred, if I didn't believe Bessie to be the sweet lovely girl she was … but I had to ask."

The two men nodded their understanding.

"When I thought you were the culprit, Wilfred, and that you were getting away with a sickening crime, I wrestled with this same dilemma—how could I make you pay? Obviously, I couldn't murder you …"

"That's a relief," Wilfred interjected with a chuckle.

"So I figured," James went on. "That I would make sure you never forgot that someone knew of what I mistakenly thought was your guilt. I was determined to forever give you a snide remark, or at the very least a distasteful expression, every time I was in your presence. I wanted to make sure as long as I was around you never felt comfortable. I hoped to might make your life a living hell."

"It certainly bothered me, but as I told you, I brushed it off with the thought that you were a bit loco."

They were silent for a while until finally James said, "Let us each think on this awhile. There is no rush. There must be crack somewhere in Arnold's story and we must be diligent in finding it. In the meantime, all we have available to us is to shun him and wish him ill."

"You're right, James," Amos said, "There are no ways to make him pay that are within the realm of the law. Now let's talk about other things. I need to, because thoughts of Bessie are always with me. I need distractions."

"How about a friendly game of poker?" James suggested.

The brothers agreed and James got the cards.

Chapter 28
A Parade

WINTER ARRIVED WITH A MAJOR snowstorm on Boxing Day that year. Mrs. Wilson stayed with James over Christmas, and because of the snow she couldn't leave until New Year's Day. He welcomed the extra days with his mother. It was great to have someone to talk to in the mornings and evenings.

When Mary came over with Rebecca, he enjoyed watching the three women talk. They truly enjoyed each other's company, which made it easy for them to make wedding plans for the coming June. The details bored him, but seemed to spark great enthusiasm in them. When they saw he was not paying attention to their schemes, they sometimes teased him by playfully asking him for an opinion. Laughter would ensue as they watched him try to cover up his ignorance.

The O'Sullivans invited James and his mother over to their home for dinner a few times that season. He knew Clancy's open—some would say coarse—manner wouldn't offend his mother. It didn't; in fact, she seemed to find him quite amusing and met each startling comment with one of her own. Mary told him she adored his mother.

James settled into a routine after the holidays. He found obsessive thoughts about Bessie came less and less as time went on. Mary's cheerful attitude and the excitement of his upcoming wedding had a lot to do with that, but he wondered if he was just feeling more relaxed because he had unconsciously allowed Amos to take the lead in seeking justice for Bessie. He had never met Arnold, and had no idea what he even looked like. He was the third wheel in this family drama now.

One day in early January, James ran into Amos at the grocery store. After they had purchased their goods they left the store together. James was blinded by the sunlight reflecting off the snow and stumbled from the step into the yard.

"Showing off now, are ya'?" Amos cheered. "Fancy dancing about without spilling the groceries? Good man."

James laughed. Amos was grinning. He wasn't sure if he had ever seen Amos smile since Bessie's death. However, the smile disappeared as quickly as it came when Amos told him, "I ran into Arnold in St. John before Christmas. I told him he was a liar, a rapist, and a killer. And that he should always watch his back, because I'll never let it rest."

"What did he say?" James asked.

"Nothing. He looked scared and walked away."

"You certainly got his attention."

"I've learned something else since then. Arnold volunteered for the army. He's going overseas to fight in the war."

James let this information sink in. Everyone was saying that the war would be over in less than a year, but war is war and people get killed. Would that be Arnold's just reward? It would serve him right.

"There is going to be a big parade in St. John in two weeks, on a Sunday afternoon. The city will be seeing the troops off. I assume Arnold will be marching …" Amos let the statement hang in the air without further comment.

"Are you going?" James asked.

"Not for Arnold, but for the other young lads, yes. I'm taking my children, and Wilfred and his family are going with us. Do you want to come?"

"Yes. Thank you. I'll do that."

Mary and James took her siblings in a sleigh to St. John to see the parade. The children were just as excited about being hauled in a sleigh as they were about going to a parade with marching bands and soldiers. James smiled at their energy and enthusiasm.

"Are they always like this?" he asked Mary. "Or is it the parade?"

"This is normal," she remarked as her siblings squealed and hollered with joy at the outing. "Anything can get them going."

"Too bad your mother and father wouldn't come."

"Mother felt it was a too cold for the baby and father wouldn't come on principle. I'm surprised he let my brothers and sisters go. I imagine mother had to talk him into it."

"I know your father doesn't favour the war, but it's just a parade ..."

"It's more than that. He calls the whole thing absolutely crazy and the young men who are volunteering to fight fools. He doesn't mince words."

"No, he does not. I somewhat agree with him. It was stupid how it all got started, but now that Germany has invaded France, what can we do? We have to honour our treaty with France. If we don't, what is the good of a promise? No, I fear we have an obligation to uphold. The whole thing *is* crazy though."

"You're not thinking of going, are you?" Mary asked worriedly.

"It never even entered my mind," said James. "I can't kill a deer. I couldn't imagine shooting another person." He was silent for a moment. "I suppose they need doctors. I never thought of that … But I'd rather not. Anyway, they say it will be all over within a year—there's no need for me to be there."

He smiled at Mary and she back at him. He took her hand in his and kissed it.

As they entered St. John and began the climb up Waterloo Street, the cacophony of noise from the children increased. But James felt excited too; it seemed parades were not only for children.

It was unusual to be able to bring a sleigh this far into the city. Usually there was not *enough* snow on the roads. But this was an unusual winter, with high snow banks and a good hard layer of snow still covering the roads. He'd read that the city carted away countless wagonloads of snow from the parade route in preparation for this day.

As he rode up the hill at the end of Waterloo Street, James soon spotted Amos, Wilfred, and their families at the north side of King's Square. Amos waved and showed him a hitching post he had saved for him. The children exchanged excited greetings. They could hear bands practising in the distance and drums rumbling short bursts of percussion so loud that one boy claimed it nearly knocked him down. His sister chided him with a declaration of, "That's not true."

Wilfred helped Mary down from the wagon. "Do you think your siblings are as excited as the MacKenzie clan?" he asked her.

"They were excited before we even left," Mary said, "so the O'Sullivan's will match the MacKenzie children in no time."

Masses of people were funnelling down King Street to find the best place from which to watch. James, Mary and the rest of their group soon joined them, managing to secure a front row station about midway down the hill.

After a while, James heard a band in the distance. As the volume slowly grew louder Tommy O'Sullivan cried, "They're coming!" and began hopping up and down.

The parade's grand marshal crested the top of the hill, his voice rising over the significant noise of the band as he barked the command to turn left down King Street. He wore full Scottish attire, including a fearsome black bearskin hat and the requisite kilt, despite the freezing temperatures. He was a large man with a huge black moustache, and he swung a huge silver mace as though it were a mere stick in time to the music. The children stood transfixed, their enthusiasm curbed by the power, severity, and strangeness of the grand marshal as he neared.

Behind him, the band played a military marching song, the percussion reverberating off James' chest like a playful phantom. The new recruits followed, their cheeks rosy from the cold. You could see the pride in their faces when the cheering grew as they marched past. "There they are!" Tommy cried.

Amos turned around and yelled in James' ear, "There he is. Arnold. On our side. Six down."

James stared. "That one?" He pointed at a fellow who was just about to pass in front of them. "Him?" James yelled incredulously. Amos affirmed without taking his eyes off Arnold.

James couldn't believe it. He was expecting a fellow with a sinister, sly demeanour. He had pictured a younger version of Arnold's father, Robert, with black hair, a thin frame, and features that reminded him of Dickens' Fagan: sharp and sly.

Arnold was nothing like that. He was short and rotund, with red hair and a round, smooth face. He looked much younger than 18 years old to James.

This boy a rapist? A killer?

James stood bewildered as he marched past. He hardly heard the next band as it marched past behind the recruits. Arnold was a boy, not a demon ready for the fires of hell. He looked as young as Bessie. *Most* of the soldiers looked young—but Arnold fit into another category altogether.

The children broke him out of his reverie with cheers for the brave soldiers. They were thrilled at the ear-splitting brass, the huge drums, and the uniforms. Some wanted to be soldiers, some drummers, some trumpeters.

Amos whispered in his ear, "So did ya' see the little bastard?"

James nodded but said nothing.

"We'll have hot chocolate when we get home," Mary yelled to her younger siblings, who were sitting in the back of the sleigh on the ride home. The sun was low in the sky and the temperature reflected that. The wind had died down, but not the chatter of the O'Sullivan kids. They seemed oblivious to the cold. They responded to Mary's comment with cheers and suggestions about what they might eat with their hot chocolate.

"You're quiet," Mary said to James. "Arnold wasn't what you expected, was he?"

James directed the horses to turn slightly to the left and to go over the bridge, though he knew they needed no such command—there was nowhere else *to* go. "You're right. He's just a kid. And I guess the shock of seeing him has opened up the whole Bessie affair again in my mind. I'm sorry," James said.

"No need to be sorry. I was shocked too. He looks so innocent. He looks younger than 18, doesn't he?" Mary placed her hand over James'. "He's leaving in a few hours to go overseas. There is nothing you or anyone can do for Bessie anymore. God will be his judge."

"You're right. I know that. It does me no good to ruminate about things I can't change. And I won't. It's out of my hands. I just watched young men march in front of me, many of whom will not come back. Like Bessie, these men will be destroyed for no reason. But it's because politicians can't sit down and talk things out. I think that may be a worse crime than murder."

"Now you sound like my father," Mary said. Then she prodded him playfully in the arm and added, "And I thought you were deciding what you were going to have with your hot chocolate!"

James laughed. She always knew how to ease his burdens, soften his reflective side and get him to take life less seriously. He needed her in his life.

Tommy poked his head up between them. "I have to pee soon," he said.

"We'll be home in a few minutes, Tommy," James yelled for all to hear. "And then hot chocolate after a good pee."

"Yeah!" Tommy cried.

Chapter 29
A Confession

THE CANADIAN EXPEDITIONARY FORCE WAS involved in their first major battle in April 1914 and suffered mass casualties. This conflict became known as the Second Battle of Ypres. It was during this battle that Germans used gas as a weapon for the first time. With the news of this new weaponry and the casualties, hatred of the Germans grew in Canada.

James threw his paper down on the kitchen table in disgust when he read about this and uttered a primitive growl. For the first time in his life he wanted to kill someone. He envisioned running a bayonet through some German's gut, or mowing down a row of advancing Huns with a machine gun. He wanted to fire the artillery shell that would send a line of Germans flying through the air, limbs detached, blood droplets mixed with mud, smoke, and fire. He wanted revenge.

He got up to pour another cup of tea from the pot before opening his office for the morning. He needed to calm down. The monthly physician's meeting in St. John had been rancorous the previous night. His normally calm, reflective colleagues were shouting about the utter horror of death by gas, the immorality of its use, and the depravity of the Germans for using it. Many called for revenge and death to all Germans, and although he refrained from adding to the furor, he felt caught up in the mass hysteria. He could feel the anger and angst build up inside him as the night went along. Today's newspaper articles evoked those emotions again.

He sat down and sipped his tea. He wondered, *how do you treat toxic gas inhalation? And what is chlorine gas?* He had no idea how he would deal with these things if he was a doctor in the field. *Symptom control, I guess. I must try to find information about treating gas exposure.* Sooner or later the men who had marched away so recently would come home sick, if they made it home at all.

James glanced at the clock on the kitchen wall. He wouldn't be able to finish reading the paper before his first appointment today, so he quickly scanned the news, turning pages until he came to the section on employment advertising. It reminded him about how Mary would soon work with him, side-by-side, doing administrative tasks while he tended to patients. The thought made him smile.

He had become quite well-known of late, and often found patients in his waiting room who he didn't know or hadn't anticipated seeing. He was getting so busy that it was common to be interrupted while with a patient by phone calls and even called inquiries from the waiting room. Further, he had no time to deal with his accounts and they were a mess. He had traditionally used an honour system for payment but he no longer had any idea of who owed him what, and he felt embarrassed asking people for money. Many of the poorer folks paid him with food or services, which was fine; but he needed to keep track and ensure that he actually got money from those who could afford his services.

Mary could see he needed help. She subtly inquired about his business and then offered to become his bookkeeper and receptionist after their marriage. He hadn't thought of medicine as a business—but of course it was, and he was very bad at that part of it. He looked forward to her help, but until then, he'd have to make the best of it by himself. It would be improper for her to work with him until they were married.

There are quite a few changes coming, he mused. When Mary assessed her future home—his house—she told him that she thought his attempt to live a true country life was both amusing and quite admirable for someone who grew up in an upper-class family.

"It's like you are atoning for your comfortable childhood, or acting out a fantasy," she said. "But does it really have to be so hard, James?"

He couldn't explain to her why he strove to live such a simple life. When he tried to, it didn't make much sense to him either, because the truth was that it wasn't that simple to chop wood, keep woodstoves going for heat and run outside into the pitch dark and cold to go to the toilet.

James smiled at the recollection of that conversation. Mary made it clear she insisted on indoor toiletry and water if she was going to live here. He took her words to heart; he could afford to live a more comfortable life, so why not? Yes, there were going to be a lot of changes in his life soon. He was in the middle of renovating and would have it all done by June.

The tinkle of his office door chime announced the arrival of his first patient, Mrs. English. She had suffered a chest infection about a month ago and James was watching her closely. She had a congested lower lobe in her right lung that was persisting. James was quite sure she wasn't contagious—she had no fever or any other symptoms—yet despite the fresh air and exercise he prescribed, the lung continued to be quite noisy when he listened to it through the stethoscope. She felt well, but he was worried she might have pleurisy, an abscess, or perhaps even cancer lingering there, silently growing.

Or maybe she'd always had a bit of congestion—a past infection might have left scar tissue. An X-ray would help ascertain the nature of it, but so far, she had refused because of the cost. Instead, she'd agreed to come in once a week and James only charged her for one visit per month. He felt better following her closely for a while.

After examining her, James informed her there were no changes that he could discern. Mrs. English good-naturedly admonished him for insisting to see such a healthy woman as herself, which made them both laugh.

James saw five other patients that morning. The one commonality was that everyone was angry about the gas attack on the troops overseas.

"It's a terrible thing to do," they said one-by-one, "to make another human suffer so. Those Germans are heartless."

James wondered at lunchtime if any local boys, those young men in the parade, had been in that fateful battle? How many had died or were suffering? Was Arnold gassed and sick, or dead? In his case, it was fitting. But what of those other hopeful, young faces? Did they need the help and care of a qualified physician?

Suddenly he started to wonder if he was right in his resolve not to serve. He may not be a fighting man, but he had something to offer.

During the Medical Society meeting in the third week of May, Dr. Peters advised the group that there were more troop casualties than the papers were reporting and that he had been asked by the government of Canada to recruit more doctors for the army. Dr. Peters said doctors would be given the rank of captain; they would not have to endure weapons or military training; and they would be immediately shipped to hospitals overseas.

Slowly, over the preceding months, James came to a painful decision: He was going to enlist in the army. Prior to the Second Battle of Ypres, he hadn't entertained the thought, but Dr. Peters' words, and the fact that the war showed no signs of abating, changed his mind. He decided it was his duty to join the war effort.

At church, Reverend Philpotts continued to try to rally the congregation to support the war effort. "We must all do our part," he said. "God is on our side." He used the gas attack as proof that the Germans were in the grip of an evil force, a force that must be defeated. It was now a righteous war.

James saw nothing 'righteous' about it, but he was starting to feel he would be remiss to not support the young men who had left their safe homes to put their lives on the line for liberty. And real or imagined, he was certain judgemental eyes were boring into his back as he sat with the O'Sullivan family up front every Sunday. There was no getting around it; it was his duty to care for the young men who were risking their lives for their nation and, as he was one of the youngest doctors in the St. John area, he was naturally expected to be one of the first to volunteer.

But what about Mary? It was only three weeks until their wedding day. It was very likely that, in making this decision, he would leave almost immediately after she became his wife. *Perhaps we should postpone the wedding … if I should be killed, she would be left a widow!*

He wasn't looking forward to informing her of his decision to join the army. This would hurt her deeply. However, he didn't want to do her the injustice of making her wait for a man who might not return. He hoped she would understand.

On a Saturday afternoon in the first week of June, James invited Mary to ride with him for a picnic. He rode over to the O'Sullivan's on Sadie, with Mary's horse in tow, to pick her up and together they rode back through Rothesay, past Reed's Point, to a pasture high above the river. From their vantage point at this spot, the river narrowed drastically, changing from a wide, sandy beach-lined waterway to a marshy, reed-lined watercourse full of birds and plant life to marvel at. The occasional billowy white cloud fled eastward along an otherwise azure sky. It was a beautiful day, and Mary was a beautiful girl.

James felt depressed despite the perfect day and Mary noticed right away. "Are you alright, James?" she asked. "You've been a little quiet this afternoon."

He let out a hesitant sigh. "I have something to tell you," he said quietly. He took her hand and faced her while they lay side by side on a blanket. Mary looked at him with apprehension. She hitched herself up higher on her elbow to look him in the eyes. "I love you," James said, "more than anything in the world." Mary said nothing. He looked directly into her eyes and told her, "Mary, I've decided to join the army."

He saw her flinch as she said, "What? You think the war is crazy. Why?"

"It doesn't matter what I think, my love," he said sadly. "The hard truth is that there are young men—most of them mere boys—getting injured and dying on the battlefield and they need help. They need all the doctors they can get over there and I feel it is my duty to help to ease their suffering as best I can."

Mary dully absorbed this information, and then asked, "But what about your patients? They have come to depend upon you."

"They did fine without me before and they will again. For me, it's become a question of who needs me more."

"You could get killed."

"I could, I suppose, but there is little chance of that, Mary. I will be far from the battle, working in a hospital in France or maybe even in England. The greatest risk I will face will be stabbing myself with a surgical blade." He risked a smile, but Mary remained grim and said nothing.

James sat up, pulled her to sitting and embraced her, but she remained stiff and unresponsive. He released her and leaned back holding onto both of her shoulders. "I know this is a shock for you. I know that this was the last thing you wanted to hear before our wedding, but please understand that this is also the last thing *I* want. I was so looking forward to you being my wife in three weeks. I imagined this summer as a dream come true. Our wedding day would have been the happiest day of my life."

"James, what are you talking about? What do you mean 'would have been'? Are you saying we're not getting married in three weeks? Are you leaving before the wedding?" Now Mary looked angry. James had never seen her angry before.

"Probably not," he stammered, a bit stiffly. "At least, I don't *think* they will ship me out that soon.

But I thought about our marriage and was afraid that if something happened to me, I'd leave you a widow. You're too *young* to be a widow, Mary. I won't leave you a widow! Perhaps we shouldn't take the chance. Perhaps we should postpone our nuptials!"

"You just said there would *be* no danger. You said you'd be far from the battlefield!" she said heatedly.

"That's true," he agreed, "But war is dangerous. I'm not likely to get harmed—but you never know."

"I'll take those chances," she said firmly. "*I* could die tomorrow. *I* could get consumption, pneumonia, or God knows what else! No one knows what each day brings! Dr. James Wilson, shipping off to the war is *not* a reason to cancel our wedding. You can't live life that way. Life is a risk every single day!" Then she looked up at him, suddenly stricken. "Unless you don't want to get married anymore … is that it, James?"

James melted. "I want to marry you so *much*, Mary. I want to spend the rest of my life with you. If you will still have me, please forget everything I just said. I will go to war, but not until you are my wife." He kissed her passionately, abandoning propriety to his emotions.

Mary was crying as she drew away from his embrace. "There will be no more talk of war until after the wedding," she said.

James promised. "I love you so much," he said.

Chapter 30

A Father's Worry

The wedding was wonderful. Both of their mothers had worked with Mary to create a white silk dress with lace piping and tulle skirting that was beautiful. Mary was the most radiant bride. They married at St. Paul's with the whole congregation in attendance as well as Frank and Marg, Robert and Isobel and Percy and his wife. The reception was at the O'Sullivan house. Rebecca and some of her women friends created a fabulous picnic-style feast and set up picnic tables outside, and Mary's siblings dashed about cleaning up dishes and making sure the guests had enough to eat. That night, an exhausted James carried Mary across the threshold of their newly renovated home and laid her down on brand new sheets he had purchased for this occasion.

He had often daydreamed about the night ahead and making love to Mary was as exciting as he had anticipated.

She surprised him by being an eager participant; she had no reticence about appearing unladylike. On the fifth night of their marriage, she whispered, "I feel like being naughty," and to his surprise, she rolled on top of him and proceeded to move her body with such an erotic rhythm that it resulted in mutual, shared, concurrent orgasm. It was a special moment, something James could never have envisioned. He was left near tears by the special nature of what they shared.

They left just days later for their honeymoon. They drove to Boston along the coast of Maine, stopping at seaside resorts along the way. In Boston, they visited many of the O'Sullivan relatives, saw a play, and attended a concert.

His surprise at the libidinous nature of his new bride never ceased and he soon found out that Mary was very open to intimate talk. One night they were lingering over wine after dinner, looking out onto the silent dark water of Bar Harbour in Maine, when Mary asked coyly, "Did you like last night?"

At first, James didn't understand she was referring to their love-making the night before, but when he noted her mischievous smile, he was speechless—shocked that she could be so open about sexuality.

"Are you blushing?" Mary giggled.

"The wine makes me flush …" he stammered.

"So, did you enjoy what we did?"

"Mary, you are the most open person I've ever talked to," he said in a hushed voice, worried that neighbouring patrons would overhear. "I'm not sure I know how to respond. I've never talked much about this sort of thing to anyone."

"*What* sort of thing?" Mary asked teasingly.

James laughed. "You are an extraordinary creature. Yes, I enjoyed last night very much. Where did you learn how to … do these things?"

"Girl talk," she giggled. "I am a very open person, James. I will have no secrets from you and I hope you won't with me. I will reveal my most innermost thoughts to you and tell you what makes me sad and what makes me happy. I think our intimate relations should be the same. Why do people try to pretend it doesn't happen? In particular, why are women supposed to pretend it gives them no enjoyment?"

"I don't know," James said. He had never really considered this before. "Maybe it's because it's associated with drunkenness, prostitution and loutish behaviour, which are considered ungodly?"

"Do you think I'm being a slut by doing what I did last night and talking about it now?" she asked.

"No! Mary, I love you so much. I'm enthralled by your candour and honoured that you trust me in this way. This is the most enlightening conversation I've ever had with *anyone.* It is a joy to know we can talk about anything. It's going to be an amazing life with you." He reached his hand across the table and touched hers.

"I'm glad you feel that way," she said. "Because I have to warn you, I enjoyed last night very much." Then she smiled and slyly whispered, "Now I know why mother had so many children."

James tried to keep his laughter under control.

They arrived home the second of July. Renovations had been finalized while they were away, and James spent the first few hours at home playfully running water and flushing toilets. Mary immediately set to work adding touches to the décor that announced her presence as lady of the house. She added or rearranged decorations and furniture, with approval from James of course. He loved her ideas and their collaboration. It symbolised a permanency to their relationship, a home that was for them.

He learned a few days later that he was scheduled for deployment to France on August 10 via merchant ship. It sounded like there would be few fellow soldiers onboard. The ship's purpose was to bring supplies to the front, and he was just hitching a ride. He had assumed he'd be going with a company of soldiers to England for further training before being sent to the front lines, but he was bypassing all that. Apparently, doctors were needed very badly. Until then, however, it was business as usual.

Mary began working with him in his office right away, and it was a delight to have her. Within the first week, he realized that with her handling the administrative tasks he'd become more efficient and focused on his patients. By the second week, Mary had setup a simple, practical bookkeeping system to keep track of accounts. He promised they would buy a professional bookkeeping ledger the next time they were in St. John.

Over the ensuing month, patients expressed their sadness that he was leaving and left many gifts and well wishes. Thomas McGarrigle, the boy he saved from a perforated appendix, brought him a wooden boat he had made. Others brought stocks for Mary to ensure she would be fine with her husband away. Even the O'Learys visited, with Frank offering to come down and help Mary with the horses, firewood and other chores in James' absence. Margaret O'Leary kissed James tearfully saying, "You saved Frank. No other doctor could have done that."

"It was God's will ..." James started to protest.

"Yes," Margaret interrupted, "but you gave him the best care and did the work. You went above and beyond. People are astounded he's still alive, especially when I tell them the bone broke clear out of his skin. But not only is he alive, he's walking and doing chores. He won't be able to go logging anymore, but he figures he may start fishing for a living."

"You don't need much legs in a boat and the salmon are plentiful," Frank cut in.

Margaret embraced James again and tearfully murmured, "Thank you." Then she shoved him and said, "You just come back, you hear? Fix the boys up and then come back." She abruptly turned her back and left the room, leaving Frank and James alone.

"Guess she told *me*," James said smiling. "I have to come back."

"Yep," Frank said, "and you don't dare cross Marg. I'd say you have no option but to come back." Frank shook his hand and limped out the office.

A few days later, on a Saturday, the rest of the gang—Charlie, Percy and Robert—showed up. They chose to stay outside on such a pleasant day to chat with James on the porch. Mary served them beer and sandwiches and left, saying, "I'll leave you gentlemen alone so you can talk about things my woman's ears shouldn't hear," as she closed the door.

"You're a lucky man," Charlie said. "Pretty, humorous—and serves beer without a sermon."

"I suppose it helps," Percy added, "that her father sells this stuff."

As they talked and laughed, James reminisced about the day he first met Frank and his friends; about the raw, cold ride along the frozen river; the anxious anticipation of what trauma he might find; and then the bewildering, incongruent discovery of the comical trio of Frank, Percy, and Robert, happily inebriated in the woods, while Frank slowly went into shock.

As they were eating, during a lull in the conversation, Robert blurted out, "I haven't heard from my son, Arnold." There was an uncomfortable silence. "Mail's bad," he went on, "I know that. We wrote to him a few times. No one has told us whether he's hurt or not, so I suppose that's a good thing."

Robert looked down at his sandwich like he wasn't sure how it came to be there, mystified, like he was searching for what words to say next.

"He's probably okay," Charlie offered. "Mail's bad, just like you say."

"He's a good boy, Arnold is. A good son. Never gave us trouble. You wouldn't find a nicer fellow. Too nice, if you ask me. I always thought he needed more grit. He's too damn placid for his own good. Isobel always told me to leave him alone and let him be. 'He's a gentle soul,' she'd say. Didn't like hunting. Didn't like fishing. But he was good with the farming and he'd do any chore you'd ask him to do without grumbling. All in all, he is a good son and I don't know what Isobel and I will do if he doesn't come home."

Robert looked miserable. His eyes glistened and his lips trembled. Then he looked directly at James and said angrily, "He didn't do anything to Bessie MacKenzie. He swears to it and I believe my boy. I don't care what she wrote."

"What do you mean—wrote?" Percy interrupted. "She wrote *what*?"

"Arnold told me she had a diary or something and accused him of making her pregnant. Wrote down she was meeting him the night she died. Police told him that. Lies. It's lies."

"Really?" Percy said. "That's why the police had him in for questioning about Bessie's death? I was wondering why they would question him about a suicide. You just said they were getting information. Seemed peculiar to me."

"Why a girl would write something like that, I don't know," Robert said. "Gets herself pregnant by some lowdown, and then makes up a story about being with someone she wishes it had been."

James shifted uncomfortably in his seat. He felt he had to defend Bessie. She wasn't like that; she was a lovely girl, wise beyond her years … but Robert spoke before he could protest. "Isobel says she can't figure it.

The Bessie she knew was a wonderful girl. A treasure to her mother, Isobel's sister—and such a comfort to her father after her mother's passing. Now Arnold's no angel. He's a dumb-ass for getting a girl pregnant before he finished all his schooling, but many a boy's done that. If a girl's willing to spread her legs, I reckon there's not a man alive wouldn't oblige. So, I can't completely blame him."

James didn't agree with that crass, simplistic statement, but he held his tongue. However, he felt his face flush.

"He's proved himself a man though," Robert went on, "because he took responsibility for the girl and his child. He married her, got himself a job, and works hard to support his family. I'm proud of him for that. And the police couldn't find where he done wrong, so that should be that."

Robert looked directly at James when he said this. James returned the stare and struggled to remain silent. He wanted to argue but was conflicted. How would he feel if Arnold was dead right now? *I'd feel guilty for calling Arnold a rapist and possibly a killer when I can't prove it, and that would be a fine last thought for a grieving father.*

And he had to admit that it had been disconcerting to actually *see* Arnold. He looked exactly as his father described him: an innocent, young, redheaded boy who should be playing in the creek instead of fighting

Germans in a foreign land. *Could that young lad really rape and possibly kill Bessie?* He remained quiet.

"Guess we better get going," Charlie said breaking the silence that ensued. "You take care of yourself, James. I'm sure if you see Arnold, please tell him to write if he hasn't done so already. And tell him his parents send him their love."

James nodded, stood up, and shook hands with each man as he bade them farewell. He held Robert's hand a little longer and reassured him that he would look out for his boy. He felt a great deal of empathy for Robert. He was worried about the well-being of a son he obviously loved and missed.

He watched them ride away and wondered if this would be the last time he'd ever see them. Unable to face Mary at the moment, he descended the front steps and marched across the yard to the barn. It was time to say good-bye to Sadie.

Chapter 31
A Letter to Mary

August 30, 1915

Dear Mary,

I can't believe it's been only a month since I left you; it seems longer than that. I think about you all the time. I miss being with you and having our little chats. I love you so much.

I'm writing you from my barracks, which I share with three other doctors. We all take shifts, so someone is always sleeping, and we must be quiet inside. To talk, we go outside and around back. It has been hot here. I hope it has been less so for you, my dear.

It is difficult to describe our barracks. It is sort of a combination of wood and canvas with a stove in the middle. There's a table and four cots around the periphery. I'm in France, close to the front lines. Don't worry; I'm not near the bombs and action. I'm quite safe. I thought I'd be at a hospital like I told you (and I was thinking of a hospital like St. John

Public), but I'm not. I'm at what they call a 'dressing station'. Ha! It's not what it sounds. We see the casualties first and triage them. If they can wait, we patch them up and send them by ambulance to a casualty clearing station, where more definitive treatment takes place. However, a fair number of our boys can't wait that long and we have to perform surgery right here. Many cannot be saved and it is our duty to make that decision here. That can be hard.

I won't go into describing the injuries to you, but let me just say, they can be horrendous.

I have been to the front lines. The major (Dr. Fisher) insists we all experience what the men are going through, and it is hell. It is hot and wet, with bugs and rats crawling around; sniper fire or artillery barrages or raids from the enemy can occur at any time. Mostly, though, it is boring. The men sit in trenches hour after hour, doing nothing. The troops are rotated from the front lines to the back for some rest every so often because, as you can imagine, it's hard for them to get a good night's rest. Despite all that, the men find ways to keep their spirits up. They are often quite comical with their jokes.

I was only there for half a day, but that was enough for me! The medics handle what they can in the trenches, mostly rashes, lice infestation and feet problems. There is a common malady call 'trench foot'. It is caused from the feet being perpetually wet. The trenches are a soggy mess, like I said. They have tried putting boards down to keep the bottom dry, but before long the boards get trampled into the quagmire and it is just as mucky as before. And it stinks!

This war is so stupid. I can see the Germans hunkered down in their trenches only about 200 yards away from our own trench. We seem to be at a stalemate. Every so often they send troops across and we mow them down and then the reverse happens a day or so later. It's absolutely crazy.

So don't worry; I've had my experience at the front line. The major's happy and now I'm out of harm's way.

They brought a wounded German to the dressing station the other night by mistake (it's hard to see who you're picking up at night in no man's land, which is what they call the ground between the trenches). Anyway, on his belt was a motto that said, 'Gott Mit Uns'. You know what that means? 'God is with us'. It made me pause. They think they're fighting for a righteous cause, and so do we. Who's right? I don't think God picks sides. I pray to Him this madness ends, but I don't see how that will happen any time soon.

The trip over wasn't bad. The ship made it in eight days. We met up with five other merchant ships in Halifax and were escorted across the Atlantic by warships. I guess that was when I was in the most danger from German U-boats, which were lurking about beneath the surface. The seas were rough only on one day, and I didn't get seasick. I was worried about how I'd fare at sea and I'm glad to report that your husband is a salty ol' pirate.

I'm writing this letter on my bunk by lamplight. I must now get to sleep because you never know when you'll be called.

I miss you very much. I had what I can only describe as a spiritual experience when we said goodbye on the pier. For a moment, everything around us melted away—your family, my mother, our friends. The whole big crowd suddenly didn't exist. Even the noise around us faded away—the conversations, the sailors shouting orders, the boat creaking, nothing. I saw only you in a mystical place without definition and I felt complete peace.

I miss you so much.
Love,
James

Chapter 32
An Order Refused

THERE WERE NO MAJOR BATTLES between the Second Battle of Ypres in April of 1915 and the spring of 1916, but there were constant failed attempts to breech the lines. Raids were often carried out just to gather information, despite the loss of life that ensued. Shellfire was used to soften the trenches before raids, to accompany and repel raids, or sometimes just at random. The troops tried to ignore the knowledge that at any moment a bomb might land on their heads; but for many, it was an impossible feat of denial. During the night, snipers tried to position themselves in spots that made the trenches unsafe, even when the men were hunkered down. Many men broke down under this stress.

James was rotated between the dressing and casualty clearing stations, depending upon need. He grew adept at amputating limbs, which was by far the most common surgical procedure needed. However, many men he worked on died from infection, even with the most successful amputations. The care and cleaning required to ensure proper healing was almost impossible to adhere to in the circumstances in which the men found themselves. Supplies such as carbolic acid often ran out and even just sterilizing water was a chore. Everyone did the best they could with what they had, but it was difficult.

When the mud, dirt, and blood were washed away, James saw the most horrendous things, head wounds that defied description caused by bullets or shell fragments and even a boy holding his intestines in his hand. James never forgot his puzzled expression as he said, "Look Doc," with bewilderment. "Look."

James did what he could, but often nothing could be done. He learned to spend his time with those who could be saved at the expense of those he deemed could not. It was hard to look a pleading boy in the eyes and tell the medics to place him 'over there'—'over there' being the place of no hope, no treatment; a waiting area for death. James made sure no man suffered and made judicious use of morphine for the boys who were 'over there'.

One evening in mid-November 1915, a rush of casualties came into the dressing station, including a soldier on a stretcher whose dark hair rose straight up from the gauze wrapped around his head and face. His uniform was soiled with mud and blood and one foot pointed abnormally inward. One watchful, alert, dark eye peered out from under the gauze on his head.

"Blast injury," the medic rapidly reported. "Massive head injury, shrapnel wounds to abdomen, and severe leg trauma. Patient still alert and responsive. Lost a fair amount of blood. Pulse 110."

"Help me undress this fellow immediately, Miss Perkins," James ordered a nurse who appeared by the soldier's side as he was brought in.

"You may want to look at his abdomen," the medic said lowering his voice.

The medic and nurse spread open the uniform and removed blood-soaked gauze to expose his abdomen, which was a confusing, pulsating, gory mess. James gently manipulated a few areas to confirm the soldier's abdomen was almost entirely ripped open. He looked up at the medic and nurse and silently acknowledged that these wounds were untreatable. There was no need to uncover the head injury, nor the severe leg wound.

The soldier emitted a groan. "God it hurts," he mumbled.

James was amazed this man was still conscious. He didn't have to ask where or how bad the pain was. "We'll get you something for that pain, soldier," he said. "Miss Perkins, five cc of morphine for this fellow as soon as possible."

He turned to attend to the fellow behind him only to face Dr. Fisher. "Dr. Wilson," he muttered, "I told you our supply of morphine is low."

"I'm aware of that, sir, but this man needs something."

Dr. Fisher brought his face close to James and whispered so as not to be heard by the soldier, "You've assessed him as untreatable, I understand."

"Yes, sir."

"And by the looks of it death will be soon. Is that not so?"

"Yes, sir, but the wounds are horrific, and the soldier is conscious and in pain. He needs relief."

"Normally I would agree with you … *hold that injection, nurse* … but not today. We might need that morphine before the supplies come."

"Dr. Fisher," James said, omitting the rank title, "it is my medical opinion that this man needs morphine now."

Dr. Fisher noted the omission of rank. "You heard my order, captain."

Miss Perkins was still holding the syringe of morphine by the soldier's side. James turned around and looked at the soldier again. His dark eye still conveyed life and hope. A vision of Bessie's face came to him, sitting on his examination table with sadness but also with hope and the determination to deal with her unwanted pregnancy. “Miss Perkins, I’ll take the syringe,” he said.

She carefully handed him the syringe.

“Captain …” Dr. Fisher warned.

James slowly turned to the soldier and injected morphine into the muscle of his upper arm.

Chapter 33
No Man's Land

MAJOR FISHER ASSIGNED HIM TO two weeks of duty in the trenches for his insubordination. He supposed being sent to the front line was mild punishment. He had heard of far worse penalties for disobeying orders. It was punishment though: He had never been so cold and wet in his life. It seemed he'd never get rid of the chill and dampness that sank into the deepest core of his being. He slept in a hole in the ground dug out from the back wall of the trench, which was braced with wooden beams. He shared the space with three other officers.

The earthen, musty walls shook and threatened to collapse with each close artillery barrage. Bits of dirt fell from the roof and often onto his head. He feared being buried alive and with a direct hit; were it to happen, that was almost a sure thing. *At least I have a roof over my head, not like the soldiers in the trenches.* Those men had to live out there for a week at a time, fending off the rats with kicks. They spent most of the time huddled up in a ball, their muscles stiff from cold, dampness, and inactivity.

The other officers in his quarters were friendly and polite, but he missed his fellow physicians who lived with him at the permanent encampment. He had more time on his hands now; injuries were quickly assessed and sent to the dressing station, leaving James with little to do. The medics inspected and treated the trench feet, lice, fleabites, rashes, cuts, and scrapes. In the two weeks he'd been here, he had only evaluated two men for permission to leave the front lines for medical treatment. One had a severe cold he suspected could be pneumonia and the other was an unfortunate lad with shell shock. He had seen a number of cases of this dementia since he'd arrived several months ago. He felt sorry for these boys. They turned into somnolent ghosts, paranoids, or hallucinogenic madmen due to the extreme violence and assault on the normal human experience that was war. In James' opinion, it was a wonder *more* didn't go mad.

He never thought he'd miss the dressing or casualty stations, but at least there he was kept busy. There was too much time to think now—and all he could think about was the cold, dampness, and the roof collapsing. Finally, to keep busy, he volunteered to go with the medics onto no man's land to retrieve the casualties and the dead.

Today was such a 'collection' day, following a night raid that followed an earlier excursion by the Germans, which had been repelled. It was a cloudy day with the wind whipping over the trench directly into their faces. From the relative safety of the trench, James heard a moan from somewhere in the distance, though for the most part it was eerily quiet.

The flag signalling a temporary abstinence of fire for medical purposes was flying. The flag was all white with a red cross in the middle. "How long has the flag been up?" asked Fred, the head medic in their sector.

"About ten minutes," one of the medics replied.

"Christ! Wave the damn thing," Fred grumbled. "Hello," he yelled. "Fritz are you awake over there?"

"There it is, Fred," the medic said.

James peered over the wall and saw a white flag with a red cross rising above the German trench in answer. He knew they had to wait to make sure all the German soldiers got the message not to fire. When Fred gave the signal, they would move.

The first time had James climbed over the wall and into no man's land, his muscles refused to relax from the anxiety, and he scurried forward in a crouched position expecting rifle or machine gun fire at any moment. It got easier each time after that, but it was never comfortable. Today, he followed the last medic out of the trench and could see the German medics doing the same.

He had gotten to know the German medics in these past two weeks, and they seemed like good fellows. They were respectful and often helpful. James had helped them with a few of their own men and they were very grateful and surprised to find a doctor out in no man's land.

"He was a bad boy," one of the Canadian medics said to a puzzled German who asked about James. The Germans laughed and from then on he was known as, 'Herr Dr. Bad Boy'.

His eyes narrowed to slits because of the bitter wind, James hurried out to find the moaning soldier, dodging craters that pockmarked the muddy field. Two medics huddled over the wounded man.

"What do we have here?" James asked when he finally reached their side.

"This is Corporal Sam Owens, and he's pissed," one said.

"Damn right I'm pissed," Sam said. "I've been lying here for hours in the cold and muck while you fellas have probably been sipping your fucking morning tea."

Sam was a hefty looking fellow. His large mud-caked hands clutched his coat tight over his chest. His upper right leg looked deformed and was covered with mud and blood.

"Looks like he's fine, except for a massive wound in his right upper leg, Dr. Wilson," said one of the medics. "I can't tell if it's shrapnel or bullets. Shrapnel, I think." Then he quickly cut the pant leg open so James could look.

"It missed a major artery," James commented. "You'll live," he said to Sam. "You're a lucky man, Sam." *Not so lucky*, he thought, *he'll need a high leg amputation.*

"Lucky?" Sam said. "You're joking right? Damn near got my leg shot off and the Doc says I'm lucky."

"Lucky to be alive, I mean."

"I know what you meant. I'm just joshing ya'."

"I'm surprised you can even joke. You must be a tough old bird," James said. Sam grinned and moaned at the same time. "We are going to turn you on your side and slide a stretcher under you. This may really hurt. Ready?"

"Is that a German?" Sam asked incredulously. A German medic had appeared by their side to help them transfer Sam onto a stretcher.

"That's Gunter," a medic replied. "He and his fellows help us all the time and we help them."

"We were just shooting at each other last night," Sam grunted between clenched teeth, "and now we're buddies. Crazy, fucked-up war."

"One, two, three!" a medic called, and they turned Sam onto his side and then onto the stretcher they'd positioned for him to lie on. Sam let out a loud groan.

Silently, James agreed. This *was* a crazy, fucked-up war.

Chapter 34
Arnold

JAMES WAS NEARING THE END of his two-week stint on the front trenches. The troops where he was stationed were falling back for rest and being replaced by fresh bodies. He was outside his quarters writing a letter to Mary when he looked up and saw a soldier pass by whose side profile reminded him of Arnold Ramsey. He watched the soldier trudge past. He had red, curly hair. *Is that Arnold?* He wasn't sure. This fellow seemed stockier than the boy he'd seen walk by that cold afternoon in St. John.

James arose and joined the line of soldiers filling in the trenches to his right, keeping his eye on the fellow ahead with the red hair. After a few minutes, James saw the red-headed soldier stop, turn around, and then tell the men behind him to halt and spread out. James walked around the men in front of him until he was beside the soldier. He studied the side of the soldier's face until the man turned his head and asked, "Is there a problem ..." the soldier glanced down at James' nametag, "... *Captain*? Is there a problem?"

"You're Arnold Ramsey, aren't you?"

"Yes, Sergeant Arnold Ramsey. I'm responsible for this sorry lot. And you are?"

"You would know me as Dr. James Wilson from Rothesay."

There was a fleeting expression of surprise on Arnold's face, which was quickly replaced by a cold glare. Nothing was said.

"I got nothing to say to you," Arnold muttered looking over the trench.

"How could you do it?" James asked with a harsh whisper.

"I didn't do anything," Arnold snarled. "If you're referring to the death of Bessie MacKenzie, the police cleared me. They told me it was you and Uncle Amos who claimed this nonsense."

"I'm sure you don't want your men to hear our conversation. Is there somewhere we can go for privacy?"

Arnold thought for a moment and then shook his head. "Nowhere safe. We got nothing to talk about anyway."

"Then I'll just have to talk here." James raised his voice and began, "When you were at that church social and you— "

"Hush," Arnold rasped. "Mike. Bob," he said, looking to his left and catching the eyes of a couple of men. Then he looked to and right he called for Frank and Stephan. When they were assembled, he said, "Me and Dr. Wilson here need some privacy. You two make sure the men are spread out evenly in that direction," he commanded Mike and Bob, pointing to his left, "and you two search that way," he said to Frank and Stephen.

"Got the crabs, Sarge?" a soldier asked, grinning.

"Trying to figure out how the doc can get rid of your stink, Frank?"

The men disappeared after a chuckle.

"They seem to like you," James said. "I see you're a sergeant now."

"Seems like I'm good at fighting. That and I'm about the only one left from my original squad, so you could say I earned my stripes by surviving."

A cold gust of wind brought a shower of dry, brown leaves over the trench and onto them. Arnold spit away a leaf that landed on his mouth. He seemed to have aged ten years from when James last saw him less than a year ago. The once smooth face was marked with stubble, scars, dirt, and lines he'd expect to see on a grizzled, rum-fuelled gunslinger. Arnold lit a cigarette.

"I know you raped Bessie," James said harshly. "But why did you have to kill her? Seems like she was keeping the secret."

"I didn't rape or kill my cousin. It was a suicide and I'm sorry she got herself pregnant. I liked Bessie. She was a good girl. Why do you and Uncle Amos continue to accuse me when the police have said I'm innocent?"

"They *didn't* say you're innocent. They said they didn't have enough proof to find you guilty."

"But *you* do."

"Bessie's diary is all the proof I need. Why would she make something like that up?"

"Maybe she was writing a book or something. I don't know. Look I didn't do it, okay? I can't say any more than that. I'm sorry for Bessie and Uncle Amos, but there's some other guy that got her pregnant, not me. I guess the shame was too much for her."

Arnold seemed sincere and acted truly sad and honest, which confused James. He'd been wrong about Wilfred. For a moment, he questioned his judgement and his memory. Had Bessie really said a *relative* raped her? After all she was upset and speaking through anguish and tears. Perhaps he'd misunderstood her.

But the diary ... James grabbed Arnold's coat and wrenched him around. "If I've falsely accused you of this horrible crime," James said in a threatening whisper, glaring directly into Arnold's face, "then I apologise to you from the bottom of my heart and damn me to hell for all time. But if I'm right and you raped and murdered sweet Bessie, then I hope you rot in hell!"

Then he pushed Arnold, turned, and walked away.

Chapter 35
A Surprise

JAMES OPENED THE DOOR TO leave his quarters and discovered the first snow of the season had fallen overnight. The early morning sun reflecting off the fresh snow blinded him, and he tread cautiously from his barracks along the path toward the casualty station, his eyes burning and tearing as he went.

He had been back from the front for almost a month and had resumed the routine of rotating between the casualty and dressing stations. It was nearing Christmas. Staff had tried to make the area outside the casualty station look festive by dressing up a sad-looking deciduous tree with ribbons, thin strips of gauze tape, and coloured paper ornaments that were now covered with snow. James smiled, remembering last night's enthusiastic carolling that was made the more raucous by a generous allotment of whiskey and rum. After the gruelling past few weeks, the staff needed to lift their spirits and Major Fisher said nothing as a week's worth of alcohol rations was consumed in a few hours. Major Fisher wasn't such a bad fellow after all, James decided.

He'd shown James his humanity in other ways as well. Soon after his return from the front, he spoke to James privately, "I'm so glad you're all right, James. I hated sending you to the front, but you were insubordinate in front of others. I had to do something to punish you."

"I understand, sir," James said.

"Doug. Please call me Doug when we're alone. You call me 'sir' or Major Fisher when we're working—protocol and such—but privately we're Doug and James. You don't mind me calling you James?"

James was taken aback by this sudden offer of friendship; it reminded him of his conversation with Dr. Peters a few years ago. *Was that really a few years ago?* "Certainly not," James said.

"I admire you for standing up to me," Major Fisher said. "You decided as a physician for the well-being of your patient. To protect yourself, you could have submitted to my order and no one would have said a thing. Orders from a ranking officer are to be obeyed; we both know it's as simple as that. But by damn, you stuck to your principles and did what was best for your patient. I admire that and I hope I'd have the guts to do what you did if the roles were reversed."

"I appreciate you saying that," James said.

"You understand my position at the time, I hope. I had to manage the supplies and I was very afraid we'd run short of morphine."

"I understand. I've run into this sort of situation before, when a physician in authority had to reign in my enthusiasm—I gave him fits, too." James snickered and Dr. Fisher broke into laughter.

Today, just as James was reminiscing about him, Dr. Fisher merged from the casualty station and said, smiling, "Good morning, Captain. You seemed to be in very good spirits last night."

James had had more than his share of rum the previous evening ... but he had good reason for it.

"I hope you're not chastising me, sir," he said. "I've found out some very good news. I'm going to be a father!"

"Well that *is* wonderful," said Dr. Fisher. "Let me congratulate you!"

"Thank you, sir," said James, shaking Dr. Fisher's outstretched hand. "Thank you!"

A package from Mary had arrived the morning before the festivities and within it was a letter:

Dear James

I am bursting to tell you this good news. I'm pregnant! We are to have a child soon!

Shortly after you left, I discovered my pregnancy but feared to tell you. First, I wanted to be sure that's why I was so sick, and so I waited until my next cycle, which never came. Then, because you had so much else to worry about and I didn't want to add to your burden, I decided to wait until I was certain I would not miscarry. Then I thought possibly you would be home before the baby was born—wouldn't that be a surprise homecoming, to see me with a baby bump? But from your letters and the news we're getting, it seems the war isn't ending anytime soon and so I can't surprise you. So, this is my Christmas gift to you—by the time you come home, you will have a child. It is only a few months until our baby arrives, and I so wish you could be here.

Your mother is doing well and was quite ecstatic over the news of my pregnancy. She has been staying with me often. Your friends go and get her and bring her here from St. John and then take her back after our visit. Amos, Wilfred, Frank, Robert, Percy, Charlie, and many of your patients do so much for me. Every day someone is here tending to the horses, cleaning the stalls, fetching me supplies, bringing me food—father says I'm going to get a reputation by having so many men around!

I have lots of female company too: The ladies from around town often come to sit with me. I am hardly ever alone. We talk of the war often, and of course baby things too. I've had so much advice I could write a book! Mother says to ignore it all except for her advice. Ha!

I miss you so much. It would be so much fun to have you near to share the joy of our new child. The darn war!

Don't worry about me, I feel fine and Dr. Peters says I'm as healthy as a horse. (I try not to take offense in being compared to a horse! Ha!).

Please take care, my love. Eat well, keep warm, and try not to be a hero. Do you get enough sleep? When I climb into my warm bed at night, I think of you lying in a cot in some cold tent and wish I could just wrap my arms around you and warm you up.

I love you so much. I hope my news brings you some Christmas cheer.

Love
Mary
P.S. In this package are some treats from all of us here at home.

It was definitely the happiest start to a day he had had since leaving Canada. He was going to be a father! The word *father* seared emotions into his soul that were a mixture of joy, excitement, and concern—but predominately pure happiness.

"Good morning, Dr. Wilson," Nurse Campbell said, as James entered the station with a grin on his face.

"That's wonderful news you gave us last night—about being a father—you were giddy with happiness."

"Good morning, Nurse Campbell. I *am* happy."

"It's so nice to hear good news for a change. God knows we all need it." She resumed changing a dressing on a soldier recovering from a leg wound.

James looked around to see what he needed to tend to. The casualty station consisted of a common room with a wood stove in the center, with the medical supplies and desks along the wall. Two areas that fed off this common room—the operating rooms to the right and the 'resting room', which was a euphemism for the dying room. In the common room, men lay circled around the woodstove in rows. James moved toward a nurse outside the resting room and asked softly for an update.

"Two soldiers died during the night and a third will likely succumb soon," she whispered back. He nodded and went to assess the situation. Generally, when battle wounds were inoperable, the men died quite quickly, but this fellow had lingered on far beyond what anyone expected. Both of his legs and one hand had been blown off, plus a shell fragment had damaged his spine and paralysed him from the rib cage down. Thankfully, the man—Private Franks—was comatose. James opened Franks' eyelids to assess pupillary function and sounded his chest. He noted congestion and periods of apnea. It shouldn't be long now.

James went back to the main ward and slowly made his rounds, checking on the soldiers who were recuperating from surgery or medical treatment. He assessed each patient and updated their progress on their charts. A few soldiers were stable enough to be transferred to the Convalescent Hospital, which a true hospital in Belgium, just across the border about 20 kilometres away.

He was writing on one man's chart when two soldiers entered the station. One was Arnold Ramsey. And he didn't look well.

Chapter 36
Arnold's Illness

A MEDIC HELD ONTO ARNOLD, who looked unsteady and pale. "Nurse," the medic called, "I have an ill soldier here. Where can I put him?"

Nurse Campbell hurried over and helped the medic place Arnold on one of the cots used for evaluations. He moaned with relief as they lowered him onto the edge of the cot. The nurse put up a screen at the end of the bed to give them privacy and then hustled behind it to attend to Arnold.

James didn't think Arnold saw him, or was healthy enough to be aware of him; but he had noticed no obvious injury, blood, or bandages to indicate battle trauma. He surmised his illness was probably viral, and hopefully not infectious. He prepared himself to speak to the boy. He would have to. He and the other two doctors he worked with rotated in eight-hour shifts and he was the only doctor on duty right now. Due to their heavy workload, he was reluctant to bother one of the others for a nonemergency. He knew he could suspend his feelings and treat Arnold as any other patient—but could Arnold suspend his? James felt uneasy. The encounter might be uncomfortable.

Soon, Nurse Campbell emerged from behind the screen and approached James. "Dr. Wilson," she said, "I have a sick soldier for you to see. He has a fever, weakness, and a productive cough. His vitals are on the chart."

"Thank you, Nurse Campbell," James said. "I'll be right there."

James finished writing a progress report he was working on and proceeded over to see Arnold. He went around the screen and introduced himself. "Arnold, I'm Dr. Wilson, as you know. I'm the only doctor on duty right now and I have no problem examining you, but I understand if you'd prefer to see another doctor."

Arnold groaned and said, "I feel so rotten, I wouldn't care if you were Satan."

James picked up Arnold's chart and looked over his vitals and the brief history of illness written there. "The medic brought you in because of weakness and general signs of illness. Is that right?" James noted the elevated temperature, the rapid pulse and respiratory rate. There was a deathlike pallor to Arnold's face and he had sunken dark eyes, dry lips and obvious weakness.

"Yes. He told me last night that he was bringing me in today. He said I wasn't in good enough condition to fight. I could have told him that—I'm too weak to climb over the wall."

"Tell me how this started," James said.

"About two weeks ago …" Arnold broke into such a strong coughing spasm that it jolted him upright. He collapsed on his back when he finished. "About two weeks ago," he resumed, "I developed a slight cough. Then after a week or so, the cough got worse with lots of phlegm. Then about three days ago I started to get fever and chills. Then I couldn't eat and now I'm weak and tired, and I have chills and fever— "

"How are you feeling right now, Arnold?"

"Freezing. Weak. Tired. It hurts to cough."

James nodded and proceeded to examine him. His pulse was rapid and bounding. He heard decreased air entry in the bottom lobes of both lungs with sounds of severe congestion. His heart was labouring. He obviously had severe bronco-pneumonia in both lungs.

"You have pneumonia," James informed him. "You need strict bed rest, clean air, hydrotherapy, and possibly poultices. I'll arrange for you to be transported to the Convalescent Hospital today. Any questions?"

"What are my chances?"

Suddenly, despite everything, James saw only a vulnerable, anxious, very ill patient lying before him. The feelings of disgust and anger he held toward this boy momentarily faded, yet he couldn't bring himself to reach out and touch his arm in a moment of empathy and reassurance as he would have done to someone else. "You have a severe case of pneumonia, Arnold. It is hard to say how well you will recover. I've seen lungs congested more than yours get better, and lungs in better shape than yours get worse. We will do what we can for you and the next few days should tell the story."

Arnold seemed to be studying him, evaluating the information. His jaw started to tremble from chill and rigors. He said, "I've managed to dodge bullets and shell fire … to think a bloody cold might be my downfall. How stupid is that?"

"More soldiers have been stricken and retired from disease than you realise," said James.

Arnold tried to wrap the blanket around him tighter. "I thank you, Dr. Wilson," he said. "I know you don't like me …"

"It's not a question of liking you—you're a sick patient and I'm a doctor. It is my job and my duty to care for you."

"But you're convinced I killed poor Bessie."

"I'm highly suspicious. And I'm convinced you raped her."

"Because of a silly girl's diary? You didn't even know her. You only saw her once."

"How do you know I only saw her once?" James asked, instantly alert.

"I … I guess the police told me," Arnold stuttered.

"I never told the police that. They have no idea how many times I saw her. They never asked. So I suppose you are the one who broke into my office and slugged me over the head. You were looking at Bessie's file, weren't you?"

Arnold started to retch, and James fetched a basin and brought it to his bed just in time for him to spit. He lay back in his cot with a weary sigh when he was finished.

"Do you need help, Dr. Wilson?" Nurse Campbell called from the ward.

"No, thank you," James called back. "We're okay."

Arnold folded up into a fetal position. "So cold," he murmured. "I'm so tired."

"I'll see if the nurse can spare another blanket," James said as he moved to the foot of the cot to write up Arnold's history, physical findings, diagnosis, and orders on the chart. Clearly exhausted, Arnold seemed to be falling asleep. James turned around and left. He had never felt this ambivalent about a patient before. He didn't like the feeling.

Chapter 37
A Visitor

THREE DAYS LATER, JAMES WAS lying on his bunk after lunch, resting up for a shift that was to start at 4:00 p.m. when a knock came at the door. "Come in," James called.

A chaplain entered. "Dr. Wilson?" he asked.

"Yes?" James got off the cot and went to shake the chaplain's hand. The chaplain was short, with a full brown beard and a nose so sharp and pinched that James wondered immediately if he had trouble breathing through that beak—a loud snorer, no doubt. "What can I do for you, chaplain?"

"I'm Reverend Philip Stone," he said.

James nodded, "To what do I owe the honour?" he asked.

"Dr. Wilson," Reverend Stone said, "you sent a Sergeant Arnold Ramsey to the Convalescent Hospital three days ago. I'm sad to inform you he passed away yesterday."

It didn't surprise James to hear this, though Arnold had died faster than he expected. The pneumonia—bilateral pneumonia—was severe, and he had noted signs of sepsis when he'd seen the boy.

"I appreciate you coming all this way to tell me," James said. "But why?"

"Sergeant Ramsey asked me to," said Reverend Stone. "He asked me to come to you with his confession."

I was right after all. He knew he was about to hear the story of how Arnold raped and murdered Bessie.

"I'm not in a habit of relaying confessionals," said the reverend. "They are strictly confidential. But he made me swear before God that I tell you. He was clear and almost frantic that I relay this story to you. It was like God granted him a few hours of reprieve from his suffering to allow him to speak to me, because for hours before that he was almost comatose, feverish, shaking and mumbling foolishness. Then suddenly the fever abated, and he became lucid. We chatted for over an hour and two hours after that he was dead."

James didn't think God had much to do with this; it was common for a two-hour period of calm to occur just before death, even after hours or days of struggle—remarkable but common.

"He was a troubled young man," the Reverend went on, "and I believe at the end he was truly remorseful for his deeds."

"Please sit," James said, offering the reverend a chair. "And let me offer you some tea."

Reverend Stone took a sip of the tea James brought him before continuing. "He told me to tell you that you were right. He said he must be responsible for a young woman's pregnancy. I believe the name was Bessie."

James nodded. *A rather cautious admission*, James thought, *'must be responsible'*.

"Sergeant Ramsey said he didn't remember much of that night because he was drunk. It started when he and his wife had a big argument and he stormed out of the house and then impulsively went to a social in a village outside his city. During the church social he met his uncle and promised to give his cousin a ride home after the party. He felt agitated because of the domestic quarrel but felt immediately better when he drank some alcohol with a few friends behind the church. He drank too much and by the time the band finished, he was quite inebriated." Stone took another sip of tea and held the warm mug with both hands before going on. "He remembers joking with Bessie as they drove home later, but he has no idea how they ended up in the woods having sex. He believes it was consensual, but he conceded that the whole event was foggy."

"Reverend Stone," James said, "I'm sorry, but that is the worst, most lame excuse of a confession I ever heard. He raped her. Did he tell you how old Bessie was?" The reverend shook his head. "Fifteen. And the most sensible, mature fifteen-year-old you'd ever want to meet. She kept a diary that chronicles the rape. Being drunk doesn't excuse Arnold. Even before God, he didn't admit full responsibility."

"Maybe he truly believed this was what happened … or maybe he was in denial," the reverend suggested.

James made a face that demonstrated what he thought about those theories.

"Are you related to this Bessie?" Reverend Stone asked.

"No. I was her physician."

"I don't mean for this to sound critical, but why are you so emotionally involved in this matter?" The reverend asked gently.

James sighed. "I swore to Bessie and God that I'd find justice for her after she died."

"Why you and not the police?" the reverend asked.

Why him indeed? He knew it would sound strange to an outsider. "I always felt responsible for her death," he slowly answered. "If I had only told her father about the pregnancy, and who I thought the rapist was, the family would have dug down and figured it out quickly and she'd still be alive. I was torn between my commitment to patient confidentiality and my responsibility to protect a child. My choice allowed her death to happen."

"That would be a hard decision to make," said the reverend. "How long did you wait?"

"Overnight. The day after I saw her in my office, I decided Bessie and I should tell her father—together—but instead I went to a meeting and put it off. The next day she was dead."

James looked at the reverend. It was the cold, hard truth and he didn't expect forgiveness, relief or sympathy.

Reverend Stone looked him directly in the eye. "You know, in Proverbs 18 it says, '*you may have to draw straws when faced with a tough decision*'." James looked blankly at him. "To me," Stone went on, "that statement suggests a number of things. First, God can't possibly direct you to make every decision—you can ask for guidance, but there are no guarantees. And second, sometimes there is no right and wrong. In your case, both choices were fair and certainly both were noble and just."

"I think I made the right choice, Reverend Stone," James said. "But I also feel the time it took me to finally decide what to do—my indecision—is what killed her."

"A most forgivable indecision, Dr. Wilson."

"A fatal one."

"Her death probably would have happened anyway, even if you'd told her father that same day."

"Why do you say that? If her father knew about her condition and the rape, he would have prevented her from going to meet Arnold the night she died."

"Are you sure about that?"

James had to admit that Bessie was a headstrong girl. She said she wanted to handle things her way. It would have made sense to get money from Arnold rather than ask her father for the money to go to Montreal.

"Besides," Reverend Stone said, "Her death was an *accident*."

James frowned. "How do you know that?" he asked.

"Sergeant Ramsey said he pushed her, and she fell back and struck her head on a huge sharp rock. At first, he thought she was just knocked out, but then her body stiffened strangely and she began convulsing. The next thing he knew, she was dead."

"He told you that?" asked James.

"I believe Sergeant Ramsey," the reverend answered. "He didn't strike me as a cold-blooded murderer."

This *did* sound plausible. The coroner thought the gash on the back of Bessie's head was from scraping on rocks as she washed ashore, but James had thought the wound was a little too bloody to have been inflicted post-mortem. And the reverend's description of Bessie's abnormal posturing and seizure sounded like a classic brain haemorrhage.

"The boy said he didn't mean to harm her. He didn't think he pushed her very hard. He was angry because she kept pushing him for money and claiming if he didn't give her some, she'd tell everyone what happened. He didn't *have* the money she wanted; he barely had enough to feed his child. She wouldn't listen and kept badgering him until finally he'd had enough, and he pushed her."

James could hear sympathy in Reverend Stone's voice. His heart softened toward Arnold a bit. He was in a tight spot. It was a tragedy. He could understand Arnold's anxiety about the situation … but he raped a young girl, and no excuse in the world could justify that behaviour.

"How did he explain the rocks in her dress pockets, and her being in the water?" he asked.

"He admitted to doing that. He said he panicked. He hoped he'd sink her to the bottom of the river and she'd never be found. People would think she ran away from home or was murdered and buried by an unknown assailant."

"So, he didn't try to stage a suicide?"

"He didn't mention that. Is that what people thought? That the girl committed suicide?"

"That was the official final police report."

"Frankly, I don't think Sergeant Ramsey was that clever."

There was not a lot more to say. James and the reverend chatted for a while about human nature and tragedies, the war and the weather, while they finished a second cup of tea. After a while the reverend left and James sat heavily on the chair by the stove.

Was Arnold a monster or not? Certainly, his crimes were not premeditated … *but does that make them any less evil?* He thought about Bessie and how he'd finally fulfilled his promise to her, but he felt no better than he had before.

He needed to clear his head. He got up and left the hut to take a walk.

Chapter 38
Another Visitor

THE SNOW THAT HAD FALLEN a few days ago was now gone, washed away by yesterday's rain. Today, the skies were dull and filled with heavy, dark, solid clouds. The improvised Christmas tree looked ridiculous in this light, without snow. James turned away from the casualty station and headed to the road beside the camp that lead to the front. When he came to it, he crossed it and climbed a short embankment to the edge of a forest and entered.

He wasn't supposed to go into the woods alone, but the need for solitude and fresh air drove him onward. He wandered past trees, feeling their bark, wanting to find a connection to something familiar. He observed withered patches of tall grass that had struggled to survive against the sun-robbing canopy of tree branches above. Now they rested until the spring, when the fight for survival would begin again. He felt something withering within him. How he missed home, and Mary.

He was tired of the mayhem, the mangled bodies, the food, the mud, the smells, the cacophony of screaming artillery fire and blasts. No end was in sight. Where was God in all this? His once-daily prayers were becoming only occasional. How could the God he prayed to, a loving, all-powerful God, allow this carnage to continue?

James felt a patch of moss on a coniferous tree, soft and yet firm, refusing to be pushed off like a piece of fluff. He looked up to the top of a tall pine tree swaying in the breeze. How could God let a sweet girl like Bessie die so frivolously after being used for a young man's wanton, carnal desires? How could such a God watch as a seemingly normal, responsible young man like Arnold destroyed his life in one night, with one drunken, evil action. How could a war start, and thousands lose their lives, simply because a fanatic killed a duke no one had heard of.

Leaders who can't resolve their differences over a cup of tea ask their young men to resort to a sickening riot of death and destruction on their behalf. Men who pray to the same God thrust bayonets to eviscerate their fellow man without hesitation or remorse. What a messed-up, fucking world!

James picked up a twig and bit into it. His belief in a life worthwhile; a life made fruitful by noble works; an idyllic, peaceful life in the countryside, had disappeared along with his relationship with God. It was heartbreaking and he felt sick in his soul.

A sparrow flew onto a small, bare tree branch not far from him. The bird seemed to be watching him, tilting its head one way and then the other, always keeping James in view. James reached into his jacket pocket and snapped off a small piece of cracker that lay in a fold of tissue there. He offered it to the small bird in his open palm.

The bird watched.

James slowly kneeled.

The sparrow's head flicked back and forth as he weighed the danger versus reward. After a moment, he flew to the pine tree beside James and looked down upon him while clinging to the trunk. He fidgeted and then dove from his perch and landed on James' index finger.

The bird was weightless, like it was made of paper. He saw a solid being sitting on his hand and he felt the gentle talons clinging to his finger, yet the bird did not seem lifelike. It gently took the piece of cracker from James' palm and looked him directly in the eye, freezing that moment in time, hanging it between this world and the next.

Then the bird fluttered away.

James arose and slowly walked back to the base. This encounter reminded him of something he had once read: '*God will come to you like a bird singing in the night*'.

No matter how bleak things became, how fed up he was, how dark his soul, how sickening the slaughter and injuries, he had Mary and his baby to think of.

He returned to the casualty station with a renewed spirit. He would see this war through to the end.

Epilogue

Dr. James Wilson arrived home April 15, 1919, five months after the war ended—late because he stayed behind to tend to the few remaining Canadian soldiers who remained in English hospitals until they were fit to sail home. He had spent nearly five years overseas and was one of the longest-serving Canadians in the war.

James and Mary reunited one sunny morning on a pier in St. John. As the ship docked, James searched the crowd on the pier to see her beloved face. He saw the familiar red hair in the crowd and as soon as he disembarked, he headed for her and they hungrily embraced, collapsing into each other with a mixture of relief and complete joy. After a few moments, James reluctantly released Mary to look at her. She had not changed a bit. She was beautiful, with her long, fair, red hair and delicate features, and a smile that always melted his heart.

"I missed you so much," James said, touching the side of her face. "I dreamed of this day."

Mary buried her face in his chest and cried. "And I missed you," she murmured.

James saw Clancy, Rebecca, and his mother standing on the edge of the crowd behind them. Clancy was holding the hand of a young boy.

"Is that boy standing with your father our son?" he asked Mary in disbelief.

Mary stepped back from him and looked over at the young boy. "Yes. That's your son—Harold," she said. James marveled at him. He was a handsome lad. The boy wore a grey coat with a matching cap, and grey trousers with brown shoes. Like him, Harold had blond hair, but he had his mother's delicate sharp nose.

James was overcome. He had to fight the tears that threatened to escape.

Harold waited patiently by his grandfather's side with a flush on his cheeks and a wide grin. "Come and see your father, Harold," Mary called, extending her arm to their son.

Clancy let go of Harold's hand and the boy ran to Mary and took her hand. He looked at James with big blue eyes and said, "You are my father." It was a statement and not a question.

"Yes," James said. "And how did you know that?"

"Mother and I talk to you every night before I go to bed."

"Your picture is by his bed," Mary explained.

"Mother says that you will teach me to ride Sadie."

James knelt down to be at eye level with Harold. "I will most certainly do that. I hear you kept good care of Sadie and Bob while I was away."

"Yes, I did." Harold said. Then he asked, "Can I learn to fish too?"

James laughed. He wanted to take the boy into his arms but refrained as he understood that his son really didn't know him. Instead he asked, "May I hug you, Harold?"

Harold raised his arms.

James and Mary had five children and lived all their lives in Rothesay. James continued as the sole physician in Rothesay until his death at the age of 75.

Shortly after his return from the war, he bought an automobile. He no longer had the idealism of the young Dr. James Wilson, the first physician to practise in this riverside village. He was older now and had seen the worst of humanity. It made him appreciate creature comforts more than he had as a youth.

He was well respected in his community and loved by his patients, and he continued practising as a physician right up until a week before his death from a massive stroke.

All was not ideal, however. As Mary reclaimed her husband, she realized that she had lost a part of James to the war. While he was a loving, caring man to her, their children, and eventually their grandchildren—gentle and even-tempered—a spark was now missing. The zest for life that once showed in his eyes, mannerisms and activity was gone.

Before the war, even in quiet moments when he read or worked in the yard, Mary noted that his mind was active and his spirit bright. After the war, it was not unusual for her to observe him dully staring out the window for long periods of time, seemingly oblivious to the present. Sometimes, when he was working out in the pasture, she would see him braced against the fence, one foot up on a lower railing, fixed and unmoving as though in a trance.

At first, she thought nothing of it, assuming that he was daydreaming or appreciating being alive and the tranquility of peace; but as time went on, she came to realize it was more than that. It was as though his mind sometimes completely froze and shut down.

At night, James often murmured in his sleep, or thrashed about and woke up sweating and crying out. She would hold him and comfort him and could only imagine what horrors he dreamed about. He said he had seen and witnessed too much in the war, and that it affected his dreams, but he never shared the specifics.

He was unable to put the daydreams and nightmares into words, for they were not stories but flashes—visions of maimed bodies; frantic, pleading eyes; limbs in macabre positions; dying eyes; horrific head wounds; exposed guts spilling onto gurneys; the smell of blood and vomit; and, the cries and cacophony of battle. He longed for peace, for quiet moments to reflect and be grateful; but idle times were the catalyst of this torment. He eventually learned to avoid being alone as much as possible.

James continued to go to church, but his relationship with God was forever changed. He didn't know what to make of his religion, but he dutifully attended church on Sundays with his family and kept his opinions and questions private. The encounter with the sparrow, which he never forgot, continued to give him hope that there was a gentle and loving God above and that life was inherently good, but most of the time he simply felt empty and was unable to rejoice in spiritual fervour or even quiet contemplation at church.

He told Amos about Arnold's confession and the two of them agreed not to tell Robert and Isabel. They both felt that the death of their beloved son was enough for them to endure. James admired Amos' strength as he supported his cousin in his grief and endured Robert's glowing reflections about his son. *How can he hear this without mentioning Bessie and her short, tragic life,* wondered

James? But he did, listening bravely and with compassion as Robert read letters from Arnold's ranking officers, who spoke glowingly of his bravery and concern for his men. In fact, Amos didn't bat an eye when Arnold was posthumously awarded a medal of bravery on the recommendation of his lieutenant and fellow soldiers, who attested to his valour. Instead, Amos quietly and respectfully listened without comment. James admired Amos so much for his control. In Amos' compassion, James saw the work of God, and it lifted him for a while. He and Amos stayed lifelong friends.

Visions of horror from the war tormented James for the rest of his life ... but so did Bessie. He often saw a vision of her that summer day in 1913, sitting on the side of his exam table, wearing an ankle-length, brown dress, her head bent, long brown hair covering her face, rocking slightly, clenching her hands, as she timidly said ...

"You see, I was forced."

Afterword

THE EVENTS IN THE FIRST part of this book took place in Rothesay, New Brunswick, Canada. In the early 1900s, Rothesay was a small town located just east of the city of Saint John, with smaller villages scattered in-between. These small villages were eventually amalgamated to create the existing town of Rothesay, and it was this modern-day version of the town that was used as the setting for this book.

In 1877, much of the city of Saint John was destroyed by a major fire, but it was quickly rebuilt because its year-round, sheltered port was an important link between Europe and the rest of Canada. In the early part of the 1900s, Saint John was a busy energetic city offering shipbuilding expertise, a vast supply of wood from the forests of New Brunswick, and a large workforce of mostly Irish immigrants, all of which contributed to its rebuilding.

I chose to use the abbreviated version of 'Saint' (in 'St. John') in the telling of this story, because in the early years, most people spelled St. John this way. However, now it is improper. The Canadian Postal Service, frustrated with mail getting mixed up between St. John, New Brunswick and St. John's, Newfoundland, ended this spelling by an act of parliament around the time of the first world war, officially changing the name to Saint John.

Saint John and Rothesay are both situated on the traditional land of the Wolastoqiyik (Maliseet) and Mi'kmaq peoples.

There was no Dr. James Wilson. He is a completely fictitious character. I wanted to explore what it would have been like to practice medicine before the advent of antibiotics. I referred to Sir William Osler's text, *The Principles and Practice of Medicine,* written in 1892, to learn how physicians would have treated certain conditions in those times. Some of these treatments might seem quite strange to us now, but I tried to stay true to the times, and to Dr. Osler's texts. For example, James asked his father if he was taking creosote tablets and Fowler's solution for his TB, as Osler's medical text recommended at that time. This treatment was discredited as worthless when medicine became more scientific and rigorous. Treatments that had been proven beneficial by unbiased studies were recommended instead.

Today, performing an operation at home would be grounds for criminal prosecution; back then, simple surgeries on patients under chloroform had to be bravely attempted because of the lack of rapid transportation, and ignorance about the importance of sterility.

During this period of history, women didn't have many rights, including the right to vote. Certificates asked if the brides could read or write, though nothing like this was asked about the groom. Further, as described in the book, the justice system was skewed to protect males from false accusations of domestic violence and rape. It was almost impossible for a rape victim to get justice without displaying evidence of major body trauma—and even that didn't guarantee conviction.

During World War I, far more soldiers died from late complications of war wounds and communicable infections than from actual combat. I used the book *Doctors in the Great War,* by Ian R. Whitehead, for reference to understand what the role of doctors was during WWI. 'Shell-shock' was the term used back then for severe cases of what we now call 'post traumatic stress disorder' (PTSD), but we now know the *overtly* shell-shocked were only the tip of the iceberg—the vast majority suffered in silence.

Our lives are sometimes shaken by random unjust events that forever change us, and the best we can do is move on.

About the Author

Dr. Shawn Jennings resides with his wife in Rothesay, New Brunswick, Canada. They have three children and three grandchildren. Shawn suffered a brainstem stroke at the age of 45, caused by a traumatic tear of an artery. He had to retire from family medicine but remains active in his community. He is dysarthric, dysphasic, tetraplegic, and uses a power wheelchair for mobility.

This is Shawn Jennings' third book. He previously wrote a memoir, *Locked In Locked Out.* The second edition of this book was released in January 2020. Shawn is also the author of the fiction novel, *The Dove's Eye,* released in 2010.

CPSIA information can be obtained
at www.ICGtesting.com
Printed in the USA
LVHW091750230320
650872LV00023B/220

9 780228 824435